SPINNERS
THE PROTECTORS OF THE BERMUDA TRIANGLE

Five teenagers from Bermuda are trapped in

The Bermuda Triangle. They must face the forces

of evil to protect the Triangle from destruction

R.C. Farrington

THE PROTECTORS OF THE BERMUDA TRIANGLE

WONDERFUL PEOPLE WHO CONTRIBUTED TO THIS BOOK:

Jason Farrington has created outstanding graphic designs
for this novel. www.gorilladesignstudio.net

Rod Ferguson of Bermuda, has made contributions
of his time and thoughts to help make this novel possible.

Visit:
www.bermudaspinners.com

ISBN: 1-894916-97-2

Production: Print Link, Bermuda
Printed in Canada

DEDICATION

This book is dedicated to all my friends in Bermuda and Louisiana who have encouraged and supported my endeavors to write this novel.

I would also like to dedicate this book to my two labs, Taz who was adopted from the Bermuda SPCA and Lexi who was a stray that came to live with us. Both labs are best buddies.

INTRODUCTION

Bermuda is the most beautiful place on earth, and whoever reads this novel should take at least one week out of their busy lives to visit one of the most incredible places on the earth. There, you will find soft pristine turquoise-colored waves gently rolling up on the pink beaches. You will also find breathtaking, the myriad combinations of arbors, shrubs, vines and flowers that reflect all the colors of the rainbow. Then, when you consider the historic forts, the village of St. George's and the most picturesque golf courses in the world... Yes, Bermuda is truly an island paradise.

Characters depicted in this novel, other than known historical persons are all fictitious. Comparisons, to people living in the past or present, are coincidental and not intentional.

CHAPTERS

Main Characters from 'Spinners the Lost Treasure of Bermuda' who continue on in "Spinners the Protectors of the Bermuda Triangle:"

The Spinners:

MICHAEL CLARK from Boston now lives in Bermuda with his grandmother. He is 16 years old and tends to be the leader of the group.

KENO MING is dark skinned and is very mature and powerful for his 16 years. He lives at the St. David's Lighthouse where his father is the lighthouse keeper.

Samantha (Sam) Savage is a beautiful and brilliant young girl. She is 15 years old and is considered the "brains" of the group. Her father is Inspector Ian Savage, a local police Inspector for the St. George's branch of the Bermuda Police Service.

Roderick (Portagee) Madeiros is the "littlest" and the youngest at 14 years old, but an "inventive" Portuguese boy who is an electronic whiz kid.

Graham Aston is dark skinned and also 16 years old. He is the "rich" kid of the group. His family is the dominant oil importer in Bermuda.

The Good:

Inspector Ian Savage: Local Police Inspector for St. George's.

Bubba, Buford and Cooter: Confederate blockade-runners during the Civil War. They are all cousins.

Jason was a British fighter pilot from the 1953 time period.

Spence was a US Navy bomber pilot on a patrol mission out of the US in 1956.

Salty was a peg-legged ship's cook that escaped from Captain Drax.

The Bad:

Cuda, Sledge, Gunner and Axil are small time thugs who used to work for Tattoo Jack in St. George's.

Alvaro is a current day pirate from Brazil who is extremely vicious and deadly.

~1~

SHOOTOUT AT THE SHINBONE

SHOOTOUT AT THE SHINBONE

That night, gale force storms were bearing in on Bermuda, no one in their right mind would be out on a night like this, no one except Tattoo Jack's ex thugs Cuda, Sledge, Gunner and Axil. They were on their way to the Shinbone Pub to spend another night of binge drinking themselves into a stupor. A year had almost passed since Tattoo's disappearance in the Triangle and the times had not been good for his goons. Although Tattoo was impaled on Drax's saber, his gang never really knew what happened to him. They had kept their little gang together, but had been reduced to petty and bully crimes. With the absence of Tattoo, Inspector Savage had obtained search warrants on Tattoo's warehouse and found unreported shipwreck relics, along with tons of stolen goods and a small stash of drugs. This was enough evidence to shut down Tattoo's operation and confiscate his property, including his warehouse and deep sea fishing boat, the "Black Shark." The Inspector was never able to tie any of Tattoo's men to the illegal crimes, but that was all right for the inspector. With the head of the serpent cut off, the rest of the serpent would soon die. At this rate it wasn't going to take them long to drink themselves to death or be arrested for some crime they would eventually commit.

With the absence of Tattoo, Axil had assumed the top dog spot of the gang. Sledge would have been the only one who could have challenged him for the spot, but he reluctantly accepted the number two spot. The thugs walked down Water Street in St. Georges, heading toward Shinbone Alley. Even though they were the only ones out that night, they still walked like they owned the village. They were on the down and outs. The locals still feared them and would stay clear. Soaking wet, they entered the dimly lit Shinbone and headed to their table in the back corner of the pub. Except for the bartender, they were the only ones in the Shinbone tonight. If it weren't for the foursome, the bartender would have probably closed the pub. As the night wore on, the booze loosened up the conversation. Although his speech was a little slurred, Axil spoke out, "Why didn't we get that lost treasure, instead those snot nose Spinners? They got millions."

Sledge chimed in, "Damn right, those kids stole the cross and the treasure right out from under our eyes. The stupid kids let the government have fifty percent of the treasure for absolutely nothing."

Cuda blurted out, "They even gave tons of money to charities and the poor. Can you bloody believe that?" The conversation went downhill from there.

Axil pulled out his boning knife and pounded it into the old wood table. He then yelled out, "If those brats dared to walk through that door right now I'd get up and make shark bait out of them."

No sooner than he finished when the two front doors blew open with the force of a grenade explosion, blowing the doors off their hinges. The rain and wind blew through the pub like a hurricane. Six dark bodies smashed through what was left of the entrance, brandishing AK47 assault weapons and spraying bullets around the pub. Cuda fell over backwards, hitting the back of his head on the hardwood floor and he passed out cold. Sledge fell forward over the table and lay on the floor, covering his head with his hands. Gunner hit the floor and tried to hide behind Sledge. Axil was the only one that had the nerve to get up and fight back. He stood up, ripped his knife out of the table before Sledge knocked it over, and went in the direction of one of the dark bodies. The next thing he saw, through the smoke of automatic weapons' fire, was the butt of an AK47 striking him in the forehead. Axil found himself flat on his back, not having a clue what had just happened.

The guns quit firing and as the smoke cleared, another single figure entered the pub. The first words out of his mouth were, "Brothers, get yourselves off the floor and greet your Brothers from Brazil." To the shock of the foursome, Alvaro, Captain of the Piranha, appeared. Alvaro was a ruthless pirate, who was a cold-blooded killer like Captain Drax in the Triangle.

With the gale force storm at its peak, the sound of weapons' fire was not heard by anyone outside of the pub. The Brazilian pirates did not care that in Bermuda weapons were banned. Alvaro walked over to Axil, helped him get up off the floor and sat him down on a chair. By now the other three were also sitting in chairs not having a clue what was going on. Alvaro then said, "Brothers, it's so nice to see you again, we've missed the treasures you used to sell us. Speaking of treasure, we've become aware that over the last year, some local kids have found a large stash of treasure. Axil, my friend, I need your help in recovering part of this treasure."

Axil looked at Alvaro and laughingly said, "You wasted a trip here mate. The treasure has been gone for a long time."

Alvaro reached over and grabbed Axil by the neck and replied, "You idiot, we're not stupid, we know about the legend of 'The Lost Treasure of Bermuda.'

There's much more treasure not accounted for yet." He then struck Axil with the back of his hand. Just then one of Alvaro men came over and whispered in his ear. With all the shots being fired and the gun smoke in the air, the bartender was not accounted for. Alvaro knew the time would be short. He must leave the island before the authorities arrived. He then turned to his men and said, "Get our brothers up out of their chairs, they're going on a little trip with us as our guests." The other Brazilians aimed their automatic weapons at the foursome and signaled them to head for the doorway. When they were all heading down the alley, Alvaro pulled out his walkie-talkie and said; "This is Alvaro. Meet us at the pickup zone in three minutes."

A voice responded on the walkie-talkie, "Roger that, boss, over and out."

Alvaro responded, "Over and out." He then turned to the group and said, "Let's get this show on the road." Within a couple of minutes they were all in the centre of the St. George's King's Square. With the severe storm going on, the square was like a ghost town. Alvaro now pointed to the sky. Through the storm clouds you could see two objects moving very fast towards the square. As the objects closed in, you could hear a distinct "whomp, whomp, whomp" sound of a twin bladed, rotor helicopter. Watching in shock Cuda, Sledge, Axil and Gunner could not believe their eyes. There were two US Huey chopper gunships that had been used in the Vietnam conflict. M-60 machine guns were mounted on each side of the Hueys. The chopper gunships quickly landed in the centre of the square. Cuda and Sledge were loaded into one chopper gunship and Gunner and Axil were loaded on the other. Within two minutes, the chopper gunships lifted off and were heading out to sea.

Alvaro was right about one thing that night. The Shinbone bartender ran straight to the St. George's Police Department. Just by luck of the draw, Inspector Ian Savage was on duty that night. After hearing the frantic bartender's story, the sergeant called for the Inspector to come to the front desk. The Inspector listened to the story and then called for four other officers to accompany him to the Shinbone. When the officers entered the Shinbone, there was an instant feeling that they had just entered a war zone. The walls, tables and bar had more bullets in them than had been fired in Bermuda in the last twenty- five years. The Inspector turned to the bartender and asked, "What the hell happened here? This place is ripped to shreds!" The bartender retold the story of how the six men, dressed in black, came crashing through the doors and started firing weapons. The Inspector then asked, "Who were they shooting at other than the walls and the bar?"

The bartender replied, "They seemed to know that Tattoo Jack's thugs were here tonight, but then again, they're here every night."

"So where are they now? I don't see any dead bodies or blood stains," queried the Inspector. The bartender then told the Inspector that when the firing started, he dropped down behind the bar to the floor and crawled out the back door. The Inspector then got on the radio and requested the forensics team to get down to the Shinbone as soon as possible to collect evidence. He thought to himself as he looked around, "What in the world would these hit men want with Tattoo's ex goons?" All he could hope for now was to find some evidence or another witness that might help make sense out of this mess. All he could do was to go back to the police department and file his reports. The next day he would put out an island wide search for Axil, Sledge, Gunner and Cuda. When he returned home, he would have to pack for a trip to the UK. The Inspector had been selected for a six-week special investigative training program with the Scotland Yard.

Meanwhile, the chopper gunships stayed under a five hundred foot ceiling to make sure the Bermuda airport would not pick them up on radar. Looking back at Bermuda, all you could see were some small lights through the storm. Alvaro was on the same chopper gunship with Gunner and Axil. As they were standing there, Alvaro stepped up from behind and put one hand on Gunner's shoulder and one hand on Axils shoulder. He then asked, "My brothers, I'll ask you one more time, how do we find the rest of the treasure?"

Gunner turned to Alvaro and said, "Alvaro shove it up your butt!" He then turned to Axil and said, "These jerks won't do anything to us. They need us to find the treasure."

Alvaro gripped their shoulders very tightly and responded, "You're right my brother, but we don't need all of you." Then, without hesitation, Alvaro shoved Gunner out of the chopper gunship door. All you could hear was Gunner screaming as he was flinging his arms and legs when the dark night swallowed him down. Alvaro then turned to Axil and said, "Sit down my brother. You can have a chat with Scarzo when we get back to the ship." Axil was still shaking. He quietly sat down and just sat there with a blank stare, looking out into the dark stormy night. He knew Scarzo was the kingpin of this band of killers and smugglers. His chances of seeing St. George's again was very slim.

The chopper gunships now flew low and fast, back to their base ship, the "Prowler." As the "Prowler" became visible, Alvaro could see Axil staring in amazement at the ship. "Yes my brother," said Alvaro, "you're about to land on the most state of the art ship in the world. We stole this stealth ship from the US Navy and they were livid. But who cares? It's a stealth ship and they can't find us. It's a Sea Fighter catamaran that has a top speed of over fifty knots. The "Prowler" can house two chopper gunships and a speedboat and yes, the tons of treasure you're going to help us get. This ship has the fire power to blow anything out of the air or water within a mile of it." With that, Alvaro laughed and slapped Axil on the back. Then he lit up his Cuban cigar. The "Prowler" had now cleared the pilot to land.

Very quickly, both chopper gunships landed on the massive catamaran and were secured. Axil, Sledge and Cuda were quickly escorted below to Scarzo's cabin. While they were waiting with Alvaro, Cuda, finally asked, "Where's Gunner, wasn't he with you, Axil?"

Alvaro smiled and said, "He swims with the sharks now, my brothers."

"What's he mean by that?" questioned Sledge.

"You idiots, he's dead!" yelled Axil. Sledge and Cuda started backing up as if they were going to leave. All of a sudden, someone standing behind them cold cocked them both. Axil turned around. It was Scarzo standing over them, laughing and holding the black night stick that he had clubbed them with. Scarzo was a huge muscular man. Yes, you could say talk and dark, but not handsome. He tried to cover up an SS scar on his face with two- day old beard. It was believed that Scarzo had been a member of the Odessa Group in his earlier years. Many of the founding members of this group were Ex-Nazi SS officers who had escaped from Nazi Germany after World War II and now lived in various locations throughout South America. Scarzo thrived amongst these brutal killers and was an excellent understudy. Years later Scarzo left the Odessa Group and formed his own mob of modern day pirates. He was much more diverse than his Nazi friends in Odessa. He had a legitimate antiquity business set up for selling treasures and collectables. Sometimes he bought the treasures legally, but most of the time he stole them from other treasure collectors who never lived to report the theft. Yes, Scarzo was a cold -blooded killer who would not stop until he got what he wanted and right now he wanted the rest of the Spinner's treasure.

As he walked over to his desk Scarzo said, "Welcome home Amigos. Alvaro I see you brought our brothers back to me."

"Yes sir boss," replied Alvaro.

Scarzo snapped his fingers. The thugs quickly picked up Cuda and Sledge and escorted them with Axil over to their chairs. "I see we lost a member of the family." Scarzo commented. " I hope the rest of you decide to join our quest for the rest of the treasure." All three of the Bermudians nodded in agreement. "Very good," Scarzo added, "I knew we could count on you boys. Now let's get down to business. You boys give me the inside story so we can get this show on the road." With that Cuda, Sledge and Axil started spilling out their guts like there was no tomorrow. Little did the Bermudians know that there might not be a tomorrow for them. They were then all escorted to separate cabins on the ship.

-2-

SPINNERS & SCOOTERS - ZOOM, ZOOM

SPINNERS AND SCOOTERS – ZOOM, ZOOM

The sun rose over Bermuda at dawn, what a beautiful day. One could never have guessed that the previous night there was a terrible storm inside and outside of the Shinbone. The morning started early at the Savage house. The Inspector had to pack for a six-week trip to the UK and then go to the police station to brief his superiors on the shootout at the Shinbone pub last night. His flight on British Air was not until that evening so he should have ample time to get all his affairs in order before his flight. Just before he was ready to leave for the station, he walked by Samantha's room to see she if she was up yet. He knocked on her door and yelled, "Day light burning, you going to get up today?" There was no response.

Sam was a usually late sleeper. If she didn't have to get up she might lay in bed until noon everyday. Her excuse was that she needed her beauty sleep. This was as far from the truth as one could imagine. Sam was a beautiful young girl. She had long blonde hair with a slender face and figure to match. Her light eyes matched the crystal blue skies over Bermuda. Sam was also athletic. As she was almost six feet tall she could "shoot hoops," and out gun any boy in St. George's on the basketball court. Sam was also a scholar. She was in the top two percent academically in her class at school. She also had a crush on her fellow Spinner, Michael.

Inspector Savage opened the door and reached over and gave Sam a little nudge on the shoulder and said, "Did you hear me Sam?"

Finally Sam answered, "Yes daddy," and then pulled the covers over her head. The Inspector was in a hurry this morning, but he stopped and sat down on the end of her bed. He then pulled down the cover from over her head and said, "Sam, I do need to talk to you before I go to the station. It's very serious."

Sam then sat up very quickly and responded, "Daddy, I'm sorry. What's the matter?"

The Inspector then began to tell her about the events of the night before. "I'm not sure what any of this means, with the Shinbone being shot up last night and Axil and his group of thieves apparently missing. I just don't know what to make of it

"Does it have anything to do with the Triangle or the treasure?" Sam asked.

The Inspector replied, "No, I don't think so. I just think Axil and his thugs have made some very bad enemies. We just can't figure out where the weapons that were used last night came from. At any rate, we're trying to track them down today and find some answers."

"Was anyone hurt or shot last night?" Sam asked.

"Not that we can tell. But I want to make sure you and the rest of the Spinners stay far away from Shinbone Alley and especially Axil and his thugs if you see them. In fact, if you see them, report it to the desk sergeant as the station as quickly as possible."

Sam gave her dad a hug and said, "I promise you, daddy, we'll stay clear of the Shinbone and we'll report the thugs if we see them."

"Very good," responded the Inspector, "I have to get going now. You enjoy your day and I'll see you tonight before its time to head to the airport." With that, the Inspector stood up, rubbed Sam's head and left the room.

Sam couldn't wait to call the other Spinners and tell them what had happened the previous night. It took about an hour, but she finally tracked them all down. They agreed to meet down by the dunking stool at the square in St. George's. There, they would plan their day and yes, maybe sneak by the Shinbone to see what all the excitement was about.

Not only were the Spinners now a year older, but they had also all changed in many ways from their adventure of last summer. Michael was now living with his grandmother in St. George's. He was six foot one inches tall with jet- black hair and very slender. His weight of one hundred fifty pounds had not kept up with his height. He played guard on the school basketball team. Michael missed American football, and he knew he did not have the frame for rugby. School in Bermuda was much more demanding than he had been used to in Boston. Thank goodness Sam was there to help him out. Michael was also very fond of Sam.

Keno was a giant for his age of sixteen. With his massive frame of six feet four inches and a weight that tipped the scales of over two hundred twenty pounds, he appeared to be much older than he was. For a big boy, he was agile and could play any sport he wanted to. The studies came hard for him, but his Spinner friends were there to help him. Keno had a close bond with his father. They both loved electronic communications. Girls were the last things on Keno's mind. His friends, his scooter and electronic communications came first.

Then there was Graham, the good- looking ladies man. There was not a girl in his school that didn't dream of a date with Graham. Graham was almost six feet tall with a medium build. His hair was done up in short braids most of the time and he had a smile that would melt the heart of any girl in the room when he made an entrance. Graham, as was Sam, was in the top two percent of his class academically at school. His goal was to further his education at university, earn a Masters Degree in geological engineering and continue on in the family petroleum business.

Roderick, or as his friends would call him, 'Portagee,' was the "odd man out," when it came to height in the group. Being younger, he may have not hit his growth spurt yet, but no one was holding his or her breath. Portagee, if he stretched, was only five feet four inches tall at the most. Being short didn't hold him back; in fact it just made him work harder at whatever he did. He was the highest scoring striker on the school soccer team in school history. He was sharp as a tack and loved electronics. Portagee had such a thirst for knowledge, but his curiosity would sometimes get him into predicaments. Because his father was a fisherman, Portagee was the junior seaman in the group.

That summer was much different for the Spinners getting around the island. Graham, Michael and Keno had all turned sixteen. Zoom, zoom, the three of them now had scooters. They were free to explore the entire island without relying on parents or the buses. Sam and Portagee were welcome passengers on the back of any of the three scooters. Although Portagee still had two years before he turned sixteen, he was already building his own scooter in his backyard. He was keeping it a big secret and not letting anyone, including the Spinners see it. They all knew he must have been making many modifications to the scooter. Yes, the Spinners were now all very wealthy. However most of their wealth was tied up in special trusts which they would not see until their mid twenties, except for Graham. He was already extremely wealthy. Much of his treasure money was used to establish trust funds to help the needy on the Island with special housing and education grants.

That morning, Michael picked up Sam while Keno picked up Portagee and Keno drove in from St. David's. They parked in the square and met at the dunking stool as they had agreed. After a long discussion of how to sneak by the Shinbone to get a peek at the damage from last night, they decided that with two police officers standing on guard in front of the pub, it would be impossible to visit without being seen. After all, everyone in St. George's knew who the Spinners were. While they were standing around trying to decide what to do, Graham pulled five sterling silver key chains from his pocket. They were engraved with the name 'Spinners.' He tossed one to each of the Spinners and said, "Our old key chains are either beat up or lost, so I thought it was about time we had some new ones."

Portagee added, "Cool, these are gyro spinners. Look how fast they spin."

Sam laughed and said, "I wish I had a scooter so I could put a scooter key on my key chain." While Portagee was spinning his key chain he accidentally dropped it on the ground. When he bent down to pick it up, he noticed some funny markings in the centre of the square.

Portagee pointed at the markings. "Look here! What are these marks in the asphalt?" he asked as he looked down at the markings.

Coming from Boston Michael said, "They look like two sets of tracks formed by a horse- drawn snow sled." Everyone laughed.

Graham said, "I'm sure you're going to say that Santa and his reindeer were lost last night in the middle of summer and forced down in Bermuda for an emergency landing during the storm last night."

There was more laughter now. Then Sam waved her arms and said, "Wait a minute you dingbats, Graham may be more right than wrong. What else has a sled type runner?"

Portagee piped in, "My brother's water skis?"

"No silly," replied Sam, "I mean what else flies that has runners?" The boys a stood there with blank looks on their faces. "A helicopter, goofballs,' Sam yelled. "What was a helicopter doing here last night in the middle of the storm?"

But there's no helicopters stationed here anymore," replied Keno.

"I know," replied Sam, "but I bet it has something to do with last night." They sat there thinking about the helicopter theory. But what did Tattoo's ex thugs have to do with a helicopter?

Keno said, "Let's go over to the Supermart and get sodas and chips. I need a snack. All this thinking has made me hungry." Everyone agreed, and they left their scooters and walked. After the soda and chips, the Spinners headed back to their scooters on the opposite side of the square. Sam pointed out all the television news crews and reporters who were beginning to show up to get a glimpse of the Shinbone.

Sam said, "This Island is so small, by now everyone in Bermuda will know what happened here last night. They all think the 'St. Valentines Day' massacre happened here last night, except my daddy says no one got shot. So where did the gangsters go? There's no point in staying here. Half the island will be here by noon." With that, the Spinners hopped on to their scooters and zipped down Water Street. It was time to leave the crowd behind and see what clues they could find elsewhere. Actually looking for clues was just an excuse for the Spinners to zoom around the island and have some fun. The Spinners shot out on York Street. As they approached Mullet Bay, Keno and Michael had flashbacks of their witnessing of the 'Battle of St. George's' on Bartram Island while in the Triangle. That was one of the most horrible days of their young lives. Although the battle that day between the Nazis and the pirates was brief, it was extremely deadly. That was a day that Michael and Keno would like to erase from their memories.

As the Spinners crossed the Swing Bridge leaving St. George's, Keno signaled the group to follow him on the roundabout and turn into St. David's. Without any hesitation, Michael and Graham followed Keno into St. David's Island. It was evident that Keno was heading to his home at the St. David's Lighthouse. When they pulled into the lighthouse parking lot and parked their bikes, Portagee quickly asked Keno, "What's on your mind dude, did you forget something?"

Keno smiled back at Portagee and responded, "All that talk about helicopters made me think that there must have been some radio communications going on last night."

Sam now popped in, "I bet you just happened to have your radio receiver on last night and recorded it, right?"

Keno smiled and added, "You got it baby cakes." Keno and his father had always been interested in radio communications of all kinds. With some of the money from the treasure Keno had purchased state-of-the art transmitting and receiving equipment. Living at the lighthouse gave Keno a very tall structure on which to mount his antennae. This was a great spot to track and pick up signals. They Spinners rushed into the lighthouse and went directly into Keno's room. Keno turned on his computer that he used to record the radio chatter each night. He started playing back the radio transmissions from the previous night. At first it was just the basic stuff you would expect, which just about had the Spinners bored out of their minds. Then when they were ready to give up they heard, "This is Alvaro, meet us at the pickup zone in three minutes."

Sam yelled, "Wait a minute! Pause that and play it again." Keno nodded and did so. "This is Alvaro, meet us at the pickup zone in three minutes."

Michael chimed in, "I don't know who Alvaro is, but I think that might be what someone might say if they were signaling a helicopter in to a pickup point." Everyone agreed and Keno continued with the recording. Soon after that they picked up, "Roger that, boss, over and out."

Keno then paused the recording and said, "That's got to be the response to the first transmission."

Graham added, "I think we can now assume that those tracks in the square were not from Santa Claus."

By now they were all talking at the same time and not paying much attention to the recording. Finally Keno yelled, "Quiet, listen to this one!" Then he replayed the recording. "This is Alvaro, permission to land these dirty birds."

A transmission came back, "Roger that, if you can find us, ha, ha."

Then a quick snap back, "You wise ass." The Spinners continued on, but that was the end of the transmissions. Sam now turned to the others and said, "There's no doubt that we're dealing with helicopters now, but where in the world were they landing?"

Graham responded, "It had to be a ship out to sea somewhere and probably not too far away."

"So what do we do now?" Asked Portagee.

Sam spoke up, "We need to burn these transmissions onto a CD and get them to my dad before he leaves Bermuda today." With that, Keno made the copy and the group hopped on to their scooters and headed back to St. George's.

The Spinners found Inspector Savage walking down Water Street towards King's Square. They quickly filled him in and took him down to the square to show him the black runner marks. After reviewing the marks the Inspector said, "I've got to hand it to you kids. I don't think we would have ever found this clue so far away from the Shinbone. Job well done." He called for a team of officers to get down to the square and preserve the newly found evidence. "Let's all head back to the police station and you can play those transmissions you recorded last night." The Spinners followed the Inspector to his office in the Police Station to play the CD on his computer. After listening to the CD, Savage agreed that it could be a communication from a helicopter to a ship, but why? He also picked up that the transmitters seemed to have Spanish accents, which would also be unusual in Bermuda.

Michael then turned to Portagee and said, "What do you know about this?" Then he winked at the others.

Portagee fired back, "Wait a minute, I'm Portuguese not Spanish, you goober." Everyone laughed. Michael then said he was just kidding.

The Inspector then spoke up, "Thanks for your help. I'll turn this evidence over to my superior. They will probably get the Harbour Patrol and maybe the US Coast Guard involved with these leads. You're all great junior officers, but while I'm off the island, let's leave the crime investigating to the police, OK?" The Spinners all agreed. However, every last one of them they had their fingers crossed behind their backs. Inspector Savage went back to work and the Spinners left the Police Station, hopped on to their scooters and zoom, zoom off they went.

That night Sam, her mum and little sister took her father to Bermuda International. The long overnight flight to London was not a trip the Inspector relished, for as tough as he was, flying was not his favorite pastime.

One at a time he said his good byes to his family. When he got to Sam he said, "Little one, you be sure to stay away from Axil and his thugs and keep the rest of the Spinners on the straight and narrow while I'm away." He then hugged Sam and gave her a kiss on the forehead.

Sam responded, "Yes daddy, we'll keep out of trouble, I promise." The Inspector left and walked through the doorway to his flight. As he cleared the doorway, he turned back and waved goodbye. A tear came to Sam's eye. She knew he was going to be gone for weeks and she was going to miss him, as she had when she was in the Bermuda Triangle. With the Inspector gone, the Spinners would be on their own, to solve the mystery of the 'Shootout at the Shinbone.'

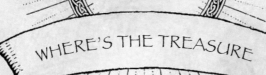

~3~

WHERE'S THE TREASURE

WHERE'S THE TREASURE

The "Bermuda Triangle" is actually another dimension in time. Some might describe it as a "Twilight Zone," or even "Never Land." The apexes of the triangle are Bermuda, Miami, Florida, and San Juan, Puerto Rico. Whatever gateway you enter the triangle, you will find yourself close to being parallel to the same space you left, before you went into the Triangle. In fact, if you entered the Triangle in the Atlantic Ocean, you would still find yourself in the Atlantic Ocean, except in a different dimension. It might take you days or weeks to realize you had been transported. The only clue you would have is that compasses would just spin around in circles and guidance and communication equipment would no longer function. You would be confined to the defined area of the Triangle and would just find yourself going around in circles. If you entered the Triangle on a landmass, such as Bermuda, you would still be in Bermuda, except you might think you were in a distant paradise. The island would be in the pristine state it was over 500 years ago, before anyone ever stepped foot on it. The wild hogs would still be running on the island and if you bothered to notice there would be other extinct animals, birds, plants and fish, to be found.

The only hope of returning to the dimension, from which you came, would be to find a gateway back. The balance of nature in the Triangle is simple. The existing life in the Triangle evolves and reproduces just like our parallel world; however, if you are a species from another dimension, you enter it sterile. Thus, you can exist in the Triangle but you cannot populate it. Interestingly, it is a Never Land in which you will remain the same age as you entered. You can be injured or killed just like anyone in our dimension. You just won't age or contract any disease of our world. While time stands still in the Triangle, it marches on in our dimension. So when you return from the Triangle, you would not re-enter in your time in history. You would find yourself in the time that had lapsed while you were gone. There are few humans alive in the Triangle today. Most people enter the Triangle from airplanes and ships, entering temporary gateways in the middle of the Triangle, the Atlantic Ocean. Most planes run out of fuel before finding any land mass, crash in the ocean and invariably the occupants drown. Most ships usually enter the Triangle through a raging storm or hurricane and are severely damaged on their arrival. They might sink soon after their arrival or even worse, because they cannot find any landmass and without any sense of direction, the sailors and passengers may simply starve to death or die of thirst. This leaves many ghost ships floating around the waters of the Triangle.

The Triangle is truly a paradise when left alone. However, at times, when evil outsiders enter the dimension, the paradisiacal balance is spoiled. In our world, Mother Nature is normally able to maintain a reasonably natural balance. However, for the past three hundred years an overwhelming invasion of evil beings has entered the Triangle.

Many things have changed in the Triangle over the last year. The Pilgrims moved from Spanish Point to the encampment that the pirates had occupied for two hundred years in St. George's. Two Post World War II pilots, Spence and Jason headed the family, who called themselves the Pilgrims. Spence was a US Navy pilot who was captured with his co-pilot by the Nazis in the Triangle. Unfortunately the co-pilot was tortured to death by their captors. Spence had never been able to forget this and was continually tortured with nightmares of his ordeal.

Jason had been much luckier. He was a British fighter pilot on a secret mission when he was lost in the Triangle. Jason was fortunate to be found by the Pilgrims and not the Nazis or pirates.

Three of the Pilgrims were from Louisiana. Bubba, Buford and Cooter, all cousins, were Confederate blockade-runners during the Civil War. They were already crazy long before they were trapped in the Triangle. Being sailors, it was hard to believe that one of them, Cooter could not swim a lick. In fact, if you threw him overboard with a rope tied around his leg, he would make a good ship's anchor. The three of them were excellent trackers and hunters, having grown up in the swamps of Louisiana. Buford tried to look out for the others, but that was easier said than done. To make matters worse, for almost a hundred years they never knew that the South had lost the war, not until Spence told them in the 1950s.

Salty was a peg-legged ship's cook who escaped from Captain Drax. After one hundred years of serving Captain Drax, Salty escaped the pirate encampment and lived in the jungles, until he befriended the Confederate cousins. Over the years their family grew with the additions of Doc, Georgette, Lynn and the pilots.

It was another beautiful day in the Triangle. Everyone in the village woke up with the smell of bacon and eggs floating through every hut. Salty was up early that morning and was feeling very good, so he decided to cook up a storm. Throw in some hot rock baked bread and some bananas, what more could one want for a breakfast in paradise? Needless to say, none of the Pilgrims missed breakfast. When everyone had finished, Jason and Spence thought it was a good time to discuss a subject that they all had neglected for months. Jason now spoke up, "Listen up everyone Spence and I have something to talk about,"

Cooter chimed in, "I hope this is going to be short and sweet, I'm going hog hunting today with Buford and Bubba."

"Don't worry boys, we'll get you out on those trails soon enough," piped back Spence.

Salty said, "You land lubbers will probably just shoot each other anyway."

Bubba fired back, "Now listen here peg leg, if you don't behave there won't be any smoked ribs when we get back."

"OK, OK," Jason said, "let's get down to business. We have this little treasure here, enough to fill up Fort Knox, and it's just sitting in a hut."

Buford asked, "What's Fort Knox?"

Jason responded, "Never mind. The point is sooner or later someone inside or outside of the Triangle is going to come looking for this treasure. We need to hide it, destroy it or just get it the hell out of here. We all saw that Drax would kill anyone who got in his way."

Doc had been quiet up until now, but he decided it was time to ask, "What about the Tucker Cross?"

Spence responded, "We have to protect the Cross no matter what. That's our lifeline with the other world."

Lynn spoke up, "I think we should hide the treasure, but we need to be very careful. It's best that only a few know where the treasure is. We all trust each other, right?" Everyone agreed that only four of the Pilgrims should know the final hiding place of the treasure. They would draw straws; the four straws with burnt ends would be the ones who would hide the treasure.

Jason adjourned the meeting by saying, "Everyone, enjoy your day. Tonight at dusk we'll meet and draw straws to see who gets to work their butts off to hide this treasure over the next few days." With that, everyone broke camp and went off as if it were just another day in paradise.

That night, everyone made it back to the village just at dusk. Georgette was the first to arrive and had already started a fire. Spence started to call the meeting to order. However, Buford interrupted him by saying, "Excuse me folks, while we were out hunting today my cousins and I decided we should be the ones to hide the treasure. So you all can forget drawing the straws, so let's put on the feed bag and eat."

"Wait just a minute!" yelled Spence. "What happened to the democratic way of deciding this?"

Bubba spoke up, "Remember we're just a bunch of Johnny Rebs, we seceded, right?"

"Now hold on to your long johns boys," Jason spoke up, "you need one more person on the team and that's me."

"That's fine with us," Cooter replied. No one felt like arguing. The treasure team had proclaimed themselves and tomorrow they would have a very busy day. As the others finished dinner and cleaned up, the cousins and Jason went off to plan where to hide the treasure.

Sitting down by the bay, Jason asked the cousins if they had any ideas where the treasure should be hidden. Cooter spoke up, "Let's load it on a ship and take the treasure to Richmond. The South needs the money, right boys?"

Jason responded, "And so does the Queen of England. So do you have any real ideas?" The group had a good laugh and Buford went on to tell Jason their idea of where the treasure could be safely hidden.

After hearing the plan Jason said, "Who ever said you boys were 'hicks from the sticks?' That's a great plan this meeting is over. Come on guys drinks are on me." With that, they went back to camp and broke out one of Captain Drax's personal bottles of rum.

The next morning everyone got up extra early to help load the treasure on to an old sailing yacht that the pilgrims had found in the Great Sound earlier in the year and had repaired. The group worked steadily not taking many breaks. By late morning, the treasure was loaded and the ship crew climbed aboard and shoved off.

As they sailed away Salty yelled, "You boys, don't get lost or forget to come back, you hear?"

Bubba looked back and waved, then yelled, "Don't wait up for us, ya hear?" Salty yelled back, a few choice words that the women folk wished they had not heard. Then it was back to their small village and they were able to enjoy the rest of the day.

Several days later at dusk, Georgette looked out over the harbor and saw the old yacht slowly making its way back to the village. She quickly ran over to the old ship's bell hanging from an old ship's rafter between two trees. She began ringing the bell to announce the ship's arrival. The old ship ran ashore. The cousins jumped off the deck and quickly tied the yacht to some old cedar trees. They greeted each other and headed back to see what Salty had made for dinner. Not much was said that night about the treasure, especially where it now was, but you could tell it was a load off all their minds not having "The Lost Treasure of Bermuda" in their village anymore. Yes, life would be good again, or would it?

With the calm and peace that had set in, also came boredom for some of the Pilgrims. The nicely rigged yacht was just docked there in the harbor day after day, causing some of the Pilgrims to get the itch to set sail and see what was over the horizon in the southern region of the Bermuda Triangle. Spence, Georgette, Doc and Lynn had finally decided to make the old yacht seaworthy and give life on the sea a try. After spending weeks of making the old yacht seaworthy, the small group thought they were ready to try out their sea legs. With the preparations complete for a voyage, the Pilgrims christened their yacht the, "Mayflower II." Spence, Georgette, Doc and Lynn had shocked the others when they informed them that they were planning to set sail in the next few days, if prevailing winds were favorable. No one was ready for them to leave. They would plot a course as best as they could for Miami. The sailboat would be equipped with enough rations to sail to Miami and back to Bermuda if necessary. Should they not make land in two weeks, they would return to Bermuda. With that, the "Mayflower II" would set sail on a southwesterly course, in the hope of finding Miami.

As the "Mayflower II" sailed over the horizon, the rest of the Pilgrims left the lookout post overlooking St. George's Island and headed back down to the village to help Salty with dinner. They all hoped they would see their friends again.

-4-

STING OF THE SCORPION

STING OF THE SCORPION

The Pilgrims were a week into their voyage relying on their gut instincts as to where they were sailing. They had the sun and the stars to guide them, but that was all. None of the navigational devices created, would work in the Bermuda Triangle. Spending a week on the open seas without seeing any land-masses can be very intimidating; especially when you only hope you're going in the right direction. The day for the Pilgrims started out being just the same as every day since they had left Bermuda. The wind was good and Spence was behind the wheel at the stern of the yacht maintaining the course on a southwest-erly direction Georgette, Doc and Lynn were at the stern of the yacht trying their luck at fishing. They were line fishing with small balls of bread from loaves that Salty had baked for them. With the stiff wind blowing across the bow, they were really more relaxing than fishing. In fact, if Doc got a hit on his line, it would have disrupted his nap. Spence was simply enjoying the breeze and like Doc, he kept nodding off into a light sleep, waking up each time his head snapped back. On one of those head snaps, Spence looked up out into the ocean where the sea met the sky and thought he saw something on the horizon. Then again, he thought he was dreaming. However, as he began to focus his sleepy eyes, he finally realized there was something out there. Spence jumped up and yelled, "Mates, look a-head. Check it out!"

Georgette and Lynn jumped up and started screaming. Meanwhile poor Doc just about jumped out of his skin. He had been sound asleep. They all strained trying to make out what was out on the horizon.

After coming to his senses, Doc pulled out his telescope and got a closer look. "No doubt it, it's a ship, but I can't tell if they're heading our direction or not."

Lynn quickly spoke up, "Let's make a small fire and hope they'll see the smoke."

Georgette then added, "Great, I'll get the fire pot and we'll start a fire."

Spence then interrupted her, "Whoa, hold on to your horses." Georgette, Doc and Lynn all looked at Spence with puzzled looks on their faces.

Spence, seeing their confusion added, "What the hell if they're a bunch of bloody pirates? Then what are we going to do? We can't outrun a dying porpoise in this old boat."

Doc said, "You're right. But what do we do now?"

Spence replied, "I think all we can do right now is to wait and watch. If they get closer, maybe we can get a closer look before we commit to alerting them."

Lynn quickly pointed and added, "I don't think we will have to wait long. Look the ship is now on a direct course for us."

Spence yelled, "Doc, look again through your telescope, can you see anything?"

Doc looked again, "Yes, I can see more now."

Spence snapped back, "Well, what the hell can you see?"

Doc replied, "It's an old ship, reminds me of the Sea Venture from the sixteen hundreds, except it's got cannons. Oh crap! There's someone in the crow's nest looking at us through a telescope. He's pointing in our direction and they're turning the ship. The cannons are now pointed at us!"

Spence yelled, "Hang on!" He quickly spun the wheel around to switch to a westerly course. He then added, "Look again Doc, do you see a ship's flag? Are they flying the 'Jolly Roger'?"

Doc looked again, "I see it. No, it's not the 'Jolly Roger,' it' much worse!"

Georgette nervously asked, "What do you mean, Doc?"

Doc replied, "It's a white flag with a nasty black Scorpion on it with its stinger dripping red with blood."

Lynn screamed, "Oh my God!"

The Pilgrims had the bad fortune of crossing paths with Scorpion, a Voodoo fanatic from Haiti. Scorpion and her crew had been trapped in the Triangle since 1622. That year, in September, Scorpion's ship the "Venom" was on a direct course to intercept a Spanish treasure fleet that had set sail from Havana. The hurricane struck the Venom sending her and her crew to their untimely entrance into the Bermuda Triangle. The hurricane continued on, sinking or grounding the eight ships of the treasure fleet. Over 500 people on the ships perished

Just then, the ship started firing its cannons at the Pilgrims. Fortunately for them, they were out of range for the moment. Spence yelled out, "Start praying for the wind to die out quickly or in a couple of minutes we'll be in range of their cannons!" But it was already too late. As Spence finished speaking, a cannon ball exploded in the middle of the old yacht. Spence was knocked off his feet. All he could see was smoke, fire and debris being blown through the air in all directions. Spence finally got his wits about him and stood up trying to see through the smoke, and fire, to find his friends, but to no avail. Just as he tried to move through the smoke, another cannon ball exploded in front of him. With the blinding light and the force of the explosion, Spence felt he was flying backwards at the speed of light. Then all of a sudden, he thought he had hit a brick wall. He had hit the water with such a force that it felt like hitting a brick wall. With that, Spence felt that his life was passing from him and all went black, as he sank beneath the waves.

Spence began to come to, but everything was black. He could hear some sounds, but they were muffled. He now realized his eyes were closed. Was he dead? Spence was scared to open his eyes. Then he felt something scratching on his face. He tried to open his eyes but everything was blurred and fuzzy. His eyes began to focus on the object in front of him. He could see an outline of a person. Am I dead?" Spence whispered.

"No, my handsome one, but you might be soon if you're not careful," responded the dark outline. Spence began to focus more clearly. Sitting on his chest was the most beautiful woman he had ever seen. She was dark-skinned with long wavy black hair past her shoulders. Her eyes looked liked black pearls and the whites were not white at all, but blood red. As she leaned over him, a solid gold scorpion necklace dangled over his face.

"What is your name?" she asked.

Spence, still a little fuzzy responded, "Spence, US Navy."

"I see," she said, "where do you hail from?"

"Bermuda," Spence sputtered out.

"Yes, the 'Island of Devils.' Now that's a place I haven't heard anyone speak of in over a hundred years," she added.

Spence began to see things very clearly now. He saw the scorpion flag Doc had described, flapping above the crow's nest. He was in trouble. Realizing this he asked, "Who the hell are you and where are my friends?"

"My, you have a temper, I like that," she replied. Spence tried to get up, but to his surprise, the woman grabbed him by his neck with her right hand and then lifted up her left hand for the first time.

"Holy crap," thought Spence. Her left hand was covered with a black leather glove with scorpion stingers sticking out from the ends of each finger.

"Handsome, my name is Scorpion. I'm the captain of this ship. If you don't settle down, these stingers will drain the life out of you," replied Scorpion. Spence relaxed. Scorpion then said, "That's better." Before she could finish, Spence grabbed her left hand and shoved her stingers deep into her chest. Scorpion let out a scream and fell over backwards. Spence then jumped up, grabbing a saber from the scabbard of one of Scorpion's pirates.

He knew he was outnumbered twenty to one but he still held his ground and screamed, "Where are my friends you murderer?" As he stood there, to his surprise, Scorpion rolled over onto her back and with her right hand pulled the stingers out of her chest, one at a time. With the removal of each stinger, blood flowed from her chest. She then looked up at Spence and smiled, once the last one was removed.

Scorpion stood up in front of Spence, drawing out her saber and said, "You fool! Your friends are gone. Didn't you realize a scorpion is immune to her own poison?" She was right. After being stung by scorpions for over two hundred years, the stings had no effect on her. She pointed her saber at Spence and said, "The choice is yours. You can taste the steel of my saber or the poison of my stingers and die a painful death. I suggest you drop your saber, now!"

Spence knew if she didn't kill him then her shipmates would. So with that he threw down his saber and said, "Each dog has his day. Today's not mine, you witch!"

"Wise decision, tie him to the yard arm!" she screamed. Before he knew what hit, him Spence was mauled by the pirates and tied up. Scorpion approached him and ripped his shirt open exposing his chest. She slid one of her stingers back and forth across his chest, while she talked to him, "The power of the Triangle emanates from Bermuda. I want you to take us there."

"Like hell I will, you witch!" Spence replied. He was not about to unleash this Voodoo killer on his friends back in Bermuda.

"I think you will change your mind. Remember my Voodoo powers, you fool," Scorpion admonished scornfully. Then she leaned forward and kissed him while at the same time digging one of her stingers into Spence's chest. Spence tried to let out a scream, but Scorpion's lips would not let him open up his mouth. After a slight struggle, Spence's head fell forward and he blacked out. Scorpion smiled and blew a strange yellow powder in his face saying, "Very good my darling, you will now slumber into the depths of the undead. You'll join the undead tomorrow and become my zombie slave. Tomorrow, you'll navigate us to Bermuda where I will harness the power of the Triangle." She then reached into her pocket and pulled out a leather necklace with a black scorpion hanging from it. She hung it around Spence's neck and began chanting and waving her arms and hands around Spence's head and body. Scorpion's shipmates quickly moved as far away as they could from Scorpion. None of them wanted any part of the spell to be inflicted upon them. When Scorpion finished her spell she turned and headed for her cabin. Just before she went below she turned and said, "Throw the slave down into the ship's hold and chain him up." Then she turned back and went down below to her cabin.

-5-

SCARZO'S QUEST FOR THE TREASURE

Scarzo's Quest for the Treasure

The next morning, Axil was escorted to the deck of the Prowler where he found Alvaro and Scarzo enjoying their breakfast in the brisk morning air. With the assistance of two shipmates, Axil was forcibly seated at the remaining chair at the small round patio table. As Scarzo began to greet the late arrival, Axil interrupted, demanding, "Where are my mates?"

Scarzo smiled and replied, "We're not sure, Axil. In the middle of the night we believe they jumped overboard in an attempt to escape." Scarzo then turned to Alvaro who nodded in agreement to Scarzo.

Axil just sat there in amazement. He hoped they had. However, he knew deep within, that Scarzo had probably fed them to the sharks the previous night. Not wanting their same fate, he just sat there and said, "Oh."

Scarzo then slapped Axil on the back saying, "Now we'll just have more treasure to divide up between us, right Axil?"

Axil replied, "Yes boss." Then he began to eat his breakfast as if nothing was wrong.

Alvaro spoke up and said, "Today, the three of us are going to take a fast ride on our little baby to St. George's and ask our young friends, the Spinners, a few questions." He pointed over to the speedboat, which was secured in place on the stern of the Prowler and could be easily lowered to the water.

Axil then spoke up, "One of the Spinners is the daughter of Inspector Savage. He's a tough cop, not to be messed around."

Scarzo gave Axil a look that could kill then screamed, "If that cop gets in my way, I'll slit his throat!" He then pulled out a switchblade from his pocket and, in a split second, the blade flipped out as he held it against Axil's throat. "Do you want to see what I can bloody well do with this knife?" Scarzo asked.

Axil shook his head nervously from side to side and said, "No boss." Scarzo and Alvaro then began laughing. Scarzo put the switchblade in his pocket. After they finished eating, Scarzo ordered his crew to lower the speedboat into the water.

The three of them climbed aboard the boat. Scarzo put his hand on the front passenger seat and waved at Axil with his other hand to sit there. Scarzo went to the stern of the boat sat down in the plush back seat, leaned back and lit up a Cuban cigar saying, "Alvaro, Bermuda awaits, let's move out." With that, Alvaro backed the boat out from under the Prowler, turned the steering wheel and threw the throttle all the way forward. The acceleration resembled being blasted like a cannon ball across the water. Axil flipped backwards out of his seat and landed smack on his back. Scarzo laughed and said, "Get off your butt and get back in your seat, or I'll throw you overboard." Axil did as he was told.

At the speed they were going, the ride to Bermuda was going to be very short. As the Island came into view over the horizon, Axil breathed a sigh of relief; he didn't think he would ever see Bermuda again. The speedboat trolled into the harbor at St. Georges shortly after noon. With all the commotion going on at King's Square, they were able to tie up at the dock without being noticed. When they were all off the boat and on the dock, Scarzo spoke up, "Axil, I'm thirsty. Take me to one of the local pubs and we'll lie low for the rest of the day."

Axil smiled and asked, "Would you like to go to the Shinbone? I don't think anyone will notice us there." At that point, Alvaro blasted Axil with a roundhouse right fist that almost knocked Axil to St. David's.

He then reached down and helped pick Axil up off the dock, saying, "Look my brother, you can either join us or join your mates, what will it be?"

Axil wasn't used to being on the receiving end of punishment. He was used to dishing it out to the locals. Axil responded, "I'm with you mates, follow me. There's some rum waiting for us over on Water Street." The deadly trio spent the rest of the afternoon and night drinking to their heart's content and telling lies to each other.

The next morning, Sam was the first one of the Spinners to awake. The Inspector had arrived in the UK and called Sam's mum to let her know he had landed safely. Sam's mum yelled, "Samantha Elizabeth! Your daddy had a good safe flight to England." Now that Sam was awake, she could not get back to sleep. If she was up, the rest of the Spinners were going to wake up too. Sam's mum had left early that morning, for the day with her sister on a church field trip to the Botanical Gardens. Sam knew it was OK to ask her buddies over for breakfast. After all she was good at fixing the "Breakfast of Champions," Cheerios and milk.

After breakfast Michael spoke up, "Well, what are we going to do today?" Everyone spoke up at the same time, pushing for his or her own agenda. Finally,

Sam banged a couple of pans together to get the rest of the Spinner's attention.

"Wait, just a minute guys!" Sam yelled. "Today, police activity around the Shinbone and King's square will be minimal, so let's go there and look for clues." Everyone agreed thinking that it was a good idea. Sam made her buds help her clean up the mess in the kitchen, and then they were off and on their way to King's Square.

The morning had come too early for the treacherous trio. With hangovers from their drinking binge, it took awhile for them to get their wits back. Scarzo spoke up first, "Where the hell are we? I don't remember leaving the bloody bar last night."

Axil replied, "Welcome to my home." It was an old deserted retail shop down at the end of Water Street just off King's Square. The windows had been boarded up from the last hurricane and never removed. The shop was dark, damp and smelled very musty. Alvaro was stirring as he lay on his side on the old wood floor. He finally opened one eye. All he could see were two beady red eyes staring back at him. Totally startled, he jumped up like a rocket and, in an instant, grabbed his long knife from his boot. In a single motion, he threw his knife at the intruder. Just as fast, the large rat avoided the knife and scrambled through a hole in the floor. Axil laughed and said, "You better be more careful. That was my pet rat."

Alvaro grumbled with disgust. He got up and went over to pick up his knife. "I've seen enough of this dump. Let's get the hell out of here and get some breakfast," Scarzo added. The trio went out the back of the shop and went over to one of the pubs on King's Square that regularly served breakfast.

Right after the trio entered the pub, the Spinners came cruising into the square on their scooters. As always, they parked next to the dunking stool, which just happened to be right across the street from the pub. To his amazement, Axil happened to be gazing out the window and saw the Spinners pull in. He then nudged Scarzo and said, "Well I'll be damned! There are those brats the Spinners just across the street. What a stroke of luck! Now we don't have to find them they found us."

"Now tell me their names and who's who," added Scarzo.

Axil quickly responded, "The big dark skinned one is Keno. Be careful with that one, he's as strong as a bear. The little small fry is Portagee. He's the tricky one to watch out for. The tall white boy is Michael. He's a bloody American. I can't stand him. The pretty girl is Sam. Be careful with her. Her daddy is the police inspector of St. George's. And last but not least, is the dark skinned rich kid, Graham. He was rich before they found the treasure."

Scarzo smiled and said, "Very good. After breakfast we'll pay these little brats a visit." He then turned back to his codfish and potatoes and began to eat.

The Spinners locked up their scooters and headed towards the centre of the square. They walked past the sled markings which were now nearly gone. When they were in the centre of the square Michael asked, "Sam what are the odds that we can get a peek in the Shinbone?"

"Slim to none," responded Sam.

Portagee then added, "Look Michael, you and Sam go to the front of the Shinbone and talk to the cops guarding the front and Graham, Keno and I will sneak in the back door. They will never know we were there."

Sam looked at Michael and asked, "What do you think Michael?"

Michael nodded, "I think it will work."

Sam agreed adding, "Listen you guys. Don't touch anything. My dad will kill me if any evidence is tampered with." Keno, Graham and Portagee proceeded. Michael and Sam went the direct route over to the Shinbone while the others took the back alley to get there.

The treacherous trio watched the Spinners as they walked off in two different directions. Axil quipped, "Aren't you guys worried we're going to lose them by just sitting here?"

Alvaro snapped back, "Look stupid, they left their scooters here. How far do you think they're going? Anyway they're now divided into two smaller groups. It will now be easier for us to catch one of the groups." Axil just sat there, keeping his mouth shut.

Michael and Sam reached the Shinbone first. As expected there was one officer watching the pub from the front entrance. When they approached Officer John, he pulled out his night stick and started shaking it at Sam and said, "Miss Savage what are you doing here? Your father warned me that I might see you. You know your father banned you from entering the crime scene."

Sam replied, "But Officer John, I would never disobey my father. We were passing by and just dropped in to say good morning."

"Good morning to you also, now be off with you," replied Officer John.

While Sam and Michael kept Officer John busy chatting, the other three Spinners arrived at the back door of the Shinbone. Graham looked around and could see that there was only one officer watching the Shinbone. Graham then said, "The coast is clear, but let's get inside."

Keno then grabbed the doorknob. "Crap, it's locked," whispered Keno.

Portagee stepped up to the door and then turned to Graham. "Give me your driver's license," he demanded.

Graham whispered back, "What do you want that for? You can't drive yet."

Portagee looked up at him with his eyes crossed and said, "Give me a break you rock head. I'm going to use your license to pick the lock. This lock is at least twenty years old. I should be able to slide the card between the door and the jamb. Then I'll easily depress the latch bolt back into the door and presto!" Graham gave him his license and in seconds the door was wide open.

Keno was amazed, "Can you show me how to open locks like that?"

Portagee just smiled and said, "We'd better get inside. We don't have much time to look around." They all crawled in on their bellies, one after the other until they were inside the bar.

Keno then whispered, "Drinks on me, what can I get you?"

Graham whispered back, "About five to ten in jail if you don't keep quiet." They then crept around the corner of the bar to get a full view of the pub. "Holy Moses!" cried Portagee. As they looked around, they saw the walls were riddled with bullet holes.

Keno added, "There was more gunfire here than we saw in the Bermuda Triangle. The three quickly and quietly crawled around the pub looking for clues, but with no success. As they were crawling out, Portagee saw a shell casing under the bar foot rail. The police must have missed it. Without hesitation he picked it up and crawled out of the pub. After exiting the pub the three walked around the block to Shinbone Alley and made their way back to the front of the Shinbone.

As they neared the pub, Officer John yelled, "Stop! If you come any closer I'm going to call for backup and have you all arrested."

Michael said, "We get the message. You just don't like us. Let's get out of here while we can." Sam waved goodbye as the Spinners walked down Shinbone

Alley. Officer John smiled and waved back.

"OK, OK, what did you guys find out?" asked Sam, as they turned the corner losing sight of the pub.

Graham replied, "Well, the Shinbone doesn't need air conditioning anymore.

It's got more bullet holes in it than a block of Swiss cheese. Other than that, Portagee found only a shell casing." Portagee pulled it out from his pocket and passed it around.

When Sam looked at it she noticed strange lettering on the bottom of the casing. She asked, "What language is this?" and tossed the casing to Graham.

Graham looked at it very closely then said, "It's definitely Russian. So, what's that tell us?"

Michael spoke up quickly, "Nothing, except I bet the guns were Russian military assault weapons. That means these were some really bad dudes who shot up the Shinbone."

Sam added, "But what would they want with Tattoo's thugs?"

"Who knows? But they have them now I'll bet, and I'll bet they're out to sea," Portagee added.

Michael then said, "Do you think they're pirates?"

Graham laughed adding, "Sure! And they came out of the Triangle just to get them."

Sam then said, "I know that's not possible, but what if they came for us and the treasure?"

Graham said, "Yes, but the treasure is gone."

"They don't know that. Plus who knows? Maybe they know there's still a lot more." Sam suggested. With their imaginations running wild, it was time to head back to the scooters.

The trio had long since left the pub on the square. They were now split up staking out three of the four corners of the square. As the Spinners entered the square each member of the trio saw them. The Spinners were moving at a pace, all talking at the same time. Sam, being the observant one, caught a glimpse of a familiar face off to her right. She then nudged Graham in the side and spoke in a softly, "Isn't that Axil standing over there by the corner of the bank?" Graham taking the hint slowly looked out of the corner of his eye and saw that Sam was right. The others never noticed Axil, but Sam and Graham made sure they picked up the pace walking across the square to the scooters. Once back at the scooters, Sam spoke up, "Look guys don't turn around, but Axil is over at the bank watching us. I think he's by himself. I don't see any of his other thugs."

"Why do you think he's watching us and where are his goons?" asked Michael.

"I don't know," replied Sam.

Graham spoke up, "Look, we've got three scooters and we can go three different directions at the same time. There's no way he can follow us."

Portagee called out, "Michael, you and Sam head west on Water Street, Graham, you head out on York Street then to Queen Street. I'll tag along with Keno and we'll head east on Water Street and then up Barrack Hill. Make sure you're not being followed. Then we'll all meet on the other side of Tobacco Bay by Coot Pond." The Spinners all agreed, then hopped on their scooters and shot off in different directions. They cleared the square in seconds. Axil was totally confused and went running towards Scarzo.

When he got to Scarzo, he started babbling. Scarzo grabbed him by the neck and said, "Shut up you idiot, they can't all get away. We'll find them. Go get your car Axil, and track them down."

With the same stupid look on his face Axil replied, "I don't have a car, I don't even have a scooter." By now Alvaro had teamed up with them. After hearing what Axil just said, he rolled his head back in disgust and started swearing in Spanish.

Scarzo said, "Let's just steal one of these cars on the square and get going."

Axil stood there in silence for a few seconds remarking, "Scarzo, they don't steal cars in Bermuda, only scooters."

Scarzo was getting very angry and retorted, "I don't give a rat's butt! We're going to steal a car right now. The cops don't scare me here. They don't even carry guns. Go find a car right now with a key in the ignition." Axil began checking cars until he found one with a key in the ignition. He then waved Scarzo and Alvaro over. As soon as Scarzo saw the car he said, "What the hell is this, a toy car?" It was a sub compact so small that Scarzo would have to sit in the back seat sideways. Axil started to get into the driver's seat only to be shoved out of the way by Alvaro.

Alvaro yelled, "You don't even have a car. I'm not going to trust your driving!" Axil then got into the front passenger's seat. Alvaro then stepped down hard on the gas pedal and blasted out on York Street.

Axil screamed, "Look out! You're on the wrong side of the road!" Alvaro swerved the car back to the other lane, just missing a head on crash with an island bus. "We drive on the left side of the road in Bermuda!" Axil exclaimed.

Scarzo quipped, "Just get this toy car going or I'll kick both of your butts." Alvaro stepped down on the gas heading west on York Street, trying to figure out which way the Spinners had gone.

Meanwhile, the Spinners were independently zigzagging their scooters all over St. George's, making sure Axil would not be able to follow them to their rendezvous point. Michael and Sam were the first to get to the edge of Coot Pond. Keno and Portagee pulled in a couple of minutes later. Graham was not so lucky. He had spun out on some loose gravel at the top of Queen Street and in the spill, his carburetor flooded with gas. It took Graham five minutes to get the scooter started again. By the time he had cut back to Government Hill Road, Alvaro had seen him and was in hot pursuit. Finally, Graham pulled in with the others. They directed him to pull his scooter over with the others, behind a boat that was on its side. Michael said, "What happened to you Graham? We were worried about you." Graham told them what had happened, but before he could finish, they heard a car spinning in the gravel, heading straight for them.

Keno yelled, "It's them! Quickly get across the pond before they get us!" With that, the Spinners ran down to the small dock, jumped into the water and started swimming for their lives. Before the trio could get out of the car, the Spinners were already on the other shoreline. They quickly ran out of sight. Seeing what had just happened, Scarzo started jumping up and down screaming, "Where the hell are they going?"

Axil half panicked, yelled back, "They're heading for the fort!" Scarzo pulled out his 357-magnum pistol and pointed it at Axil.

Axil knew his life was now over, but to his surprise Scarzo yelled at him, "I hope you can swim, you have two seconds to go in after them." Without hesitation, Axil jumped off the dock and started swimming after the Spinners. Scarzo turned to Alvaro and said, "Let's get in the car and see if we can cut them off."

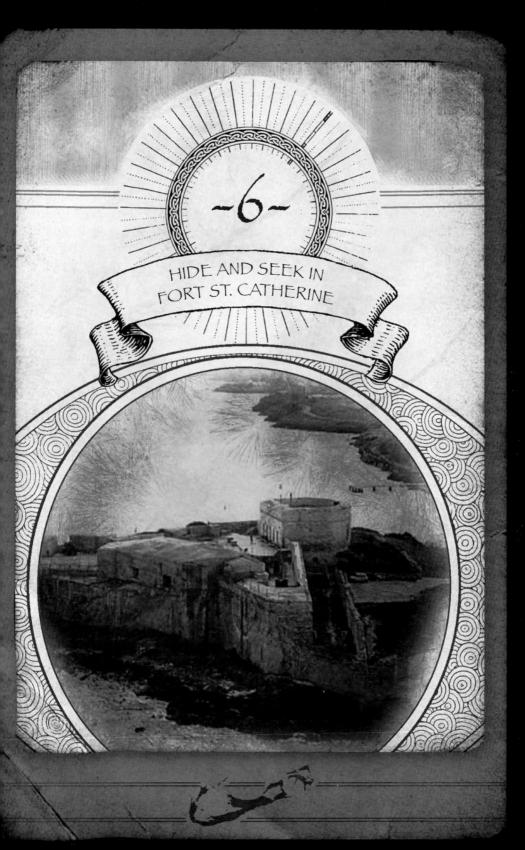

~6~

HIDE AND SEEK IN FORT ST. CATHERINE

HIDE AND SEEK IN FORT ST. CATHERINE

The Spinners knew their only option was to head for Fort St. Catherine. They quickly paid their entrance fee and entered the fort. Instead of going through the main entryway, which would have taken them underground in the long passages, they stayed on the above ground level portion of the fort. The fort was almost four hundred years old and was a massive stone structure. This fort sat on the north shore of St. George's, surrounded on two sides by the ocean. The fort had many dark and confusing underground corridors. Although it was only one hour before closing, there were still lots of tourists. This helped the Spinners to mill around the fort without being noticed. They quickly ran for the southwest wall of the fort and sneaked a peek over the wall to see where Axil was. At first they saw nothing. Then Sam pointed down to the green on the golf course and there was Axil huffing and puffing trying to catch up with the Spinners. Portagee already had his miniature telescope out looking for the car. By the time he spotted it, the car had already turned up the road heading in their direction. To their surprise, the car pulled over into the beach parking lot down below the fort. The two men in the car quickly scrambled out, one of them walked halfway up the road to the fort while the other one walked down to the beach looking up at the fort. The Spinners now sat down behind the wall. Michael was the first to speak up, "They're just going to wait us out and get us when we leave the fort. With the three of them spread out, we don't have a ghost of a chance."

Graham added, "Speaking of ghosts, do you think Ghost George will help us out?" The fort was believed to have been haunted by a ghost named George. No one really knew of his origins, but the Spinners believed he was one of the British soldiers who died on that fateful day of the "Great Hurricane of 1780." It was on that day that Captain Drax hid the treasure in Tobacco Bay. A fierce gun battle broke out between the pirates and the British shore patrol. A musket ball striking his temple fatally wounded the young soldier. At the moment of death, the explosion in the cave occurred, in addition to the vacuum of the Bermuda Triangle. This caused the poor soul to be trapped in an unending earthly existence. Apparently the soldier's ghost still occupies Fort St. Catherine, where he haunts the fort and protects it and its treasures from pirates and thieves.

Sam said, "Very funny. Not to change the subject, but who are those other two guys down there? They look pretty vicious." With only about thirty minutes before closing, the Spinners knew they were going to have to go down into the underground passages and hide until the fort closed. Then they might be able sneak out under the cover of darkness.

Once they were down in the dark hallways waiting for the fort to close, Graham reminded the others, "Did you forget that tomorrow morning the Pilgrims in the Triangle will be opening the gateway and sending out a GPS message?" They agreed that they had all forgotten which made matters worse. Being down in the corridors, they had over twenty feet of stone, masonry and brick above them. Needless to say their cell phones, which were still working after the swim in the ocean had nothing to offer, but black screens.

Axil knew he could not go into the fort. The security guards would instantly know him. Scarzo now signaled the other two to come down to him. Once they arrived Scarzo said, "It's evident they're not coming out until after the fort visiting hours are over. Alvaro, take the car and go back to Tobacco Bay and make sure their scooters are still there and then hurry back here. Axil, you stay up close, but just out of sight to see if they try to sneak out." They moved out and waited for the fort to close.

The fort had now closed and all the employees had been gone for more than thirty minutes. Alvaro had returned from Tobacco Bay to tell Scarzo that the scooters were still there. It was clear to Scarzo that the Spinners were hiding somewhere in the fort. The treacherous trio now openly walked up to the front gate of the fort. The entrance had a heavy wood, padlocked gate opening to a bridge over a ten-foot deep empty moat and then another heavy wood padlocked gate. Scarzo was not concerned about the two padlocks. He could destroy them both in a couple of minutes. He was more concerned about a passerby or a nighttime security guard seeing that the front gates had been opened. He looked around to see how they might enter the fort without going through the front gate. Scarzo soon found the way. He pointed to the northwest corner of the fort and said, "There we are brothers. We'll slide down the outer wall into the moat, then at the outer corner we'll crawl up the inclined wall. It's only about ten feet high there, let's go." They slid down the outer wall into the moat, and walked down to the end of the moat. The rocks and ocean were thirty feet below. Any fall from here would be certain death. Scarzo said, "Don't look down while you're climbing up the wall. It might just be the last thing you see." He then climbed cautiously up the wall with the others slowly following him.

Once inside the fort, they spread out checking every nook and cranny they could find. By now it was getting dark and very hard to see. Axil was sure that the Spinners must be down below in the network of corridors. Scarzo asked, "Look, all the gates and doors are padlocked, how do we know which one to go down and then how to find them?"

Axil had a trick up his sleeve to locate the Spinners; the shell lifts. He walked over to one then said, "Look here, these are old shell lifts which were used years ago to bring up shells from below to be used in the cannons. They were never sealed off so they're a perfect listening device to hear anyone talking below."

Alvaro replied, "Now I know why Scarzo did not kill you, you're a keeper." They quietly split up and went to every shell lift to listen for voices. Finally Scarzo heard voices below. He was listening at the shell lift door between gun three and gun four. He snapped his fingers for the other two to come over and listen.

After Axil listened he said, "Well I'll be damned if it's not the Spinners." Axil showed them the exit doorway that tourists would use when coming up from the corridors below. Just like the other doors, it was padlocked. Scarzo quickly put his silencer on his pistol and blew the lock open. They noise of the door being blown open echoed down through the passageways below.

The noise startled the Spinners and Keno asked, "What the heck was that?"

Sam shushed him, "Be quite and listen," she said. No sooner had the trio blown open the first door, than they came upon a second padlocked gate.

Scarzo was fuming now, "How many more damn gates are there?"

Axil replied, "This is the last one boss." Scarzo then pulled out his pistol and blew the gate open. Because it was at the opening of the corridor going downstairs, it made twice as much noise.

The Spinners shuddered at its noise and Michael said, "Oh crap, they're blowing open the doors and will be down here any second." All went silent, not knowing what to do.

The door opening was now wide open for the trio, Scarzo gave Axil the go ahead to lead the way. Axil just stood there frozen in his tracks. Scarzo looked at him and asked, "What's the matter now?"

Axil finally looked up and said, "This fort is haunted. There's a ghost down there."

Alvaro just stood there shaking his head as he asked, "What the hell did you just say?"

"It's… it's ghost George, he's down there," quivered Axil.

Scarzo grabbed Axil by the shirt collar and shoved him down several stairs muttering, "Well, no matter what, he'll get your sorry soul first."

He started to pull out his pistol, but Axil, seeing what he was doing yelled, "O-K, O-K, I'm going!" The other two started down the stairs behind Axil. It was not completely dark since a few low wattage lights were always left on. This made the corridors spooky, with the shadows and dark spots flickering like a spider web on the corridor walls.

The Spinners knew they might easily be trapped. They were in the corridor closest to the main entrance of the network, which was padlocked from the other side. Their only way out was through the exit corridor, but to get there they would have to face Axil. The Spinners agreed to split up. Two of them went along the corridor and turned into the Shell Corridor to see if Axil was heading in that direction. They quickly slipped past the Way Out Corridor. They knew Axil would be coming down that corridor by this time. They turned into a room called the Cartridge Store for gun six and seven that was directly above them. Here, there was a very small doorway passage called the Issuing Hatch, which would get them back to where they had left the other Spinners. Portagee was part of this group. He decided to check out another room just across the corridor. When he turned the corner, he was so scared he froze. He thought he saw a ghost, but after a few seconds, he realized it was an old suit of armor standing in the corner. After getting his composure back, he turned around and went back to the Cartridge Storeroom and waited with his friends. The other three Spinners were now on the other side of the thick wall so they could see and communicate with each other through the Issuing Hatch passage. The Deadly Trio was now in the Way Out Corridor and quickly came to the Shell Corridor. They had to turn right or left. They went right, going towards the Cartridge Storeroom. The Spinners heard them coming and quickly shot through the Issuing Hatch passage. By the time the trio entered the room the Spinners were gone. The trio went on to the third room at this end of the Shell Corridor. It was the Antique Weapons room. Scarzo and Alvaro were amazed at the small collection of rifles, muskets, swords, knives and pistols. Scarzo turned to Alvaro and said, "We will come back another day and visit this room." Alvaro knew what he meant and nodded his head in agreement. They then turned to the third room in the corridor and Scarzo asked Axil, "What's in that room?"

"That's Ghost George's room," Axil replied.

Alvaro laughed and went in. After a few moments he came back out and said, "You fool. That's just a haunted house display."

The trio headed back up to the other end of the Shell Corridor, checking all the rooms as they went looking for the Spinners. Just as they turned the corner to enter the Entryway Corridor, the Spinners heard them coming and all quickly went though the Issuing Hatch passage back into the Cartridge Room. Scarzo heard some footsteps. He knew they were being eluded. He sent Alvaro down the Entry Way Corridor to see what he could find. Scarzo told Axil to go through the Issuing Hatch passage while he backtracked down the Shell Corridor. The Spinners were not expecting Axil. They moved into the Ghost George room where it was very dark making it easy to conceal themselves. Axil thought he heard a noise in the Ghost room, but was too scared to enter. He knew though if he didn't go in, Scarzo would kill him. Axil mustered up the courage to enter the room. It was lightless. He just stood there listening, but there were no sounds to be heard. Then, all of a sudden, the most ghastly screaming erupted from all sides.

A damp gust of wind almost knocked Axil off his feet. He staggered briefly and then went running out of the room screaming, "Help, help! George is trying to kill me!" The Spinners, who were extremely frightened, sat there and did not move a muscle until Axil was gone. Axil ran down the corridor so quickly that when he turned the corner he ran smack into Scarzo and knocked both of them flat. The Spinners decided it was a very good time to leave Ghost George to himself. They found their way back to the Cartridge Room. Having now lost all sense of where the trio was, they made the decision that Portagee and Keno would try to escape out the Way Out Corridor and try to get back to the surface of the fort. The other three would stay where they were and use the Issuing Hatch passage if needed. Portagee and Keno made it to the upper level and found the doors had been busted open. They realized this would become their escape route. They had to go back and get the others. Back tracking down the winding stairway, they heard Scarzo and Axil talking around the corner. They had to stop and wait to see what would transpire. The other three Spinners had also heard Scarzo and felt it was time to go back through the Issuing Hatch passage. Sam went through first. Michael and Graham were not watching her. Instead they were watching their backsides for any hint of Scarzo. They turned around and saw that Sam was already through the passage and out of sight. Michael went through. As he looked up he saw Alvaro standing there holding Sam with a knife against her throat. It was too late for Michael to retreat, but Graham was still on the other side. He turned to run, but was stopped quickly by two large bodies: Axil and Scarzo. Alvaro escorted Michael and Sam the long way through the corridors back to the Cartridge Room.

Portagee and Keno now realized that Scarzo had captured their friends. They had heard how Scarzo had demanded to know where the others were. Michael was quick to tell him that there was no one else. Portagee signaled to Keno to follow him out of the corridors and back to the surface of the fort. No sooner than they were outside, Keno spoke up, "What can we do for our friends trapped down there?"

Portagee responded, "Let's wait it out. When they come out we'll follow them and at that point try to figure out what to do."

Keno said, "Ok, but where can we hide?" Portagee looked around the corner and pointed to gun seven which was a large cannon in a dark corner of that bunker.

"There's the spot. We'll hide under the cannon and wait for them," said Portagee. Both boys crawled under the cannon and waited.

Meanwhile Scarzo, loosing patience with the three Spinners said, "I'm getting bored with this. Take the brats to the surface. We'll deal with them there." The Spinners were escorted to the surface with Alvaro in front and Axil behind them. Once back on the surface of the fort, Scarzo pointed to the north-east corner and said, "Take them over there. I'll ask them a few more questions." From this spot in the fort, the only thing that was between the Spinners and thirty-foot drop to the rock and the ocean was a one-inch steel guardrail. Scarzo asked, "Where can we find the rest of the treasure?"

Michael spoke up, "There is no more treasure."

Axil was quick to respond, "Bull, there's more and it's hidden in Shark Hole. They have the entrance barred up."

Michael added, "You're a liar. There's no treasure in Shark Hole." Michael was correct there was no treasure in Shark Hole; it was in the Bermuda Triangle.

Scarzo added, "Enough of these games. Show these kids we mean business. Use the girl as an example." Axil and Alvaro then grabbed Sam. They flipped her upside down and each thug held her by an ankle over the edge of the fort wall.

Scarzo smiled saying, "You have 30 seconds to be honest with me or my friends will let her drop to her death. I want to know everything, now!" Michael and Graham knew he would drop Sam if they didn't speak up.

Graham spoke first, "OK, you bastards. Bring Sam back in and I'll tell you what you want to know." Scarzo nodded. Axil and Alvaro quickly brought her back in and then dropped her on the concrete. Michael and Graham picked Sam up and made sure she was OK. Then, for the next thirty minutes, the Spinners reluctantly told Scarzo most of the details of Shark Hole and how it was the gateway to the Bermuda Triangle.

Scarzo now knew a limited amount of details concerning the triangle and that the next day the gateway would be open. He had no concept of what to expect on the other side. He seemed to think it was going to be wall-to-wall treasure. Scarzo had heard enough and said, "Escort our new friends out to the car. We need to get back to the boat and prepare for tomorrow." The two thugs shoved the Spinners in the direction of the main gates to the fort. On their way to the gate they all passed gun seven where Portagee and Keno were hiding. They remained as quiet as church mice as the others passed by.

At the gate Scarzo declared, "Now I don't care if the gates are blown open." He then took his pistol out and blasted the padlocks off both gates. Just before the group left the fort, Scarzo turned around, threatening, "Listen up you two cowards, I know you're still here and I know you can hear me. So help me God, if one word of this gets out to the authorities, your friends will be dead in a minute." He then pulled out his pistol and pressed the barrel to the temple of Graham and said, "BANG!" Graham dropped to his knees thinking he had just been shot. Scarzo laughed and yelled at Graham, "Get up you dog!" Alvaro jerked Graham back to his feet and shoved him towards the gate. The rest followed quickly. As Scarzo walked away he said, "Don't forget what I said and don't underestimate me if you want to see your friends alive ever again." The group left the fort and went down to the car.

Keno and Portagee were quick to follow at a safe distance behind. When they reached the car it was evident to Axil that not everyone was going to fit into the tiny car. Axil asked, "Who's going to ride back to the harbor and who's going to walk?"

Scarzo laughed saying, "Nobody is going to walk. In fact, Alvaro, open up the trunk for Axil to ride in." Axil just smirked and climbed into the trunk once Alvaro opened it. The Spinners crowded into the back seat while Alvaro and Scarzo got into the front. They sped out on Coot Pond Road and headed back to the harbour. Portagee and Keno heard where they were going and quickly ran back to Tobacco Bay to get Keno's scooter.

~7~

TERROR IN THE HOLD

TERROR IN THE HOLD

Life in the Triangle had been eerily quiet since Doc, Spence, Georgette and Lynn had set sail for the southern region of the Bermuda Triangle. The cousins and Jason needed to get out and find some action. As usual, Salty had fixed the boys their favorite Bermuda breakfast, codfish and potatoes. They had never had potatoes there before now. The Spinners had sent a 25-pound bag through the Shark Hole gateway the previous month. Salty was planning to start growing them the next season using some of the spuds. After breakfast, Jason asked the boys, "Who wants to sail over to the Great Sound and see what the last storm has washed ashore?"

Salty replied, "I don't have time for such nonsense, that is, unless you find some nice mellow Puerto Rican rum to bring back."

Cooter added, "You bet Salty, we'll even bring you back Long John Silver's peg leg." Jason, Buford and Bubba all laughed while Salty said a few choice four-letter words as he shuffled back to his hut.

Buford said, "The winds look favorable for sailing today. Let's clean up this breakfast mess for Salty." Everyone got up and cleaned the dishes, throwing the leftovers out in the tall grass as a treat for the wild hogs and chickens.

Bubba added, "I wish we had some hunting dogs to feed these leftovers." The three cousins all missed the companionship of their dogs back in Louisiana. No one else said a word. Jason just smiled to himself and they all kept working.

Within the hour they were sailing for the Great Sound in their old Bermuda sloop. They had been lucky a few months before and found the old sloop tied up in Mullet Bay. Salty had figured that Captain Drax had hidden it as his escape vessel if he ever needed one. The morning was a perfectly clear day for sailing. The turquoise ocean had ripples of wind whisking along the surface. The old sloop was slicing through the water as if it were butter. Surely if she had feelings, today she would feel she was in her prime. The sloop sailed into the Great Sound at a record speed. Jason signaled the cousins to slow her down so they could watch out for the tricky reefs and any signs of new ships in the Sound. Everyone was watching different shorelines for new ships hung up on the shore or even just floating around the Sound like ghost ships. Cooter was getting impatient. After about an hour of looking he said, "All this looking is making me mighty hungry. Did Salty pack us any grub today?"

Buford responded, "If you spent as much time looking for lost ships as you do thinking about food, we would have found one by now."

Cooter smirked back at him saying, "Shut up, or I'll make fish bait out of you and I'll catch my own lunch."

Jason added, "You may have to do that Cooter. We left port before Salty could bring us any food to take. So I guess we're going to dine out for lunch today. Anyone have a favorite restaurant they want to patronize?"

Cooter was just about to get up and throw Jason overboard when Bubba yelled out, "Ship astern. It's a new one. It looks like it's hung up on a small reef." Everyone turned his or her attention to the ship. It was not an old ship at all. In fact it was very new. Maybe it had entered the Bermuda Triangle during the hurricane in the last month.

Jason spoke up, "Let's be careful boys. We don't know if the ship is abandoned or not." This was always the most dangerous way of finding a new ship. If you found someone on board you never knew if they were going to be friend or foe. The ship could even be 'booby trapped'. The cousins tied up next to the ship. It must have been a fishing ship. It was not very large, but still much bigger than a sailboat. Being hung up on the small reef had taken its toll. There was a pretty good gash in the starboard gunnel of the ship just below the water line. The ship would probably sink in the next twenty-four hours. Once the sloop had been tied up to the ship, Jason, Cooter and Bubba climbed aboard to look around. Buford stayed aboard the sloop for security reasons and kept a wary eye out for surprise visitors. His musket was cocked and ready for action. The three on board did not take their muskets. It would be too dangerous when climbing around the ship. Jason had his saber and Cooter had a dagger he had taken from one of the pirates last year. Bubba had a Bowie Knife, which he had fashioned from an old Arabian sword he had found. The Bowie Knife was a hunting knife that was almost the size of a saber, except much more intimidating. Jim Bowie, who had fought and died in the Alamo, had created the Bowie Knife. He was one of Bubba's heroes.

The ship was rocking from being hung up on the reef, so it was hard to maintain one's balance. The deck was deserted with only debris scattered across, nothing of value, just old ropes, shredded sails and sea trash. Jason checked the cabin area and ship's galley. They would be able to salvage some items from the ship. The only place they had not checked yet was the ship's hold. Since it was apparent that this was an old fishing boat there was not much hope of finding anything of interest down there. It was left for last. No survivors were found; in fact there was no evidence that any one board had survived the storm that had brought them into the triangle. The Pilgrims were on their way over to check out the ship's hold. The ship's hold was not covered. The storm must have blown the cover away. All three of the Pilgrims leaned over the edge looking down into the large black hold but it was hopeless to see anything down there. Jason was the first to speak up, "It looks like a fifteen foot drop down there. Who wants to go down first?" Cooter and Bubba looked at each other.

Then finally Cooter spoke up, "I reckon that will be me."

"Good idea," added Bubba.

Jason paused and said, "Did you guys hear that?"

"Hear what?" Cooter replied.

"That noise down there, something moving around down there in the water."

Bubba yelled, "Who's down there? Speak up before we torch this old tub." They heard some more movement, but no response.

Jason said, "Bubba go back to the sloop and get your musket." He picked up an old rope on the deck of the ship and threw it to Cooter. Cooter was on the opposite side of the ship's hold from Jason and just as he reached over to grab the rope, the ship rocked violently from a wave and Cooter fell into the ship's hold. Jason heard the splash as Cooter hit the water that was flooding the ship's hull. Jason turned and yelled, "Bubba forget the musket. Get back here. Cooter just fell in the ship's hold. See if you can find a rope." Jason turned back to the ship's hold, but it was still too dark down there to see anything, but he could hear Cooter splashing around in the water. "Cooter, can you hear me?" asked Jason.

Cooter, in a panic replied, "I can't swim! Get me out of here!"

"Cooter, listen to me," Jason said. "Stand up. The water won't be that deep." Cooter calmed down when he realized he could stand up.

Now that he was standing, he yelled up to Jason, "Dag nab it Jason, get me out of here."

"Hang on Coot, Bubba's getting a rope," answered Jason. Cooter looked around in the darkness. He could not see anything but he could hear something. He heard growling on either side of him.

Cooter yelled up, "There're bears down here. I can hear them."

By now Bubba had returned with a rope. As he threw one end down to Cooter he said, "Coot, you're not in Louisiana, there's no black bears here." Before Cooter could reply, the large figures jumped at him out of the darkness.

Cooter screamed, "They're attacking me, they're clawing and biting me!" Without giving it another thought Bubba jumped down into the hold to save his cousin and Jason quickly slid down the rope to catch up with him. In the confusion of pushing off the dark attackers, Jason realized he wasn't being bitten, instead he was being licked.

Jason yelled out, "Hold on guys, stop you're scrapping!" He pulled a match out of his pocket and lit it. To the shock of the Pilgrims they realized that their attackers weren't bears as Cooter thought. Instead they were two large Labrador Retrievers. Although they were large dogs, they had also lost quite a bit of weight. They weren't attacking the Pilgrims; they were just excited to see them. Jason said, "Look guys, these are big Labs, not bears." Cooter was embarrassed. All he could do was hug one of the big dogs.

Soon after, Buford boarded the ship and helped pull his friends and the labs up out of the dark ship's hold. Once they were all on the ship's deck Jason knew it was a miracle that these dogs were even alive. They had evidently lived for who knows how long by eating old fish that had been netted by the previous occupants. The labs had also found other supplies to eat in the ship's hold. One of the labs was chocolate in color while the other was a black one.

As they played and made friends with the labs, Buford spoke up, "These big pups need names, anyone got an idea?"

Bubba spoke up very quickly, "Yes, let's call the big chocolate one 'Grizzly' and his black buddy 'Bear.' That will wake people up when we call them."

Cooter added, "Yep, I can see it now. Here Grizzly Bear, then hearing a rumble through the jungle, that would scare the hell out of anyone." They all laughed and so it was that their newfound friends were to be called Grizzly and Bear. The Pilgrim took what they could find worth salvaging, but the pickings were pretty slim on this ship. At the rate the ship was taking on water it would not be afloat by this time tomorrow.

As they threw off the ropes from the ship Jason said, "Guys take a look at that, talk about a real mind popper." He pointed at the ship's name painted on its side, 'The Labrador.'

Cooter responded, "Well hot damn fellows, the ship was named after you." Then he reached over and petted both Grizzly and Bear.

Jason just laughed and then yelled, "Let's set sail for home mates, daylight is burning and our new shipmates are mighty hungry." The sloop cleared the Great Sound in about fifteen minutes, as they made their way out into the ocean and set coarse for St. George's. Jason had time to reflect about his friends who were on the Mayflower II and wondered how their voyage was going. Little did he know that the Venom was on a direct course for Bermuda now, with his good friend Spence onboard.

Grizzly and Bear were having a great time with their newfound friends. They were up one side of the sloop and down the other. You could tell they felt at home on a ship just by the way they handled themselves. When they weren't running about, they were checking out every "nook and cranny" on the sloop. Jason and the others were enjoying the trip back to St. Georges, because the dogs added so much life and excitement to the sloop.

It was dusk by the time they docked in St. Georges. Bubba could see smoke coming from the mess hut, which indicated that Salty was cooking dinner. The cousins decided to let Grizzly and Bear off the sloop. They knew as hungry as they were, the dogs would smell Salty's dinner and head straight for the mess hut. Salty just happened to look up and saw two large dark figures on a dead run to the hut. He didn't have a clue what they were, but wasn't going to take any chances. He quickly moved over to the wall to grab his musket. Grizzly and Bear charged through the doorway barking at Salty. The barking startled Salty, causing him to trip and fall before he could get to his musket. As he tried to pick himself up, the dogs were all over him barking and licking him. By now the others were on the scene and all ran over to help get Salty up. Grizzly was busy licking Salty in the face while Bear thought his peg leg was a bone and was chewing on it. Finally Salty was back up and figured out what had just happened. He then said, "These big dogs scared the hell out of me. Thank goodness they're friendly." He then reached over and started rubbing the sides of both dogs. The other Pilgrims apologized to Salty for the big surprise. Salty had been roasting a hog for dinner. With the help of Cooter and Jason, they brought the fixings for dinner. Salty then said, "Boy, there's plenty to go around so give these skinny pups all the hog they can eat." Grizzly and Bear must have thought they were in heaven with all this food and newfound friends. After dinner Cooter, Bubba and Buford took Grizzly and Bear to their hut to spend the night.

~8~

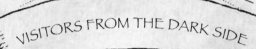

VISITORS FROM THE DARK SIDE

VISITORS FROM THE DARK SIDE

The Venom was sailing by the sun and stars. Scorpion had the ship on a direct course for Bermuda. During those times over the last week, when Spence was fading in and out of the zombie state, Scorpion was extracting navigational information from him. Spence, a trained military pilot was able to resist some of the brainwashing and drugs that he had been given. He had prayed that when the ship arrived in Bermuda, he would be able to somehow jump overboard and warn his friends of the impending danger that was soon to be unleashed upon them. Scorpion was a seductive and beautiful woman. She had taken a liking to Spence. He was much taller than most men of her time, plus she thought he was very handsome. Now that she was on course for Bermuda, this was probably the only thing that was keeping Spence alive. Spence had asked one of the crew members why there were no other women on board. His reply to Spence was that Scorpion was a very jealous woman and would kill anyone who might threaten her status.

Each night on the ship for Spence was a blur. Scorpion would have him brought up to her cabin from the hold, to have dinner. His hands were always chained together so he was helpless to protect himself when she would blow the powder in his face. While the room was spinning he could hear music and the crew chanting from the deck and he assumed drinking rum. Spence had not a clue what was happening on this ship of death from Haiti. Nor could he figure out what the draw was for Scorpion in Bermuda. She was not a treasure seeker, but a power seeker. Maybe she knew something about harnessing the power of the Bermuda Triangle. If so, she would be looking for a gateway, which was a tremendous source of power. Spence thought they must be less than a day out of Bermuda. If he could, he was going to get Scorpion to sail into the Great Sound. When they passed Saltus Island he would jump over board. Spence would then head for the shoreline at Soncy Cove, which had a hidden entrance to the Sound. They would never find him. He could then travel across the interior part of the island and warn his friends. Spence had the feeling they were closing in on Bermuda, but in his zombie-induced state he just couldn't be sure.

That morning, Spence woke up abruptly hearing yelling and the sound of footsteps running all over the deck of the ship. He wanted to get up, but he knew he was chained to a rafter in the ship's hold. He stood up and moved towards the stairs to try to get a closer look at what all the commotion was about. To his surprise, when he edged along with caution, the chain wasn't holding him back. He looked back, and to his amazement, the chain was not padlocked to the rafter. Someone had unlocked his chain in the middle of the night. Spence quickly picked up the excess chain, threw it over his back and scurried up the stairway. As he was clearing the stairs, he could see the entire crew was at the bow of the ship looking forward. Before he could reach the bow he heard a voice from the stern of the ship. "Good morning my darling. Come back here and be with me as we near Bermuda." Spence knew it was Scorpion speaking. He also knew he'd better obey her. Scorpion smiled as Spence joined her. She added, "Soon we will be able to see the shoreline of Bermuda. I will then need you to point out the safe channels and a safe landing port." Spence nodded approval and kept gazing at the horizon.

Spence had another problem. With these heavy old chains draped on him, what chance did he have trying to swim to shore? He would probably sink, like a rock, to the bottom of the Sound. The ship was nearing the Island. Scorpion put her arm around Spence and asked, "Where is our safe harbour, my slave?" Spence pointed in the direction of a small narrow tip of the Island. He called this spot the old Nazi encampment, whereas the Spinners would have called it the Royal Naval Dockyard. Scorpion then asked, "Is this where your friends are?"

Spence replied, "No, they're further up the coast, but it's going to be dark soon and we need to set ashore. In the dark, the reefs surrounding the Island are extremely dangerous."

"Very well," replied Scorpion. She commanded her crew to turn the ship toward the old Nazi encampment. Turning back to Spence, she added, "If you have any tricks up your sleeve, my mate, you will find yourself buried alive." She kissed him on the cheek and dug her stingers into his face, causing blood to flow. Spence jerked back. He was sure she meant what she said.

As they lay off the shore of the encampment, waiting for the crew to lower several longboats, Scorpion asked Spence, "Where exactly are we going to find your friends?"

Spence thought for a split second, turned and pointed, "Over there on the other side of the bay." He was pointing at Spanish Point. He added, "See that point on the land? That's the Pilgrims' home." He really meant that used to be the Pilgrims' home before the pirates burned it to the ground.

Scorpion replied, "That's good. Tomorrow morning we will pay them a visit." Spence thought to himself, if that happens then he'd find himself buried alive. He was going to have to escape before dawn.

Spence then asked Scorpion, "What is it you want with my friends anyway and what do you really expect to find here?"

Scorpion replied, "You fool, I care very little about your friends, but I may need them just as I have needed you. What do I expect to find here? Power you fool, I can already sense the power of the Triangle here. The source of the Triangle's power is here, I can feel its energy. In fact, I can feel the life force of a very evil man on this Island right now. He's waiting to become a slave of mine. Once I find the source, the power of the world will be mine!"

Spence thought to himself, "Oh crap, this lady is nuts." Spence boarded the longboat with Scorpion. After he sat down he raised his arms up to her and asked, "Would you please remove these damn chains from me? I'm not going anywhere, or at least take off this six foot long chain from around my body." Scorpion smiled then signaled one of her cutthroats to remove the long chain from him.

She then said, "I trust you about as far as I can throw this chain, but remember you're my zombie slave." She leaned over as if she was going to kiss Spence. Instead she quickly blew a puff of the mustard colored powder into his face. She laughed and said, "Relax, enjoy your ride ashore." Spence's head was spinning now. All he could do was fall over onto the floor of the longboat to help stop the spinning. Scorpion recognized that Spence was a very strong willed man and, unlike most, he could not be manipulated like a zombie, as most men could. However, the zombie powder still had an overwhelming effect on Spence, making him unable to function.

When the longboats ran ashore, one of the crewmembers yelled, "Look Scorpion, there's a grounded whale over there. It's huge!" After the longboats were secured, they all walked slowly over to the whale. They were all being very careful just in case it was still alive. Needless to say, what they thought was a beached whale, was really the old Nazi s submarine. The only way the old sub was going to move was if a hurricane moved it.

As they got closer to the sub, Scorpion knew this was not a whale. She then said, "Idiots, this isn't a whale." She drew out her saber and banged it with the butt end of the saber's handle. Not only did it sound like iron, it sounded hollow. "See, its some type of ship wreck. Let's make camp. I'm tired. Tomorrow, we'll look closer at this ship and then we'll discover the secrets of the Bermuda Triangle." Everything was still a blur for Spence. He knew that he was running out of time to escape, so he had to make his move soon.

The next morning, the Venom's crew were breaking up camp and getting the longboats ready for a departure to Spanish Point. Meanwhile, Scorpion was still engaged with the idea of viewing a close-up of the grounded ship. She went over to Spence and began tapping on his side with her foot. Spence finally rolled over, looked up and said, "What the hell do you want missy? I'm trying to sleep." Scorpion instantly reacted by kicking Spence in the side as hard as she could. Spence screamed in pain, but this was part of his new plan to escape by upsetting Scorpion.

She then said, "Get your sorry butt up, I want to see this shipwreck now!"

Spence got up slowly and said, "Follow me up this ladder and I'll give you a tour of the old U-boat."

Scorpion replied, "That's more like it, get moving." Even though Spence had his hands loosely chained together, he still scrambled up the ladder. While Spence waited for Scorpion and three of her crew, he looked around and noticed that the hatch was already open. What luck!

When they all stood on top of the sub's platform, Spence pointed down at the hatch opening of the sub and said, "Scorpion, just climb down that ladder with your torch and you can see what the inside of this old iron ship is like."

Scorpion replied, "That's good, but my crew are going down first just to make sure there are no traps down there. You come down after me." She pointed to Spence. Within a couple of minutes the four were down on the first level of the sub. Scorpion then looked up yelling at Spence to get down the ladder. Spence acknowledged her and then sprung his trap. He quickly reached over and pulled the hatch down to seal off the sub entrance. It was old and rusty, but he got it closed. As the hatch was closing, he could hear Scorpion cursing at him. Once closed, he spun the hatch's wheel, which sealed and locked the hatch. Next, he grabbed the Nazi flagpole and jammed it through the wheel. Spence knew he had ten to sixty minutes before Scorpion on the inside, or one of her crew on the outside, would figure out how to unlock the hatch. With the deed being done, Spence slid down the backside of the sub and slipped off into the tall grass and out of sight.

Once he crawled through the grass, Spence jumped up and was on a dead run down the shoreline on the other side of the small island. Spence knew from his experience with the Spinners that if he could clear the four small islands, Ireland Island North, Ireland Island South, Boaz Island and Watford Island in a couple of hours or so, he could easily disappear on Somerset Island, and then get lost in the interior of the main island.

Spence was correct in his thinking that Scorpion was so upset that she would blow the top off the sub if she could. She had her crew on the inside trying to figure out how to open up the hatch while she was pounding on the side of the sub with the butt end of her saber. Scorpion's crew outside finally heard her pounding on the wall of the sub. They quickly climbed up to the hatch on the top of the sub. Like her cutthroats inside the sub, they were at a loss as how to open the hatch. They did get the Nazi flagpole removed.

After about fifteen minutes, one crewmember tried spinning the wheel. To his surprise the hatch unlocked. Soon after that, the crew in the sub pushed on the hatch again and it slowly opened. Scorpion yelled at them to get off the ladder so she could climb out first. Although she had buried others alive, this was the closest for her to being buried alive. She did not like it! Once on top, Scorpion screamed, "Where's my slave?" No one answered. Scorpion was getting more upset by the second. She pointed down at two of her crew and yelled, "You two go find him now and don't come back without him or I'll turn you into zombies!" The two went charging off through the tall grass in search of Spence. They had not seen Scorpion so livid in over fifty years.

Spence did not have the head start he wanted to have. He had only gotten to Ireland Island South. He needed a rest, so he thought he had enough lead to take a fifteen-minute breather. The two cutthroats were closing in on Spence. They had made it to Ireland Island South and were now tracking him. Spence was getting up to move on. He could hear some commotion in the jungle behind him. He knew it was too late. He was going to have to stop and fight his pursuers. Not having any weapons and being chained didn't help much, plus he didn't know how many there were. Spence hid behind a large rock. He was able to see that there were only two pirates following him, at least for now. There was about a five yard spread between the two of them. Spence knew he would have to overpower one pirate quickly. He would only have seconds before the other one turned and would be back to assist his companion. Spence let the first one run by. As the second pirate ran by, he jumped out and threw his chain around the pirate's neck. Then he jerked him back violently and cracked his head against the large rock where he had been hiding. He never knew for sure, but the pirate was probably killed instantly. The other pirate turned around to see the struggle or lack of a struggle. He removed his musket from his shoulder and took aim at Spence. Before he could fire, Spence had taken the dead pirate's dagger from his belt and, with extreme precision, threw it hitting the other pirate in the chest.

The pirate fell back, falling to the ground with a sudden jolt, causing his musket to fire harmlessly in the air. Spence could see that that pirate was dead by the time he hit the ground.

Meanwhile back at the Nazi encampment, Scorpion and the others heard the musket shot. She said, "It sounds like our mates scored a hit. Let's get off this Island of death and visit Spanish Point." With that they all loaded into their longboats and rowed back to the Venom.

Spence was now in fear that the musket shot might bring more of Scorpion's cutthroats or at least, if they did not return, more would follow. He took the other pirate's musket and belt. Then he sat down on the ground and slid the belt between the musket trigger and the trigger guard and cocked the musket. He put the ends of the belt into his mouth and laid the barrel of the musket right over the chain between his hands. Spence knew this was dangerous, but he had no choice. With his mouth, he jerked back on the belt and "bam" the musket fired snapping the chain in two. He felt an instant pain in his left hand. As soon as the smoke cleared, he could see that fragments from the chain had cut through the topside of his hand. The cuts weren't too bad. The good news he now had freed his hands. Spence got to his feet. He looked around to make sure there were no other surprises. Next, he picked up the musket from the other pirate with his saber and dagger. At the last moment he also remembered to take the pirates powder horn and musket ball bag. Although he was at the opposite end of the island from his friends, he still felt Scorpion would spend days trying to locate the Pilgrims. This should give him ample time to get to St. George's and warn the other Pilgrims.

While Spence was making his way to St. George's, Scorpion had landed at Spanish Point. Scorpion and a search party of her cutthroats made the long hike up to where Spence said the Pilgrim settlement was. The small band reached the entrance to the settlement after an hour's hike. The front gates were charred but still standing. They all stood there starring at the gate in a trance. Suddenly, Scorpion yelled out, "You idiots, don't just stand there. Bust the gate open!" After a couple of minutes of pushing and shoving, they got one gate to swing open. It then fell off its rope hinge and fell flat to the ground. With Scorpion in the lead, the pirates entered the settlement. Scorpion looked around and said, "We've been tricked. This settlement was destroyed a long time ago. Keep looking for clues." She went to the centre of the settlement, drew a circle in the dirt, and sat down chanting. Ten minutes later she stood up and yelled to the others, "There's no death here. No clues, we're wasting our time. Let's leave this burnt out hellhole and get back to the ship. We'll keep looking for the power source." Scorpion kicked the dirt with her boot and abruptly walked out of the settlement.

~9~

SHOCK AND AWE
AT SHARK HOLE

Shock and Awe at Shark Hole

Upon their return to at St. George's, the stolen car was conveniently dumped into Convict Bay. From there, Scarzo, Alvaro and Axil escorted the three Spinners back to the dock by King's Square. Portagee and Keno had lost the stolen car, but luckily for them, they saw the others walking down Water Street on their way back to the dock. As they neared Scarzo's speedboat, Scarzo commanded, "Get those kids into the boat ASAP!"

Axil was glad to comply. He smiled at Sam, Michael and Graham and said, "You heard the man, get your butts into that boat before I beat you every which way but loose." The Spinners knew he was serious. Graham had told the others about his run in with Axil and his goons a year ago, when they almost killed him trying to extract information. The three quickly stepped into the back of the speedboat and sat down. Alvaro went to drive the boat while Scarzo sat in the other front seat. Axil untied the boat and threw the ropes onboard. He stood there on the dock, hoping that they would pull away without him.

Alvaro turned to Axil and pulled his 357 magnum from the holster inside his jacket, saying, "My brother Axil, are you sure you want to stay behind?" He pulled back the hammer on the pistol and aimed it at Axil.

Axil quickly replied, "No boss. I was just catching my breath." He jumped onto the back of the boat with the Spinners. Scarzo and Alvaro laughed while Alvaro threw the throttle forward and the speedboat shot away from the dock like a rocket.

While the speedboat was zooming out of the harbour, Portagee and Keno were dashing to the dock. "What do we do now?" screamed Portagee.

Keno replied, "Well, one thing is for certain. We're not going to swim after them. They must be going to their ship offshore somewhere."

Portagee responded, "Well, if I were sixteen we would be on my scooter and we could follow them."

Keno looked surprised, and asked, "Are you telling me your scooter can ride on water?" Portagee nodded his head and smiled. Keno added, "Even if what you say is true, they're long gone now. What do you want to do? Go report the kidnapping to the police?"

Portagee thought for a minute, and said, "Sure and get our friends murdered. With Inspector Savage off the Island I wound not trust anyone else with this information. I think we should call all the parents and tell them you're having a sleep over. That way, no one will ask us any questions as to where the others are?"

Keno replied, "Great, but then what about tomorrow?"

Portagee smiled adding, "Surely tomorrow they'll show up in St. George's. They'll have good cover then. It's the start of Cup Match." This is a two-day holiday celebrating Emancipation Day on the first day and Somers Day on the next.

Keno said, "You're right. They will be able to sneak around and get lost in the crowds tomorrow. We'll be waiting for them." The boys were right. The next day was the beginning of the two-day cricket match on the Island with the Somerset team facing the St. George's team in the annual classic. Since the match was at the St. George's Cricket Club this year, almost half the Island would be there watching the match. Not only would this be the best cricket match of the year, there would also be dozens of food vendors selling delightful local dishes to locals and tourists alike. There is also Crown and Anchor featured. This is an old dice gambling game invented by sailors a couple of hundred years ago. Cup Match is the only time of the year that gambling is allowed on the Island. Keno and Portagee knew that there was nothing else they could do, so they headed back to Portagee's house to play video games for the evening.

The next morning was another beautiful day in paradise on both sides of the Triangle. In the Triangle, Salty had already rounded up the rest of the Pilgrims for breakfast. As they sat around eating, Jason spoke up, "Well, who wants to go with me today to Shark Hole to send our monthly message to the Spinners?"

Salty was first to speak up, "Let me go this month, I never get a chance to get out of camp."

Cooter then added, "Well if Salty's going so am I."

Bubba responded, "That is fine with me, Buford and I will go hog hunting instead."

Salty popped up, "Not until you clean up the breakfast mess first."

Buford laughed adding, "Salty, don't you trust us? We're men of honor."

Salty retorted, "I trust you two Johnny Rebs about as far as I can throw an anchor."

Jason interrupted, "Now come on boys, this will all work out." He laughed along with the others.

Within the hour, the three Pilgrims had set sail in one of the longboats they had rigged with a sail. It would take then a couple of hours to get through Harrington Sound and over to Shark Hole.

The Spinners had spent the night aboard the Prowler in one of the crew-member's cabins. Sam, Michael and Graham had been awake most of the night planning an escape. Just after dawn, there was a banging on the door. Michael quickly jumped up and hid behind the cabin door with a small chair in hand. Sam moved over to the other side of the door and waited. Graham then jumped up and whispered toward the door, "Just a minute we're not quite presentable yet." Within a second the door flew open, the crewmember started yelling at Graham as he stomped through the doorway, "You little son of a…" Before he could finish, Sam stuck her leg out and tripped him. As he was falling forward, Michael quickly kicked the door shut with his foot and struck him in the back of the head with his chair. The goon hit the floor with a thud and was unconscious. The Spinners then gave each other a "high five." Sam turned to the other two and asked, "Now what?"

There was a long pause before Graham finally spoke, "Let's get up to the ship's deck and see if we can find a boat or raft to throw overboard and escape." With that, they left the cabin and quietly crept up the stairs to the topside.

No sooner than they stepped out on the deck they heard, "Well, good morning my friends. It's time to visit Shark Hole." Scarzo had his pistol pulled and aimed at the Spinners. He took his other hand and pointed down to the speedboat. The Spinners climbed down the side of the Prowler and sat down in the back seat of the speedboat. Scarzo, to the Spinners' surprise, sat down in the pilot's seat while Axil sat in the front passenger's seat. Four other crewmembers climbed in the back and sat down in the seat facing the Spinners. They were all armed with AK 47s and were wearing military vests with bullet clips and four grenades. They were wearing large Hawaiian shirts so that their vests would not be noticed if they passed other boaters on the way to Shark Hole.

The Spinners looked at each other. They were thinking the same thing. This is going to be a very bad day. Before they pulled away, Scarzo looked back up at the Prowler and shouted to Alvaro saying, "Be sure to keep track of the boat on radar, I don't want to get lost in the Bermuda Triangle. We'd better get going. There's a storm going to hit Bermuda later today and I want to be on shore or back here by then." Alvaro nodded his head and gave Scarzo a "thumbs up." Scarzo threw the throttle full forward and laughed as if he still thought the idea of entering the Bermuda Triangle was a joke. Axil was the navigator and had Scarzo on a course circling around St. George's and the North Shore, then on to Harrington Sound through Flatt's Inlet.

The Pilgrims, from within the Triangle, had already entered Harrington Sound and were now half way across the Sound. As they were getting closer, Jason said, "OK, guys, here's what's going to happen. Cooter, you're going to stand on the left side of the cave and aim the Tucker Cross at the entrance of Shark Hole. Salty, since there's a storm brewing, you stand on the right side of the cave and take this life preserver. Be ready to throw it to one of us if we fall in and need help."

Salty looked at the antique cork and canvas preserver saying, "If my life depends on this old hunk of cork then tell Davy Jones I'm on my way."

Jason smirked and replied, "You old sea dog! Just take it or I'll stuff it in your big mouth."

Cooter retorted, "Just remember I can't swim a lick."

Salty replied, "How could I ever forget?" Cooter saw that they were getting very close to Shark Hole and dropped the sail. The water was starting to get a little rough with the storm closing in. Before they knew it, the longboat bumped onto the rocks on the left side of the cave. Cooter, without hesitation, jumped out on the rocks. He didn't want to take any chances of falling in the Sound. As soon as he got his balance, Jason yelled, "Catch!" Cooter looked up just in time to catch the Tucker Cross.

Cooter shouted back, "You crazy fool! You're lucky I didn't drop this in the water."

Jason replied, "Just don't forget which way to point the cross." He turned to Salty and said, "Let's row this old tub over to the other side and get you ashore." They both rowed the longboat to the other side of Shark Hole. Jason jumped out of the longboat and held it close to shore to make it easier for Salty to disembark the rocking longboat.

Salty scoffed, "Just cause I've only got one leg, you think I'm a cripple. Well I got news for you, I don't need your bloody help."

Jason snapped back, "Hurry up, peg leg, and get your sorry butt out of the boat." Salty stepped out as Jason jumped back onboard. As he began to row Jason saw Salty had forgotten the preserver. Jason whistled at Salty, then threw him the preserver.

Salty yelled back, "Thanks, you land lubber." Jason rowed away from the entrance of Shark Hole so he could throw the GPS disk through the gateway when Cooter opened it with the Tucker Cross. As he rowed, he looked up at the sky. The storm was moving in rapidly. This meant the gateway would be wide open today because of the way the power of the cross, reacted with a strong storm. It was going to take Jason a few more minutes to get ready to throw the disk.

The storm was also brewing on the outside of the Triangle. The rain and gusting winds had just begun as Scarzo's speedboat entered the Flatt's Inlet. He thought lady luck was on his side today. With the storm, everyone on the shoreline had taken cover, so they were able to enter Harrington Sound without being noticed. Once he cleared the narrow inlet into the sound, Scarzo threw the throttle fully forward. The boat cleared the rough waves like a flying fish. Axil was quick to point out the way across the sound to Shark Hole. The Spinners were keeping quiet in the back of the boat. As the speed of the boat increased and the boat smashed through the rough waves at high speed, Sam, sitting in the middle, took the hands of her friends.

Meanwhile, back on the Prowler, Alvaro was in the ship's bridge watching Scarzo's progress on the state-of-the-art tracking equipment. Alvaro could tell that they were in the Sound now and on a direct course towards Shark Hole. He really didn't believe in the Bermuda Triangle. He did believe that the treasure was hidden somewhere near Shark Hole.

The speedboat was within fifty yards of the entrance of Shark Hole. Axil signaled Scarzo to stop the boat. Scarzo did just that and turned to Axil asking, "Are you kidding? You want me to blast this boat into that small cave? Plus, what about that massive gate just beyond the entrance?"

Axil turned to the goons in the stern, pointed at Michael and said, "Throw that one overboard. He knows the combination to open the gate." Before Michael knew what hit him, he was in the water swimming towards Shark Hole.

Sam yelled out, "Michael, get out of here and fetch the police." One of the thugs quickly backhanded her and told her to shut her mouth. Michael knew he would have to open the gate or his friends might be killed. He quickly keyed in the combination. The massive locking device dropped open and Michael opened up the gates. He swam back to the boat and was helped aboard by Graham.

Axil spoke up, "Now, when you see the green lights and fireworks emanating from the cave, it's time to go."

Scarzo was beginning to think twice about this adventure, so then snapped back at Axil, "You know, if you're wrong were all dead, don't you mate?" Axil nodded his head. He understood.

Graham could sense their reservations and playing on their fears added, "You know, sometimes the gateway only opens part way. This boat might be too large to enter."

Scarzo turned around, pulled out his pistol, pointed it at Graham and said, "Listen you little jerk, if I want a comment out of you I'll ask for your opinion, understand?"

"Yes sir," replied Graham.

Scarzo felt he was ready to go for it, otherwise why would Graham try to scare him?

He turned back to Axil and said, "Just tell me when, and we'll be through that gateway like a rocket." He told his thugs in the stern to get their weapons out and to start blasting as they cleared the gateway. He wanted to make sure that whoever was on the other side would be dead as they cleared the Triangle. Two of the thugs pulled out hand grenades, one for each hand. The other two trained their AK 47s at the Shark Hole entrance. Time seemed to be standing still.

Back in the Triangle, the storm had really cut loose now. In spite of that, Jason was ready to throw the GPS device through the gateway when it opened. He signaled Cooter to aim the Tucker Cross at the Shark Hole entrance. He did. Within seconds the fireworks display kicked in. The green lights began emanating from the entrance while lightning began to strike at the cave. The gateway was now wide open with the storm and all the green explosions going on in the cave. It was next to impossible for any of the Pilgrims to see through to the other side. Poor Cooter was shaking so hard from the force of the cross, Salty worried that he was going to drop it and fall into the sound and drown.

Axil could see that the gateway was wide open. He quickly tapped Scarzo on the shoulder and yelled, "It's now or never!"

Scarzo hesitated for a second or two, and then he yelled, "Let's kick butt!"

He gunned the throttle as hard as he could. Within seconds the boat was blasting through the gateway. The force of the speedboat entering the Triangle caused a huge explosion on the Triangle side of the gateway. The explosion blasted out towards Jason as he was throwing the GPS device through the opening. As the boat ripped out of the gateway, a massive vacuum was created causing every-thing close to the entrance of Shark Hole to be sucked in the gateway. With no chance to move out of the way Cooter and Salty were also sucked into the vacu-um of the gateway. In a split second they were gone from the Triangle. All Jason could see was a massive object blasting out of the gateway at him. The thugs were throwing their grenades and shooting their weapons every which way. Just as the speedboat cut the longboat in half, a grenade exploded in the longboat. Jason never had a chance. He was gone in an instant. The front of the speedboat lifted about five feet out of the water after colliding with the longboat. This generated so much force, combined with the vacuum of the gateway, that the Spinners flipped out of the back of the boat. By the time they were drawn back to the entrance of the cave, the gateway had closed. Michael had been knocked out by the hard impact of hitting the water. Sam and Graham grabbed Michael just as he was sinking below the surface. They quickly swam to the shore and pulled Michael up into the heavy brush.

The speedboat ran more than a hundred yards out into the Sound before Scarzo was able to shut the engines down. As they idled, Scarzo eventually got his wits back and began to look around the boat. He asked, "Where the hell are the brats?" He also noticed one of his thugs was missing too. With the storm raging, all they could do was to try to find a place to go ashore.

The Spinners could no longer see the speedboat. They thought it would be safe to come out of the bushes and look around. Graham was stunned. He was the only Spinner who had never been in the Triangle before. As he looked around, he saw something floating in the Sound about twenty yards out from shore. Graham grabbed Sam by the arm and said, "What's that out in the water?" Sam looked. Without a word she dove into the Sound and swam towards the floating object. Graham started yelling at Michael while pointing at Sam swim-ming in the Sound. Michael was still a bit out of it, but he could tell Sam was trying to save someone.

Michael snapped, "Go help her. There's someone out there!" Graham ran down to the shore, jumped in and started swimming after Sam. Sam had already reached the body and was trying to pull the person back to the shore. Graham caught up to her quickly and helped her pull the body ashore. As the pulled the body up on shore and turned it over, Sam was shocked to see who it was.

"It's Jason!" screamed Sam. She immediately began performing CPR. It was clear he was cut up and bruised, but there were no gun shot wounds. After working on Jason for what seemed to be an eternity, Jason began to cough up water from his lungs. A few minutes later he was able to sit up and talk. Jason asked Sam if she had seen Cooter and Salty. Everything happened so fast that none of the Spinners had seen them.

With all the confusion, Jason finally looked over at Graham asking, "Who's this young man who helped save my life?"

Sam replied, "This is Graham. Remember he's our bud who got left behind on our last visit to the Triangle?"

Jason stood up to shake Graham's hand saying, "It's nice to finally meet you Graham… and by the way thanks for helping save my life." Jason then added, "Let's look around for Cooter and Salty, but I fear they were drawn back into the gateway. If they were, Cooter had the Cross with him." This added to all the confusion. The group looked all around Shark Hole for the missing Pilgrims and the cross, but with no success.

Sam finally said, "Jason, I think we'd better get out of here before Scarzo comes back looking for us." Jason agreed. They would head back to the Pilgrim's encampment on land to tell Bubba and Buford what happened. They hoped to regroup tomorrow. The Spinners and their companions walked though the jungle towards North Shore without noticing a lone figure that was watching everything that was taking place.

Back on the other side of the Triangle, aboard the Prowler, Alvaro watched the system monitors in amazement. One moment Scarzo's speedboat was a blip on the screen, then the next minute it was gone. Alvaro began to yell, "What the hell just happened! Where did they go? Don't tell me they're in the Bermuda Triangle. That's BS." He looked around the bridge. No one attempted to give an explanation. "Check all the equipment to make sure there hasn't been a malfunction." The crew checked every piece of equipment. It was clear that everything was in perfect working order.

Alvaro spoke up, "Make damn sure you find out where they went off the screen. We're going to take a boat out and find then just as soon as the weather breaks." Alvaro sat back in the captain's chair, lighting up his Cuban cigar.

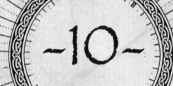

~10~

BLAST FROM THE PAST

BLAST FROM THE PAST

Fortunately, the gates to Shark Hole were already wide open because the explosion that came out of the cave would have blown the gates off their hinges. If someone in Bermuda had been passing Shark Hole on Harrington Sound Road at that exact moment, they would have thought an earthquake had struck. Just as the explosion occurred, two bodies were flung out of the cave through the smoke and they hit the water with such speed, that they must have skipped across the water for fifty yards. One of the figures began to swim to shore, after skimming along the surface. The other figure just kept splashing in the water like a wounded penguin. Indeed, it was Salty and Cooter, sucked out of the Triangle and blasted back into the real world. Was Bermuda ready for such a blast from the past?

Salty could hear the splashing behind him. It dawned on him that it must be Cooter and he remembered that Cooter couldn't swim a lick. He quickly turned around and started swimming in Cooter's direction. When Salty got closer to Cooter, he yelled, "Stop that bloody splashing! You're going to attract every shark in the Sound."

Cooter blurted back, "I can't swim you knucklehead."

Salty yelled, "Grab this, and I'll pull you ashore." He kicked out his peg leg for Cooter to grab. Salty knew that with only one leg he'd better hold on to the preserver to keep him afloat. He would kick back to shore with his good leg while Cooter hung on to his wooden peg leg. After swimming for several minutes, they made it back to the rocks on the north side of Shark Hole. Both of the Pilgrims were exhausted and just barely crawled ashore before collapsing. While they were lying there trying to recover, they kept hearing sounds above that puzzled them.

Salty spoke up first, "What in the world is that godforsaken sound?"

Cooter replied, "I'll be danged if I know. It almost sounds like a train engine, but if that's the case, there must be a bunch of them up there on the same track."

Salty fired back, "What the hell is a train?" Cooter started to explain, but he was still pretty exhausted so he told Salty not to worry about it. Right now, they both needed a power nap. Both of the Pilgrims were in for some big surprises. Salty disappeared into the Bermuda Triangle in 1780 and Cooter entered the Triangle in 1862. The world was going to be a very different place for this pair of old world throwbacks.

Portagee and Keno had been milling around St. George's all day waiting for signs of Scarzo's speedboat and their friends. Keno finally turned to Portagee as they waited from under the portico of a local shop on Water Street and said, "Do you think the storm has kept them away?"

"Maybe so," replied Portagee, "but the storm is breaking up now so maybe we'll see some sign of them soon."

"I guess so," replied Keno. The rain had slowed to a drizzle, so Keno and Portagee left their dry spot, headed down Water Street and crossed over to Kings Square to check out the docks again. While they walked along the docks scanning the bay for Scarzo, Portagee heard his GPS phone go off. Keno's went off a second later.

Portagee got excited. He thought that maybe Sam, Michael or Graham had sent them a message.

As he looked down at the screen on his phone he was shocked, "Oh crap, we forgot all about the message from the Pilgrims today," Portagee lamented.

Keno said, "Now what do we do? We only have five hours to pick up the GPS disk before it self destructs." The two were now in a predicament. If they left to recover the device, they might miss Scarzo and the speedboat. The other problem was that only Keno could drive, so if Scarzo showed up and Portagee was there watching by himself, then Portagee could not follow them.

Portagee finally came up with the only feasible solution. "Keno you stay here. I'll run up to the York Street bus stop and catch the next bus to Shark Hole. You can stay here with your scooter and watch for our buds. Call me on the cell if they show up."

Keno agreed and added, "Little guy, you'd better get your butt moving. It's going to be hard to find the GPS disc floating around after this storm." Portagee threw back a few choice words in Portuguese as he began to run towards the bus stop. Keno had no idea what Portagee had said, but he smiled anyway. After all, they were best friends and he knew Portagee was only kidding. Portagee made it to the bus stop in less than three minutes and luckily only had to wait another ten minutes before the bus pulled up. He stepped on the bus and handed the bus driver his zone three ticket. Portagee went midway down the aisle to sit down. He pushed his tracking button, which would now keep track of the GPS disk to help make it easier for him to find. These special phones the Spinners had were made just for this occasion. They could recover the GPS disk each month when the Pilgrims had thrown them through the Triangle gateway. Portagee called Keno on the cell phone. Keno answered, "What's up dude, did you get on the bus yet?"

Portagee replied, "Yes, and the disk is being tracked on my phone as we speak. There's only one hitch that I can see."

"What's that?" replied Keno.

"It looks like the storm is pushing the disk along the shoreline towards Devil's Hole. It's going to be much harder to find," Portagee added.

Keno, now quite worried, said, "You'd better be careful, dude."

Portagee closed by saying, "I will. Keep in touch." Then he hung up. Portagee decided not to get off the bus at Shark Hole since the disk was already quite a ways from there. He would now get off at one stop after that.

Salty was the first to wake up. In a flash, a thought popped into his head. He jumped up and started shaking Cooter yelling, "Coot, Coot, wake up! What happened to the cross?"

Salty kept shaking Cooter until Cooter finally jumped up and said, "What in the hell is the matter with you Salty? I was having the best sleep I've had in days. Why did you wake me up?"

Salty replied, "What happened to the cross? You were holding it, remember?"

Still a little fuzzy Cooter said, "Come to think about it, I did have the cross. Oh yeah, when I was drowning I dropped it in the Sound."

"You did what?" Salty questioned.

Cooter smiled and said, "You old horned toad, I'm just kidding. I managed to stuff it into my front pocket when I grabbed your old rotten wooden leg." Then he pulled out the cross to show Salty.

Salty said, "This old wood leg saved your sorry butt. You'd better not scare me like that again, you blasted idiot."

Cooter added, "Don't you remember, Sam told us the cross was stolen, back in this world. If we were caught with it, they would probably hang us from the gallows."

Salty answered, "What do you mean us? You're the one who has the cross. I'm just kidding Coot. I think we'd better hide it until we find the Spinners and get our butts back home."

"So where are we going to hide the dang cross?" asked Cooter.

Salty said, "Let's hide it in one of the caves over in the jungle."

Cooter agreed and added, "Let's get moving. I have to admit to being mighty hungry. Do you think there's a saloon in these parts?"

Salty replied, "We're not in the bloody colonies. They have pubs here."

Cooter looked back at Salty cross-eyed and said, "Dang it Salty, who cares? If I can get some grits and biscuits that's all that matters."

Salty laughed and added, "Move it." He pointed up the hill. Both the Pilgrims started climbing up through the dense brush. Surprisingly enough, they stumbled across an old set of steps leading upwards.

The bus was now on Harrington Sound Road and was approaching the bus stop at Shark Hole. Portagee had fallen asleep and had no idea how close he was to the bus stop. Cooter and Salty had just stepped out on Harrington Sound Road and, by chance, the pink bus stop post was by the stairs. Neither of the Pilgrims could believe their eyes. They were standing on a solid rock road. Cooter spoke up first, "We doggies. How do you think they made a road out of solid black rock?" They had no idea that the road had been paved with asphalt not rock.

Salty answered, "Beats me." Just then, the large pink bus rounded the corner and stopped in front of the two Pilgrims. Salty was so startled that he tripped backwards down several steps before catching himself by grabbing a small tree.

The bus driver opened the door, which hit Cooter in the arm as he said, "You mates going to Hamilton?"

Cooter, still trying to get his wits about him stuttered, "No, no sir." Before he could say another word the door slammed shut and the bus took off down the road. Cooter just stood there in shock.

By now Salty had climbed back up the stairs and asked, "What was that? How did it move without any horses?"

Cooter replied, "I haven't the foggiest. That was the biggest covered wagon I've ever seen in my life. It sounded like a train when it left."

Salty said, "There you go, talking about trains again." Just then three scooters zoomed by them, only missing them by about two feet.

Cooter regained his footing saying, "Well look at that! A metal horse on wheels, what will they think of next. I wonder what they feed them." Salty just stood there in silence not knowing what to say. Cooter said, "Let's get the hell out of here before we get killed." With that they moved across the road as quickly as they could, through the bushes and out of sight.

When the bus had started up Portagee woke up and happened to look back as the bus pulled away. "Crap," Portagee thought, "that was Cooter and Salty. What in the world were they doing here?" He quickly pulled out his cell phone and called Keno. When Keno answered, Portagee whispered, "Keno, you will never believe this I just saw Cooter and Salty at the Shark Hole bus stop."

Keno replied in shock, "Are you sure?"

Portagee answered, "Yes, I'm not seeing ghosts. I'm getting off at the next stop. You'd better come pick me up so we can find them. I'll wait here. Don't forget my helmet."

"Roger that, I'll see you soon," replied Keno. He then ran over, picked up Portagee's helmet, jumped on the scooter and zipped out towards Shark Hole.

While Portagee waited for Keno, he decided to go down to the shoreline of Harrington Sound to recover the GPS disk. The signal was still blipping on his cell phone screen so he knew he was getting close. After walking along the shoreline for about fifty yards he spotted the top of the device glimmering from the sun's rays shining through the breaks in the clouds. Portagee was hoping to find the device close to shore so he could avoid a swim. But today this was not going to be the case. He quickly removed his shirt and sandals, emptied his pockets, dove into the Sound and swam out to the floating device. After returning to shore, Portagee without thinking to check it for a message stuck it into his pocket and hiked back up to the road to wait for Keno.

Cooter and Salty had now climbed up the hillside through the brush and entered into a clearing. Salty said, "Will you look at that? They must have a ton of sheep to keep this field trimmed so short. Look over yonder. There's a flag sticking out of the ground." Before he could say anything else, a small white ball went bouncing towards him, hit his leg and rolled to a stop. Cooter yelled, "What the hell just hit me? Salty, I think I just got shot."

Salty laughed and said, "Look over there. That hard egg just hit you Coot."

Another one went zooming over their heads on a beeline towards the flag off in the distance.

Cooter pointing at the flying egg said, "Where's the chicken that's blasting these eggs?" He walked over and picked up the one that had hit his leg. After holding it for a few seconds he tossed it to Salty and said, "That is the hardest boiled egg I've ever seen in my life."

Salty tried to crack it open and said, "I don't think this is an egg." Before he could finish, a small covered cart came over the hill moving just like the big pink covered wagon except it wasn't making any noise. Half way down the hillside the wagon stopped. Two men jumped out of the wagon and began to run down the hill screaming at Salty and Cooter. Salty dropped the egg and grabbed Cooter by the arm saying, "Look those men are swinging sticks at us, I think they're going to use them on us for messing with their eggs. Let's get out of this pasture before we get killed." Cooter nodded his head and began running with Salty down the pasture towards the flag.

As they were running, Cooter yelled to Salty, "I wish I had my musket. I would show them who's boss around here."

Salty breathlessly said, "Shut up you bumpkin and keep running, or in your case, hobbling." They quickly passed by the flag and darted down the other hillside into the bush. Once they felt they had run far enough, both of them collapsed on the ground and lay there exhausted.

After almost ten minutes, Cooter spoke up, "Salty why do you think those two farmers back there were ready to beat the tar out of us for picking up one of those hard boiled eggs?"

Salty replied, "I don't know, but it looks like it might be awhile before we eat." With that, they heard something moving through the brush just about twenty feet from them.

"What now?" said Cooter.

Salty answered back, "Shut up you big dumb reb, looks like it's a wild chicken."

Cooter replied, "I hope it's not the one that laid those eggs back there. If it is, it's going to be tough as nails to eat." He jumped up and started chasing the wild chicken. Just when he was about to give up, the chicken trapped itself in a thorny bush. Cooter reached in grabbing the chicken by the neck and with a snap and spin of his wrist, the poor chicken's neck was wrung before the chicken knew what hit him. As he walked back to Salty Cooter said, "Momma taught me how to catch chickens."

Salty smiled and added, "Let's see if we can find the caves over in the jungle where we can be safe for the night. Meanwhile, if you pluck that chicken, I'll cook him tonight." So off they went heading towards Walsingham Nature Reserve to find shelter for the night. As they walked Cooter whistled "Dixie" and plucked out the chicken's feathers.

Meanwhile Keno had been in such a hurry that he zoomed right past Portagee. Portagee waved both arms high in the air and yelled in Portuguese trying to get Keno's attention. Keno caught a glimpse of Portagee in his side-view mirror and quickly turned around. As Keno pulled over, Portagee asked him if he had seen Cooter and Salty. Keno replied, "No! It was clear sailing all the way here. There was no one walking along the road."

Portagee said, "They either got on a bus, which I doubt, or got off the road and into the bush. I bet they were pretty overwhelmed by what they had seen already."

Keno questioned, "If they're in the jungle, how are we going to find them on my scooter?"

Portagee answered, "I'm guessing they're heading up by Tom Moore's Tavern. There they can find shelter in the caves and it's an area that will look more familiar to them." Keno agreed, so Portagee put on his helmet and jumped on the back of the scooter. Off they headed towards Tom Moore's Tavern.

By now, Salty was getting pretty tired of hearing Cooter whistling "Dixie." He turned to Cooter saying, "If you don't change that bloody tune to something else I'm going to stuff that darn chicken down your throat."

Cooter smiled and said, "Come on Salty, that's the only song I can whistle."

Salty barked back, "I don't give a damn, just quit it." Cooter then stopped and started walking a little faster forcing Salty into a faster pace. "All right you Johnny Reb, slow it down." Cooter slowed down. He really did not want to wear him out. He was only giving Salty a hard time. They were heading on a northeasterly course. Soon they cleared the heavy brush and came out onto the shoreline of Castle Harbor. They sat down to rest on the small rocky beach and as they looked around, they could not believe their eyes.

Cooter pointed out across the bay and said, "Well dog gone it. Have you ever seen anything like that in your life before? Look Salty, those boats are moving across the water faster than if they had a sail."

Salty had already seen them and could not believe his eyes. He added, "There's a man being jerked along behind that boat holding on to a bloody rope with his feet in barrel loops."

Cooter added, "What more can we see in this strange new world? Now we have boats without sails. You know what, Salty? I bet they have steam engines in them just like trains do. I remember back in the war with the Yankees I heard there were some new boats being built like that."

At that point, Salty heard this ear shattering noise in the sky. He looked up and said, "Hot damn, Coot, here's one more thing we ain't never seen before. It's a flying monster."

Cooter's jaw dropped open. He added, "You know what Salty? That must be one of those flying birds that Jason and Spence used to tell us that they would ride in." As they were talking, the flying bird dropped down out of sight on the other side of the bay behind some fort or settlement. Cooter then continued, "Salty, that big bird just landed in that fort over there. Look there's a bridge going over to the other side of the bay."

Salty then spoke up, "With all those crazy boats and ships running all over the bay, I think we'd better cross by the bridge tomorrow."

Cooter added, "Yes, but look at all those wagons crossing the bridge, they're going as fast as the boats." Both agreed that they had seen enough for one day. It was time to move along the shoreline and then back into the jungle and see if they could find a cave to sleep in for the night. Within a couple of hours they had found a very small cave that would suit them. Cooter went and found some wood to make a fire, while Salty sharpened a stick into a skewer for roasting the chicken. It was now dark, and while the chicken was roasting over the small fire, Cooter pulled out the cross from his pocket and said, "Salty, I don't think it's a good idea to leave this cross here in a cave that we don't know much about. What to you think?"

Salty replied, "Watch this, my rebel friend." He reached down and untied the strap on his peg leg and stood it up in front of Cooter. He lifted off the padding off the top of the peg leg, which revealed a large hollowed out area in the top of his leg.

"Well I'll be dog gone," smiled Cooter.

Salty then passed the leg over to Cooter and said, "Drop that little prize in my leg. No one will find it there."

Cooter asked, "Where in the blue blazes did you ever think of doing that? Were you smugglings gold and jewels in it?"

Salty replied, "No, no, no. Back in the days with Captain Drax, on the high seas, I would hide limes in my leg and sneak them out of the galley and give them to sick shipmates. Captain Drax would have hung me from the yard arm if he ever caught me doing that."

Cooter countered, "Well, I reckon it will be safe there for my friend." Salty tapped the wood plug with padding back over the top of the peg leg and strapped it back on to the stump of his leg. The chicken was now roasted to perfection. The two relics from the past would stuff themselves and then call it a night. Tomorrow they would hopefully be off to find the Spinners in the old village of St. George's.

Keno and Portagee had missed Salty and Cooter. Since it was dark now, they wanted no part of the Nature Reserve at night. It was spooky enough during the day. They would go spend the night at Keno's place at the St. David's Lighthouse and begin their search again the next day.

~11~

DOUBLE THE TROUBLE

DOUBLE TROUBLE

Scarzo's speedboat had found refuge in Church Bay in the Sound. The speedboat had received slight hull damage from the collision with the longboat, but not enough to affect its sea worthiness. As Scarzo ran the boat up on the beach, he started screaming, "I have never been so ticked off in my life!" Axil knew to keep his mouth shut. He jumped out of the boat and signaled for the others to help drag the boat ashore. Scarzo was only just getting started, "Axil, where the hell are we? What happened to those kids?"

Axil looked around and replied, "Well boss, I know we're in Harrington Sound except there's nothing else here that should be, houses, roads, boats cars. It's like we stepped back into the past. Don't get mad, but I think we're in the Bermuda Triangle, Scarzo."

Scarzo snapped back, "You're full of it. That's impossible! The Bermuda Triangle doesn't even exist!"

Axil added, "Oh no. Then look at the compass on your boat." Scarzo looked down and to his amazement the compass was spinning out of control.

Scarzo replied, "That doesn't prove anything. It was broken in the collision with the other boat. I'll prove it. I'll call you and prove it to you." He then reached into his pocket and pulled out his cell phone. He flipped the phone open and dialed Axil. Nothing happened. The phone was dead.

Axil said, "I know now you're going to say your cell phone is broken as well, right?" Scarzo didn't say a word. He just climbed out of the boat, walked up on the beach and sat down. He reached into his jacket, and pulled out his pistol. He took aim at Axil and pulled the trigger. A shot blasted out grazing Axils' ear. Axil fell to the sand screaming in pain.

Scarzo laughed saying, "Well, at least my 357 still works. Tomorrow we'll find those kids and the treasure." Scarzo, Axil and the remaining two crewmembers spent the night on the shore recovering from their wounds and making minor repairs to the speedboat.

Scorpion and her crew had managed to avoid the effects of the storm by anchoring the ship in Stovel Bay at Spanish Point. She was still furious with Spence for escaping and vowed he would be doomed to be a zombie forever, once she found him. Not being familiar with Bermuda and having lost her guide, Scorpion would have to rely on her Voodoo powers to find the mysterious power source in the northern point of the Triangle. She was all set to sail along the north shore of the island looking for signs of life or the power of the Triangle. Without wasting any time she had three longboats tow her ship out of Stovel Bay and then they set sail along the north shore.

Jason and the Spinners weathered out the storm in Crystal Cave. They had not been there for a year. Michael and Sam had shown Graham around the cave. Jason was exhausted and spent the night lying by the fire.

The next morning Jason knew that they must leave early. Being without a longboat, they would have to swim across to Coney Island and then on to St. George's Island. Jason was worried that they would be exposed during that that leg of the journey if Scarzo and his speedboat caught up with them at the entrance to Castle Harbor. The small group had been hiking along one of the hog trails through the jungle for about an hour. As they neared the intersection of another trail, Jason signaled the group to stop. They would watch the other trails for a few minutes to make sure there were no surprises waiting for them. While they waited quietly, Jason heard someone or something coming down the intersecting trail. He reminded the Spinners to remain silent while he quietly drew out his saber. Jason's musket remained strapped to his back. He thought it might make too much noise if it were fired. As the sound grew closer, Jason knew it was someone walking down the trail. Just as the figure neared the trail crossing, Jason jumped out and began to swing his saber at the intruder. The intruder quickly yelled out, "Whoa, whoa there partner, I come in peace!" To Jason's shock it was Spence, he had almost killed his friend.

Jason dropped his saber, grabbed Spence and shook him. Then he yelled, "Where the hell did you come from?"

Spence replied, "It's a long story and we don't have a lot of time. I'll tell you as we return to the village." He looked over seeing the Spinners and in a state of shock said, "Holy smoke, when did you kids come back?"

Sam spoke up first, "Oh just yesterday, but some pirates came with us." She then smiled, turned, and introduced Graham to Spence.

Jason asked, "Where's Doc and the others?"

Spence replied, "They were lost at sea when the pirate ship, Venom, attacked us. They're here now looking for the power source of the Triangle whatever that is. The captain is a Voodoo witch whose name is Scorpion. She is a ruthless killer. She blew our boat out of the water."

Jason asked, "You mean Doc, Lynn and Georgette are gone?"

Spence dropped his head, "Yes."

Jason replied, "They'll be missed. They were family to me. Spence, do you think this Scorpion is close by?"

Spence replied, "I don't think so. I escaped from them yesterday at the Nazi encampment. They probably went to Spanish Point looking for you. I gave them misleading information. Scorpion will now be very upset and she will be out to kill me."

Jason added, "Well, don't worry my friend. We'll protect you."

Spence asked, "Is everyone else back at the village?" Jason told Spence the bad news about Cooter and Salty. He thought that they were drawn back into the other world when the gateway was closing. The Pilgrims and the Spinners knew that they had to get back to the village on St. George's Island to warn the others before Scorpion or Scarzo found them. They moved quickly down the hog trail that led to the North Shore. At this point, Jason felt that the greatest danger was in the ocean and they would be gambling that no one would be watching them from the jungle. He was almost right, except for the fact that someone out in the jungle was matching their movement stride for stride as they progressed along the trail.

Scorpion was now much closer than Spence thought. The winds were blowing in Scorpions favour and she was going to pass by Coney Island in a couple of hours. As she stood on the deck of the Venom, she was beginning to feel faint vibes from the power of the Triangle, but that was soon interrupted by a new sense of an evil on the island. Scorpion could feel the evil that someone was emanating. She could tell that this evil being was a vicious killer. She could also feel that this person was the type that could be controlled to do her bidding with her Voodoo powers. If she could get within a hundred yards of this evil being, she would sense it and could cast a spell on it to do her bidding.

Back at the village in St. George's, Bubba and Buford were beginning to get worried. Their friends were a day overdue from their trip to Shark Hole. If it weren't for Grizzly and Bear, the village would be lonely as hell. The two cousins had kept themselves busy training the two labs with southern style hunting techniques. As the two were walking back to the village with the dogs, Buford asked Bubba, "Do you reckon there's a problem? Cooter, Salty and Jason should have been back by now."

Bubba replied, "I think so. They didn't take extra food or ammo to go hunting. I think when we get back to the village we should set sail in one of the longboats and head over to Shark Hole."

Buford agreed and leaned down to Grizzly and Bear saying, "You boys want to go on a boat ride?" Both dogs jumped up and down and began barking.

"Well, there's your answer Buford," replied Bubba. They stepped up the pace to get back to the village faster. Once they got back, they quickly picked up their muskets, ammo and sabers.

Bubba and Buford headed down to the harbor. As they got near the longboat, Bubba turned around and yelled for Grizzly and Bear. They came running down the path like there was no tomorrow. They quickly jumped into the longboat. The two cousins pushed the boat offshore. They raised the sail and tacked across St. George's Harbor, over to Ferry Reach and up to Harrington Sound. With the strong breeze, they were making good time. They sailed up the narrow Stock's Harbor and on to Coney Island.

Bubba and Buford were sailing in the direction of Coney Island with their new pals Grizzly and Bear. They were close enough to see some figures moving across the southern portion of island. As they neared the island Bubba spoke up, "Look it must be Jason, Cooter and Salty."

Buford responded, "That may be so Bubba, but I can see five people out there." Bubba started waving his arms and yelling. Buford finally grabbed his arm and said, "Cuz, they can't hear you! Let's fire our muskets over their heads to get their attention." With that they both loaded their muskets and fired them one after the other. Their plan worked. Sam and Michael were first to turn and see the longboat, but they were not the only ones who had spotted them.

The Venom had also spotted them. Scorpion's first mate screamed at her, "Captain, Captain that longboat just fired on us!"

Scorpion turned toward the longboat and said, "Blow those fools out of the water." With that, the Venom turned broadside and fired one of her cannons at the longboat. Buford heard the cannon fire, looked up and saw the ship for the first time. The cannon ball exploded about twenty yards in front of the longboat.

Buford yelled, "Bubba, turn this boat around before we get clobbered by that pirate ship!" The longboat turned quickly, but it was too late. Scorpion commanded her cannon crew to fire again. This time the cannon ball exploded just ten feet in front of the longboat. Buford and Bubba knew that they were now marked. The next cannon ball would probably hit them. Bubba and Buford grabbed the two labs and just as they were getting ready to jump overboard, a third cannon shot hit directly into the longboat blowing it into a million shards. Sam pointed at the longboat and started screaming. Meanwhile Spence turned towards the other direction and saw that the ship was the Venom.

Spence grabbed Jason and said, "That's Scorpion's ship! It destroyed the Mayflower II and killed our friends. Let's get over to St. George's Island quickly before that witch sees us." Without a second thought Sam, Michael and Graham dove into the water with Spence and Jason right behind them. Luckily for them, the waves were rolling in high enough that the pirates on the Venom could not see them. As they swam, Jason looked over to his right to see if anyone in the longboat had survived the direct hit of the cannon ball. All he could see was smoke, fire and debris floating in the water. They soon reached the shoreline and were into the bush in seconds, out of view of the Venom.

Meanwhile, back at the wreckage of the longboat, Buford's head was the first to pop up out of the water. With all the smoke in the air and the high waves, it was hard to see. He finally saw Bear who was swimming in circles acting very confused. Buford, not knowing who was around him, said in a low tone, "Bear, Bear, come here boy." Bear instinctively turned around and headed straight to Buford. "Good boy," cried Buford. Then the two of them turned and headed for St. George's Island.

A little ways away, Bubba was floating lifelessly face down in the water. Grizzly had seen his body and swam over to him. He grabbed Bubba by the shirt collar and started dog paddling towards the shoreline. As Grizzly with Bubba in tow cleared the smoke, Buford turned around and saw the two heading in his direction. He then stopped and said, "We doggies! Bear, will you look at that? Our good old buddies are still alive. Let's go back and give them a hand." Both turned around and went back to give Grizzly a hand. As they got closer, Buford became worried; he had not seen any movement out of Bubba. When he got to Bubba he patted Grizzly on the head and took over the rescue effort of getting him to shore. Within a few minutes, Buford dragged Bubba up onto the shore and turned him over on his side. He began pushing on his back with as much force as he could. Both dogs immediately sat down next to Bubba and waited.

Finally, Bubba came to life coughing and spitting out the seawater he had swallowed. As soon as he could, Buford sat up and said, "Cuz, you almost bought the farm this time. In fact, we may still get killed if we don't get off this beach." They got up and limped off the beach into the bush, together with the labs. No sooner than they had traveled fifty yards Buford stopped and said, "Bubba did you hear the noise up in front of us?" Bubba shook his head from side to side indicating he had heard nothing. Buford knew they might be in trouble. They had lost their muskets and sabers in the explosion and only had their hunting knives for protection.

All of a sudden, both Grizzly and Bear bolted through the bush barking. Buford sighed and said, "Oh hell, those dogs are going to get themselves killed and us too." Both men pulled out their hunting knives and moved as quickly as they could through the bush. The barking stopped as quickly as it had started. Both cousins feared for the worse as they entered a small clearing. To their surprise, the Spinners and the labs were getting acquainted with licking and petting all over the clearing. Spence and Jason ran over to Bubba and Buford to see if they were all right.

Spence said, "I sure didn't think I would see you Johnny Reb's again."

Buford responded, "That goes for us too, you Yankees." They all laughed.

Then Jason said, "Well, it's easy to see Sam. Michael and Graham have already made friends with Grizzly and Bear."

After sitting down for a while resting from the ordeal, Jason spoke up, "Listen those pirates may try to follow us. Why don't you kids and the labs head back to the village and wait for the rest of us to follow later on. If you have to, you might want to lie low up in the hills until we arrive. The four of us will find a good ambush spot and wait to see if those bloody pirates try to follow."

Bubba, feeling better, added, "Give me a musket and I'll blow that witch out of the water."

Spence replied, "Don't worry. You and your cousin are the best shots. You take the muskets and Jason and I will back you up with the sabers." He turned to the Spinners and added, "Get moving. Daylight is burning and right now we don't have a clue where those pirates are."

Michael turned to his friends and said, "OK, OK, we get the message. Let's go. Come on Grizzly and Bear show us the way." The Spinners waved goodbye and headed off towards the village with the labs taking the lead.

Spence signaled the others to follow him saying, "Let's move back into the trees where the island narrows at Whalebone Bay. We can hide in the bush on the Ferry Reach shoreline and nail them as they pass through." They moved off into the bush to set up their ambush.

Back on the Venom, Scorpion was barking out commands as she pointed to her first mate, "You take seven men with you and get your butts down in that longboat. Head to shore and track down those bloody cutthroats." They lowered themselves down into the water and began rowing towards St. George's Island. Scorpion then turned and yelled at her crew, "Raise that anchor and let's set sail. We're going to sail around this island and see if we can surprise those cutthroats on the backside of the island!" Scorpion was feeling a little better, having blown the Pilgrim's longboat out of the water, but she was still nervously clicking her scorpion stingers on her left hand. The Venom sailed down the North Shore of the island, just out of sight of Jason and the other Pilgrims. They had no idea that the majority of the pirates were on a collision coarse with the Spinners.

~12~

CROWN AND ANCHOR

CROWN AND ANCHOR

Back in Bermuda, Salty was surprised to be awakened by a wild rooster crowing noisily. Salty lay there for a couple of minutes making sure he wasn't having a nightmare. He sat up and reached over to Cooter, shaking him and saying, "Wake up you old sardine, we got to figure out how to get the hell out of here." Cooter jumped up in a panic only hearing "get the hell out of here." Salty grabbed him by the arm and said, "Hang on there, mate, you're not being eaten by sharks. I was just waking you up."

Cooter stopped in his tracks. He looked back at Salty and said, "Dang you Salty, you scared the grits out of me you old sea dog. I thought we were being overrun by those damn Yankees."

Salty laughed and said, "Don't worry Coot, I would have protected you. Here, since you're up, have some leftover chicken from last night." Cooter sat down grumbling and began to have his breakfast with Salty. After eating their leftover wild chicken, they crawled out of the cave to discover it was a beautiful day. The sun was out and not a cloud in the sky. The two Pilgrims decided to make their way up the shoreline at Castle Harbour and try crossing the causeway bridge to get over to St. George's Island. With Cooter's swimming skills non-existent, a land route no matter how dangerous was better than a water route. The two finally approached the entrance to the causeway and Salty stopped and asked Cooter, "Do you think it's safe to cross that bloody bridge. It looks longer than the Great Wall of China."

Cooter replied, "How would you know how long the Great Wall of China is? Anyway, I reckon it's safe as long as we don't get killed by one of the horse-less wagons." With that, they started across the causeway, single file, trying to stay out of the way of the speeding wagons and wheeled horses.

It was the second day of Cup Match so the traffic across the causeway was bumper to bumper. Just by chance coming from the other direction on a scooter were Keno and Portagee. About half way across the causeway they passed Cooter and Salty, walking in the opposite direction. Portagee taped Keno on the back and said, "Did you see Salty and Cooter back there?"

Keno replied, "Yes, but I can't stop. There's too much traffic. We'll have to turn around and wait for them back on the other side of the bridge." They zoomed on across looking for a spot to turn around. The traffic was so backed up that they had to go all the way down to a bus stop to turn around.

Meanwhile, Salty and Cooter were almost across the causeway when a wagon stopped and a friendly Bermudian yelled across the front seat, "Hey mates. You going to Cup Match?" Salty and Cooter just stood there and looked at each other not having a clue as to what he was talking about.

Finally Salty spoke up, "Yes captain." He thought anything was better than walking on this bridge and getting killed.

The man reached over and opened up both doors on their side and said, "Hop in mates, we're blocking traffic." Salty jumped into the back seat and Cooter jumped into the front seat. The wagon moved out to catch up with the wagons in front of him. Both Salty and Cooter fell back into their seats with the rapid acceleration of the wagon.

Cooter yelled out, "Wee doggies. What makes this wagon move like this?"

The Bermudian, being very proud of his car replied, "This little baby is brand new and it's packing over a hundred horse power under the hood."

Salty leaned forward and whispered into Cooter's ear saying, "Be careful I think our mate may have been drinking some rum for breakfast today. I didn't see a hundred horses under this wagon did you?" Cooter shook his head no.

The Bermudian then added, "Are you mates part of a show at the Cup Match? Those costumes are sharp." He looked over at Cooter and asked, "Something must have died out there on the road. Do you smell that foul odor?"

Cooter turned his head and discreetly smelled his old jacket. Realizing it might be him, he responded, "Yeah, I think we just passed the skinned carcass of a wild hog back there lying by the road."

The Bermudian, said, "You're right." He took a double take at Cooter, saying, "You're a hoot! You'll do well at Cup Match."

Salty chimed in, "He's not a Hoot he's a Coot." They all laughed as they approached the St. George's Cricket Club.

Meanwhile Keno and Portagee passed the area where they had seen Salty and Cooter earlier. They were nowhere to be seen. Portagee tapped Keno on the back and said, "Do you think someone gave them a lift?"

Keno yelled back, "Yes, I bet someone picked them up."

"Where do you think they're going?" asked Portagee.

Keno replied, "I'm guessing they're on their way to Cup Match."

"O.K. let's go," replied Portagee.

Meanwhile, back on the Prowler, Alvaro was ready to send out a small search party to find Scarzo and/or the Spinners. With both groups now missing, he didn't care whom he found first. Alvaro was on the bridge checking out all the radar for any sign of his boss. Alvaro turned to one of the night watch crew and asked, "Did you spot any blips from Scarzo or any other unusual activity?"

The crewmember replied, "No sir." Then he thought for a minute and said, "I forgot. Last night reviewing the GPS recordings from yesterday I noticed something very strange."

Alvaro snapped back, "Well, what the hell did you see? Don't keep me waiting amigo."

The crewmember replied nervously, "Just at the same moment in time and at the exact same location that Captain Scarzo disappeared from sight, a new and different bleep appeared on the screen. The object moved extremely slowly like it was just floating in water. Then after an hour, it picked up speed and headed for St. George's. Then four hours later it simply disappeared once more. It was like it was a signal device of some sorts."

After Alvaro thought for a minute, he said, "I bet those bloody kids tried to signal the authorities somehow with one of their phones. I want a small party to go check out the last known location of Scarzo and track the other GPS signal to wherever it was when it blacked out. Tonight we'll take the choppers out just before dusk and check out the coastline for signs of the missing. We'll just have to make sure we stay below the Bermuda radar system."

Alvaro had no idea how close he was in his thinking about the blip on the GPS radar screen. He was seeing the GPS disk, which Jason had thrown through the gateway. Portagee had totally forgotten that the GPS disk was still active when they had returned to his house for the night. Alvaro's thugs would be able to track them there from the saved recording. Alvaro dropped off two of his men at the docks in St. George with instructions for them to rent scooters and head over to Harrington Sound. If need be, they would follow the GPS recording back to St. George's to track down the Spinners.

The Bermudian driving Cooter and Salty was lucky enough to find parking just out side of the Cup Match entrance. The three left the car as they neared the entrance. The Bermudian stopped and pointed to the volunteer entrance saying, "Come on boys. We're all working in booths at the match so we get in for free. Follow me." Cooter and Salty had lucked out. They would never have been allowed in the normal entrance without any money. Salty did have some old Spanish pieces of eight and Cooter had a few old Confederate dollar bills.

Once through the gate, the Bermudian waved goodbye and headed off to his booth. The Cricket Club was now filling up with spectators. Salty and Cooter would not be so noticeable with so many of the locals being dressed up in various and sundry holiday costumes. The match had been going on for a while by the time the two found their way up to the spectators stand. The stand seating was already full so the two had to stand off to one side and watch the spectacle. Salty and Cooter were in awe. Salty had never seen so many people and the only time Cooter had, was at the Battle of Bull Run in the Civil War. Salty asked Cooter, "What on earth is going on down there? All those men are standing around while a couple of them walk around with big flat clubs."

Before Salty could continue, Cooter started yelling, "Look, look, they're going to fight each other. Did you see that guy charge at the other side then stop and throw that big round rock at the guy with the club?"

Salty replied, "That man hit the rock back at him. Now look, those two blokes are running at each other with their clubs. Someone's going to get clobbered."

Cooter said, "I'll be damned. They just ran by each other. Look now, they turned around and are charging towards each other again. Oh hell. They missed each other again." The two looked at each other shaking their heads. Cooter added, "Let's go Salty. These guys don't know how to fight." They turned around and walked away from the stands to mingle into the crowd.

As the two walked around, Cooter said, "We doggies, I sure do smell some grub, I'm getting mighty hungry Salty."

Salty replied, "Right now, if it weren't talking you'd eat it."

Then they heard another voice off to their side calling them, "Hey mates! How about coming over here and playing a little 'Crown and Anchor?"

"Play what?" questioned Cooter.

"You know, 'Crown and Anchor,' everyone's a winner," replied the gamer.

Salty said, "Come on Coot forget your belly, let's see what this hot shot is talking about." They stepped inside the gazebo, slowly making their way through the crowd of spectators crowding around the gaming tables. Both Cooter and Salty bellied up to a large white game table that was about three by five feet. It was painted with eight one- foot square boxes trimmed in black. Two of the boxes had a symbol of the black spade, two had the symbol of the red heart, one had a symbol of a red diamond, one had a symbol of a black anchor and the last box had a symbol of a crown in it.

"Hot damn," cried Cooter, "this looks kind of familiar, how do you play?" One of the bystanders leaned over and explained to Cooter that there were three die; each die had one each of the six symbols from the board on them. He told Cooter how simple the game was to play. You just place your bets on a symbol and however many of the same symbols appear on the top of the die will show how much you can win. So if you place a dollar on the anchor and roll three anchors you win three dollars. Salty just smiled as he heard the game being explained to Cooter. He used to play the forerunner to the game called 'sweat cloth' a couple hundred years ago. He knew exactly what to do.

He yelled over to Cooter, "Come on mate. Let's play." Both men pulled out what money they had; Cooter dropped his out on the table first.

The game operator looked at Cooter's confederate dollars and said, "Sorry mate, we can't play with that old funny money here."

Cooter was about to get mad when Salty nudged him over and flipped out one of his old Spanish gold doubloons, "Hey, what's this worth?"

The operator picked up the coin. He knew the coin was worth thousands, but said "Well mate, I can give you a hundred dollars for this."

Salty, not knowing the value of money replied, "Pay up mister. Let's get this game on the road."

"Ok, here's your money and here's your dice," replied the game operator.

Salty smiled and said, "Coot put fifty down on that black anchor."

Salty then shook the cup with the dice and rolled them out on the table. Salty yelled out, "Blow me down mate, three anchors, pay up!" Cooter kept placing the bets where Salty told him to and Salty kept rolling and rolling and winning and winning.

Salty and Cooter's luck went on for over an hour. Finally the game operator dropped to his knees and said, "Please stop playing. You're breaking me. What can I do to get you to stop?"

Cooter looked at him and said, "Well Cuz, I'm getting mighty hungry."

The operator said, "Deal. I'll take you over to my mate's booth and get you the biggest fish dinner you ever saw."

Next Cooter said, "That's good, but one more favor."

"You name it mate," replied the operator.

Cooter looked over at Salty and said, "Here take this hundred dollars and give my friend his coin back." Cooter then threw the rest of his confederate dollars out on the table and said, "Oh yeah, you can have these dollars from my beloved country." The operator didn't want to give the coin back, but if Cooter and Salty stayed any longer he would be cleaned out. He grudgingly took the money, gave Salty his coin back and bought Cooter and Salty their codfish and potato dinners.

After eating Salty and Cooter knew it was time to "shove off" and find their friends, the Spinners. As they left Cup Match, the buzz of this year's 'Crown and Anchor' stall was how two crazy throwbacks just about broke the bank in a little over an hour.

GUN SHIPS AND GHOST GEORGE

GUNSHIPS AND GHOST GEORGE

Salty and Cooter were walking down Wellington Street on their way into the Village of St. George's. The two were beginning to get used to the strange surroundings and did not seem to be bothered by passing vehicles. As they walked down the street, Cooter was having a grand time swinging his new club he had bought with some of the winnings. He was really swinging a cricket bat he picked up at a souvenir tent at Cup Match.

Portagee and Keno had spent most of the day driving up and down Wellington Street and in and out of the Cup Match field and tents without any success. The two had given up for the day and were on their way out of St. George's. They were heading to St. David's to spend the night at St. David's Lighthouse where Keno lived. While they were zooming down the road, Keno looked over to the side of and saw an old wooden peg- leg hobbling down the road and instantly knew it was Salty. He did a quick U-turn and pulled up beside their two lost friends. Keno said, "Hey mates, been to the Triangle lately?" Both Salty and Cooter took a quick double take, not expecting to hear anything about the Triangle.

Cooter realized it was Portagee and Keno. He yelled out, "Well I'll be dog gone! If it ain't our little Spinner buddies." Cooter went over and hugged Keno and Portagee.

Salty then spoke up, "I hate to break up this reunion, but we've got to get the hell out of this crazy place and go back home."

Keno added, "We're confused. We lost Michael, Graham and Sam at Shark Hole and now you two have appeared. Plus, we think some pirates are on the loose and may be looking for us."

Salty said, "I wish we could help. All I remember is Jason opening up the gateway to the Triangle. Then there was a mammoth explosion and the next thing I knew, we were in this crazy world."

Portagee replied, "Look we'd better get out of here before Scarzo, Alvaro or their thugs find us. We can go hide out at Gates Fort and try to figure this out. Keno, you're going to have to make three trips on your scooter to get all of us there."

Keno nodded and said, "Come on you old sea dog, you're first." Keno was looking at Salty.

Salty piped up, "I'd walk the plank before I'd climb on to that horseless what ever it is."

Keno replied, "Come on Salty we need to get going." He tossed Salty Portagee's helmet saying, "Portagee help Salty put your helmet on." Once Salty had the helmet on, Portagee helped Salty get on the back of Keno's scooter. Keno yelled back at Salty, "Hang on Salty, we're ready to 'crank her up." With that the scooter took off. All anyone could hear as the scooter sped away was Salty screaming out every curse word in the Old English language. Portagee and Cooter laughed as the scooter disappeared in the distance.

Portagee said, "Coot, let's keep walking towards the fort until Keno comes back for us." They started walking down the road heading towards Gates Fort. About a hundred yards down the road, Alvaro's thugs saw Portagee walking as they passed by them going in the same direction. They overshot Portagee and Cooter by about fifty yards, then slammed on their brakes and spun around. They both quickly fired up their scooters and went on a collision course towards Cooter and Portagee. Portagee yelled, "That's the pirates! They're going to get us. What should we do Cooter?"

Cooter smiled and turned his back to the oncoming scooters saying, "Portagee, you might want to back up about two or three feet."

Portagee screamed, "Cooter they're going to run us over!" Cooter kept smiling and winked at Portagee. He waited a couple of more seconds for the scooters to close the gap. Then, in an instant, Cooter spun around with his cricket bat packing more power than a cricket batsman would ever dream of. In a split second, Cooter's bat smacked across the chest of the first thug, stopping him dead in his tracks, while his scooter continued on. As Cooter completed his spin, he caught the other thug in the middle of his back with the bat, knocking him off his scooter sideways. Both thugs were sprawled on the road unconscious. Portagee's heart was pounding at two hundred beats a minute. He couldn't believe what had just happened.

After recovering, Portagee yelled at Cooter, "Quick grab that one's helmet, we'll take one of their scooters and get out of here before they come to."

Cooter reached down removed one of the pirates' helmets, and put it on his head. He remarked, "I reckon these boys will be sleeping for awhile." Portagee had a helmet on, picked up a scooter, and signaled Cooter to hop on back.

Portagee said, "I hope we don't get stopped by the cops. I don't have my driver's license yet. I'm under age."

Cooter looked at him and said, "I don't know what you just said, but make sure this contraption doesn't buck me off." Without losing another second, the two zipped down the street, leaving the pirates still out cold on the road.

Several minutes later, the two pirates came to their senses. One had some fractured ribs while the other was going to have back problems for months to come. The goon with the cracked ribs called Alvaro with his cell phone to report what had happened. He embellished telling Alvaro that the Spinners, as well as several gorillas, had ambushed them. Alvaro thought he was getting double talk, but he didn't have the time to get down to the truth. He instructed the two thugs to make their way back down to the dock to wait to be picked up and returned to the Prowler.

It was almost dusk now, so Alvaro commanded the chopper gunships to be fitted for a nighttime low-level flight to the Island. He was going to find the Spinners and their accomplices and make them pay for the trouble they had caused Alvaro and his thugs so far.

Keno and Salty zipped down Cut Road on their way to Gates Fort. This very small fort overlooked one of the entry channels to St. George's Harbour. The tiny fort, no more than a twenty by twenty foot block structure was built out of native limestone. Keno dropped Salty off at the entryway to the fort and said, "Salty, wait inside, I'll be right back as soon as I pick up one of our buds." Before he could turn the scooter around and get back out on Cut Road, Portagee and Cooter pulled in next to him. Keno, amazed at the sight asked, "Where did you get that scooter? Don't you know you're not even old enough to drive?"

Portagee laughed saying, "Sorry about that. The two pirates trying to run us down didn't give us much time to think twice about the law."

Cooter got off the back of the scooter. He released the strapped cricket bat from his back and said, "I like this game called cricket. I especially love the batting."

"What's he talking about?" asked Salty.

Portagee replied, "Never mind, but Cooter kicked butt back there."

Keno said, "Let's get these scooters inside before someone sees us. We can start to work out how to get our friends back into the Triangle." They went inside thinking they were safe for at least the time being. No sooner than the door closed than they heard a 'whomp, whomp, whomp' sound from behind Higgs Island, just across the channel from the fort.

One of Scarzo's chopper gunships now rose above the trees. The pilot aboard called Alvaro on his radio, "Alvaro, Alvaro, I've got our targets tracked to a small fort at the northeast tip of the island. I'll await your orders. Over and out."

Alvaro replied, "I'm on my way. If they try to leave, fire some rounds towards them and keep them pinned down."

"Roger that," replied the other gunship.

Inside the blockhouse Portagee asked, "Keno, what's that noise outside? It sounds like engines."

"Hold on, I'll look," replied Keno. Keno opened the door and looked out. Before he could slam it shut again, bullets came ripping through the door. Keno fell over backwards, rolled to the opposite wall and just missed being hit by the fire.

Portagee ran over to Keno yelling, "Are you O.K.? What's happening?"

Keno caught his breath and quickly answered, "There's a helicopter gunship shooting at us."

Salty asked, "Is that one of those flying contraptions like Jason and Spence fly?"

Keno replied, "Sort of. Not to change the subject, we have to get out of here before they level this fort to the ground."

"You're right, but what's the plan?" asked Salty.

Portagee thought for a minute and said, "Look guys, these goons probably only think there's two of us in here. They already talked to the guys Cooter thumped. Cooter and I will shoot out the door, zip up Barry Road and try to lose the chopper between here and Fort St. Catherine. Hopefully, the darkness will play in our favour. Once we're gone, wait a minute and make sure the chopper is after us. Then you two get out of here on Cut Road and head for the Unfinished Cathedral." Portagee then looked over at Salty and asked, "You do have the Tucker Cross, right?"

Salty smiled and tapped his peg leg saying, "As long as I don't lose my trusty leg."

Portagee turned to Cooter and said, "Let's go Coot. Hang on. It's going to be a rough ride. Oh, keep that bat on your back. It won't be much use against that gunship out there."

Cooter replied, "Let's ride partner." Portagee and Cooter jumped on the scooter. When Keno kicked the door open, the scooter shot out like a rocket.

The gunship pilot quickly called on the radio, "Alvaro, they're making a run for it. I'll await your orders."

Alvaro responded in a nanosecond, "Take them out, I'll be right behind you." The gunship tilted forward and whisked to the right out over the ocean, looped around the fort and back to the shoreline trying to find the scooter. Within seconds, the gunship spotted the scooter and began firing in its direction. Portagee was resourceful. He pulled under a palm tree while the gunship flew past them.

Back at Gates Fort it was evident that the gunship had not only left, but also, quickly afterwards, a second gunship also passed over. Keno turned to Salty urging, "Are you ready to 'rock and roll' Salty?" Salty nodded yes so Keno yanked on the throttle. They spun sideways then straightened out and shot down Cut Road.

Meanwhile Portagee was thinking he had lost the gunship. Just as he was getting ready to turn the scooter around, another gunship came up from behind them and cast a spotlight on the scooter. Cooter looked up and explained, "My little friend, I think we have double trouble now."

Portagee screamed back to Cooter, "Grab hold!" They shot out from under the palm tree and not a moment too soon. Alvaro pulled the trigger and released about one hundred rounds of bullets that ripped the trees to pieces. Portagee and Cooter were running out of luck. They were on a section of the road where there was no cover, in which they could hide. Alvaro, from his gunship could see the scooter down on the road trying to outrun them. Alvaro had the scooter in the cross hairs of his gun sight and was about to pull the trigger when his copilot started screaming and pointed right in front of them. It was the other gunship, which had slowed down trying to locate the scooter. Alvaro released the trigger and turned the gunship almost ninety degrees, just barely missing the other gunship. This gave Portagee enough time to shoot out in front of both chopper gunships. Portagee turned back to Cooter and yelled, "I think we can loose these goons for good!"

Cooter yelled back as he took a quick peak over his shoulder, "I wouldn't count your chickens before they hatch. They're back on our butts again." Portagee mumbled something in Portuguese and rolled on the throttle to give the chopper gunships a run for their money. As luck would have it, just when the scooter spun around a sharp curve onto Coot Pond Road, one of the chopper gunships shot the back tire out from under the scooter. Portagee lost control of the scooter as it flipped off the road onto the golf fairway and into a sand pit. The sand pit saved their bacon. Except for a little 'road rash' they were both unhurt from the spill. Cooter was first to get up. He leaned over and picked up Portagee saying, "Yee haw, what a ride! You OK?"

Portagee replied, "I'm O.K., but we'd better hide quickly since we're sitting ducks if we stay here." He looked around and said, "Let's get up to Fort St. Catherine and hide inside the fort." They ran up the road towards the fort. While they were running, the chopper gunships were hovering around the wreck site trying to locate them. The fort had long since been locked up for the night. Portagee was quick to figure out the same way to get into the fort that Scarzo had. He pointed to the northwest corner of the fort and said, "We'll slide down the outer wall into the moat and then we'll crawl up the inclined wall. Be careful Cooter. One slip and it's a thirty foot drop." While Portagee and Cooter were climbing, Alvaro guessed that they had escaped to try to find protection in the fort.

Alvaro called the other gunship and said, "I think our friends are trying to hide in the fort over there. You cover the east side of fort and swing around to the north. I'll do the same from the west side and we'll meet on the northern side of the fort."

"Roger that," replied the other gunship pilot.

Cooter was now climbing up the inside slanted wall of the fort. As he neared the top, Portagee was just starting his climb. At the moment that Cooter reached the top of the fort's wall, Alvaro's gunship located the two climbers. He called on the radio advising, "Quickly move into position on the northwest corner of the fort. I have located our prey." Within seconds, both chopper gunships were almost in position to attack. Alvaro was anxious and fired at Portagee. His shots missed their target. With stone sparks flying everywhere, Portagee let go and slid down the wall. At the final second, he grabbed the last protruding block between him and the rocky ocean coastline below. With the storm raging on, it made the old stones that much more slippery.

Portagee, hanging on by one hand, yelled up to Cooter, "Coot, please help me! I can't hold on much longer."

Cooter yelled back, "Here take this." He had taken the cricket bat off his back and was stretching down far enough for Portagee to grab it.

While Portagee and Cooter were struggling to survive, Alvaro called the other gunship and said, "Go ahead. Take the finishing shot on these losers."

"Roger boss." The pilot moved into position and began to fire. The first shots were off the mark. But before he could aim again, he received the surprise of his life. While the gunship firing was blowing away huge chunks of the fort, Portagee and Cooter heard the most blood-curdling scream they had ever heard. Within a split second, a ghostly image blasted out of the wall of the fort heading directly up towards one of the chopper gunships. At the same moment that the pilot squeezed the trigger trying to finish off Portagee, the ghostly image of Ghost George engulfed the cockpit of the chopper with ear shattering screams while swinging his saber all over the place. The pilot was so taken with fear trying to avoid the invader; he jerked the gunship to the starboard causing his firing to rip dozens of holes through Alvaro's gunship. Alvaro was now wrenching in pain with the wounds he had just received. Alvaro was trying to retake control of his gunship while the other gunship ran totally out of control, spinning in circles. As Alvaro pleaded for his life, the two chopper gunships crashed into each other with the rotors of the second gunship ripping through the cockpit of Alvaro's gunship. Both choppers exploded and crashed into the ocean and sank out of sight.

As Portagee was being pulled up the wall by Cooter, the ghostly image turned back and came howling down towards Cooter and Portagee. Cooter was able to reach down and grab Portagee by the arm and pull him up. Before they could get out of the way, the image passed through Cooter and into the wall of the fort. Cooter yelled out, "Holly smoke! That was the most bone chilling fear I ever experienced."

Portagee was now on the top of the wall. Cooter immediately asked him, "What kind of monsters do you have in your world?"

Portagee smiled and retorted, "That wasn't a monster. That was good old Ghost George. I don't know if he was saving us or just the fort."

Cooter replied, "Who cares? We're alive anyway." He gave Portagee a big hug and said, "Let's get the hell out of here and go find Keno and Salty." Portagee giggled as they both slid back down the wall and left the fort. They began walking over to the Unfinished Cathedral. As they walked across the edge of the golf course Cooter observed, "They sure do keep these fields' grass short around here. I don't see the sheep that would keep them so well trimmed."

Portagee laughed, "This is a golf course. People play special games on this grass. The game is played with golf clubs and balls."

Cooter replied, "Hot damn. If the clubs are as good as my cricket bat, I can't wait to try this game." They both laughed as they walked along. The rain and thunderstorms didn't bother either one of them. They were just happy to be alive.

-14-

SCARZO HITS THE JACKPOT

SCARZO HITS THE JACKPOT

Back in the Triangle, Jason, Spence, Bubba and Buford were setting a trap to ambush any pirates who might try to follow them. The narrow part of the peninsula between Whalebone Bay and Ferry Reach was where they were going to set the trap. Since there were only two muskets between the four men, Jason had decided to give them to the rebel sharpshooters Bubba and Buford. They each would also have a saber. Jason and Bubba would hide on the Whalebone Bay side of the peninsula while Spence and Buford would take up positions on the Ferry Reach side. Their plan was to catch the pirates in a deadly crossfire. Jason knew the plan was viable except for one small problem. If the pirates came through in large numbers they might have trouble reloading the muskets for a second volley. Who knew what they would be using for weapons: muskets, pistols or sabers? The group was all in place. All they could do now was wait.

Scorpion's men had landed on Ferry Point. As they pulled their longboat ashore, the Venom sailed past them, also searching for the Triangle's power source and for those who had fired on the Venom. With the longboat being secured on shore Scorpion's first mate barked at the crew, "Listen up mates. Get those bloody muskets loaded and be ready for some killings. Spread out in a long line and we'll head inland looking for those cowards. If you see something, shoot first and ask questions later." The eight pirates quietly moved into the bush with their muskets loaded and cocked.

Jason and the other Pilgrims didn't have long to wait. The pirates entered the clearing within ten minutes. The Pilgrims waited patiently to make sure all of the pirates had entered the clearing. This was Jason's worst nightmare. All eight pirates had muskets and sabers. If they opened fire on them they were outnumbered and could find themselves in serious trouble. If they let them pass, the Spinners might find themselves trapped and in a deadly situation.

After a minute of hesitation Jason finally yelled, "Fire!" Bubba and Buford fired and instantly dropped two pirates dead. While the pirates went into panic mode trying to figure where the shots were coming from, Bubba and Buford reloaded. They both fired their muskets again and dropped two more pirates. However, by now, the four remaining pirates knew where the musket shots were coming from. Two of the pirates immediately trained their muskets on Spence and Buford. In a split second the pirates fired their muskets at them. Buford was grazed in the temple and fell over backwards. Spence wasn't so lucky as he was hit in the chest. He stumbled out of the bush swinging his saber at the pirates only to get shot again by another pirate. Spence fell down, face first, and lay motionless on the ground. Jason and Bubba ran over to help Spence and started dragging him back to cover. Two of the pirates reloaded their muskets and were taking aim on Jason and Bubba when suddenly, an explosion of bullets came ripping out of the bush. All four of the remaining pirates were dropped dead in seconds. The Pilgrims fell to the ground covering their heads. As soon as the automatic fire stopped and the gun smoke began to clear, four men brandishing automatic AK47s stepped out of the bush. Jason, Bubba and Buford lay flat on the ground covering their heads. Bubba and Buford had never seen automatic weapon fire.

Bubba cried out to Jason saying, "There must be a whole battalion out there shooting at us."

Before Jason could respond Scarzo spoke up, "Sorry gentlemen. It's just the four of us. Oh, by the way, please stand up leaving your muskets and sabers on the ground. If not, you'll end up like your pirate friends: dead!" The three stood up with their hands over their heads.

Bubba asked, "My friend is hurt pretty bad can I go to him?"

Scarzo replied, "Don't worry about him, he's gone. Just do as I tell you or the same might happen to you. Axil, go tie these gentlemen's hands up and make it tight." Axil went to each of the Pilgrims and tied their hands behind them with plastic ties. Axil pulled the tie so tight on Bubba's wrists that they began to bleed. Scarzo spoke again, "Now that nasty chore is over, let's get down to business. We're here for the 'lost treasure', and I believe you fellas know where it is. I want it."

Buford responded, "The treasure is long gone. Besides we're not about to help a cold blooded killer."

Scarzo walked over to Buford and said, "That's not the answer I wanted." He took his right fist and struck Buford in his stomach as hard as he could. Buford doubled over, grimacing in pain. Scarzo kicked up his right knee in Buford's face as hard as he could. Buford flipped over backwards and hit the ground like a ton of bricks, spitting out blood from his mouth. Scarzo walked up to him and kicked Buford in the side several times and screamed, "My patience is wearing thin, you country bumpkin!" Scarzo turned and started walking back through the bush. He turned around and said, "Bring these fools back to the boat. We're wasting time." Scarzo lit his cigar and walked back to the boat.

Axil yelled at the two other goons to pick up Buford and haul him back to the boat. Next, he then turned to Bubba and Jason and said, "Get your sorry butts moving, or you can expect the same treatment as your stupid friend."

Bubba turned and started to lunge at Axil, but before he could get close, Axil raised his AK47 and pointed at Bubba and said, "Go ahead. Make my day you throwback."

Jason yelled at Bubba, "Let it go Bubba, we've lost too much already today." Bubba backed off. He and Jason headed through the bush towards Scarzo's speedboat.

The Spinners were now entering the village. Grizzly and Bear had already run ahead and were running in and out of all the huts looking for their friends. Sam and Michael were amazed at the changes the Pilgrims had made to the village in the last year. Instead of looking like run down military camp, when Drax and his pirates had occupied it, it now looked like a small village that normal settlers would live in.

Everyone, including the labs, went over to Salty's mess hut to find some food. It had been almost a day since any of the Spinners had eaten. Sam looked around and found some bananas, jerky and coconuts. She made three plates of food for Michael, Graham and herself. She also gave Grizzly and Bear some jerky. Michael had asked Sam for another banana. She reacted by throwing it across the table. Her aim was a wee bit off, and the banana bounced off the end of the table and hit the floor. Bear quickly ran over to the banana and began peeling it with his muzzle.

Graham just about fell out of his chair at the sight, and said, "Well I'll be darn. These dogs like bananas. Look, Bear even knows how to peel one. Sam, throw one to Grizzly. I'll bet he wants one too."

Sam said, "O.K.," and then threw a banana to Grizzly. Grizzly jumped up and caught the banana in his mouth. He placed it on the floor and began to peel it just like Bear did. Within a minute both labs were begging for more bananas. Sam gave each of them several more.

Later, while Michael was showing Graham around the camp, Graham turned and asked Michael, "Did you hear that noise before we came into the village?"

Michael replied, "Yes, it sounded like musket shots. I hope Jason and the others are O.K."

Graham asked, "Should we go back and check on them?"

Michael replied, "I don't think that would be a good idea. We could go up to the lookout post and see if we can spot them." Michael then pointed up to Fort George Hill. He added, "We'd better go tell Sam. Maybe she might want to go with us." They went over to the Mess Hut and, sure enough, Sam wanted to join them. In fact even the labs wanted to go. The hike up the hill for the Spinners was made even longer. Graham insisted on trying to find the spot where his house would have been in the parallel world back home. After finding the approximate location they continued their hike up to the lookout post. Once at the lookout post, they all jumped over the cedar rails and looked back to the west to see if they could see the Pilgrims heading their way. Michael looked down to see an old ship's telescope tied to one of the rails. He grabbed it and handed it to Sam saying, "See if you can spot them now, Sam." Sam started panning the west end of St. George's Island with no luck. Finally, she turned in a northerly direction and got the shock of her life.

She screamed, "Oh my God! The pirate ship is just off the North Shore." Michael and Graham turned around to see the ship. At the exact moment they turned to face the ship, three cannons onboard fired one after the other, in the direction of the lookout post. Sam screamed, "Run for your lives! They're shooting at us." With the speed of greased lightening, the three Spinners and the labs took off down the other side of the hill. The first cannon ball hit the ocean side of the hill and exploded while the second cannon ball scored a direct hit on the lookout post blowing it to smithereens. The third cannon ball overshot the lookout post and exploded within twenty yards of the Spinners. The force of the explosion sent all three Spinners flying head over heels rolling down the hill. Fortunately for the Spinners and the dogs, there were no injuries.

Back on the Venom, Scorpion was watching through her telescope on the bridge. When she saw the lookout post explode she screamed, "Yes, the Voodoo power is strong today. We must be getting close to the power source of the Triangle." She started chanting and throwing a sparkling powder into the air. The crew of the Venom always stayed clear of Scorpion when she was in her Voodoo state. While she was in this state, all work and progress on the ship would come to a standstill. Finally, after about an hour, she collapsed on the bridge. Scorpion would be out of it for another hour, but when she recovered, she meant business. With Scorpion out of it for the next hour or so, the Spinners would now have a little extra, unexpected time to escape.

The Spinners finally made it back to the village. Sam spoke up first, "What are we going to do? That pirate ship will clear one of the channels very soon."

Graham responded, "I know one thing for sure. We can't go back the way we came in."

"So what do we do then?" asked Sam.

Michael thought for a minute and said, "I think our best bet is to launch a longboat, row around the northwest corner of Smith's Island and make a bee line to Emily's Bay on St. David's Island."

Sam added, "You're right. At least there we will have some options."

Graham added, "O.K. Then we're set. Sam you get some food while Michael will help me get the longboat into the water."

Sam grabbed whatever she could find that was lightweight and as much dry jerky for Grizzly and Bear. She also knew that if push came to shove, the dogs were hunting dogs and could probably fare quite well for themselves. Plus, there were lots of banana trees producing this time of year and the labs loved bananas. Sam found several medium sized leather water bags. She filled them up from a water barrel Salty had rigged up to catch rainwater. After all, the Bermuda Triangle was just like Bermuda where there are no rivers or streams. You have to get your water from the rain. She now had enough supplies to last several days on their own. Sam called Grizzly and Bear and they headed down towards the longboat.

Graham and Michael had the longboat ready to go, s they walked around the village for anything they might find that would be helpful. They entered the hut where Bubba lived, and Graham said, "Wow, this hut is like an antique weapons' museum. Look, there are muskets, cap and ball pistols, sabers, daggers, cutlasses, powder bags and horns and musket ball bags. Plus look there's old wooden boxes stuffed with surprises."

Michael replied, "I think Bubba is waiting for the South to rise again." They both laughed, Michael continued, "Let's take three sabers and three daggers."

Graham added, "Why don't we take a couple of those pistols also?"

Michael smiled and responded, "First of all, we don't even know how to load them. Secondly, if we shoot at a pirate we'll miss and only make him madder. No, we'll stick to the daggers and sabers for self defense and survival."

Graham then said, "I get it. We'll stick with the daggers." They both laughed and left Bubba's hut with their newfound weapons.

They all arrived at the longboat at about the same time. Grizzly and Bear were the first to jump in. They loved to be out on the ocean. Sam was next. Once in, she turned and said, "Let's shove off you land lubbers."

As Michael and Graham were pushing the longboat out into the harbour, Michael said, "Yes captain, raise the mainsail." They both jumped in and began rowing for Smith's Island.

Sam said, "Not to put any pressure on you boys, but if that pirate ship spies us before we get to the leeside of Smith's Island, we'll find ourselves in Davy Jones Locker. These pirates seem to be pretty good shots with their cannons."

Michael and Graham replied in unison, "Yes, captain." Then they began to row a lot faster. After about ten minutes of hard rowing, they passed between Hen Island and Peggy's Island. They were close to being out of sight if the pirate ship entered St. George's Harbour. Grizzly and Bear kept moving back and forth in the longboat. They were very excited to be out and about on what they must have thought was a little picnic excursion.

Finally Michael said, "O.K., O.K. guys, can't you two sit down and rest for awhile? My face can't stand another lick."

Sam spoke up, "Be nice to those puppies, they're just thanking you for taking them along for the ride."

Michael replied, "They won't be thanking us much if we get blown out of the water."

Sam added, "Oh Michael, chill out! We're going to be just fine." She called for Grizzly and Bear to come to the bow of the longboat to be with her. She said, "All right puppies, you sit up here with me. Those grumps rowing the boat don't appreciate your help." They could now see the tiny Burt's Island with Emily's Bay nestled just behind it. They would be able to run ashore on St. David's Island and have the longboat hidden by Burt's Island. As planned, they ran the longboat ashore on St. David's Island, pulling it as far out of the water as they could. They hastily tried to camouflage it with branches and palm leaves.

Graham pointed to Michael and said, "Michael, why don't you get a couple of palm leaves and try to wipe out our tracks in the sand as we leave the beach?"

Michael replied, "Good idea." Then he did just that as they left the beach and entered the bush.

As they made their way through the bush Graham said, "I think we should make for higher ground to see if we can spot where the pirate ship is heading."

Sam replied, "I agree. In fact we might have to warn Jason, Spence, Bubba and Buford that they might be walking into a trap." This might have been a great idea except for the fact that the Pilgrims had already fallen into Scarzo's trap. Spence was already gone and the others might not live to tell about it.

Across the island at Ferry Reach, Scarzo was waiting in the speedboat for Buford, Bubba and Jason to join him. The first to arrive was Buford. He was still dazed and in a great deal of pain. Scarzo's goons just dropped him in front of the speedboat and left him. While on their way through the bush, Jason and Bubba exchanged thoughts. Bubba spoke first, "I'd rather die than tell this pirate where the treasure is."

Jason responded, "With that attitude Bubba you will die." Bubba was shocked at Jason's comments. Jason continued, "Who cares about the treasure? It really means nothing to us, and the Spinners will never need any more of it."

Bubba thought for awhile and said, "I reckon you're right Jason. So now what?"

Jason replied, "The problem is how can we survive once we give them the treasure?"

"That's a good point," agreed Bubba.

Jason added, "OK then. We'll take our time getting Bozo and his thugs to the treasure and hopefully we can figure out how to escape before it's too late."

Bubba replied, "That's good. But his name is Scarzo, so let's not piss him off until after we escape."

"You're right my good friend. We'd better get going and make sure Buford is OK," added Jason. They cleared the bush and found Buford lying on the rocky beach. Scarzo was just sitting there smoking a cigar. Bubba and Jason went over to help to get Buford up off the rocks.

Scarzo watched them for a while and finally said, "When you fools get your friend back up on his feet we need to get going. I want to get my hands on that treasure and get the hell out of this world." Jason looked up at him and nodded in agreement. Then it hit him like a lead balloon. Jason thought to himself, "Scarzo wasn't going anywhere right now without the Tucker Cross. Let him have the treasure and float around the Bermuda Triangle for the next hundred years."

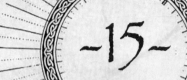

-15-

WHICH WAY IS THE TRIANGLE?

Keno and Salty had been at the Unfinished Cathedral for quite some time. They had their eyes focused in Fort St. Catherine's direction since they had arrived. With thunder and lightening filling the sky, they could not tell if they were hearing gunshots or thunder. Keno pointed out to Salty some time ago how unusual it was to see the sky light up over the fort. It was like a double lightening bolt had struck the fort. While they were waiting, Keno looked over at Salty and saw his peg leg was shaking uncontrollably. He said, "Salty, I didn't know thunder storms made you that nervous. I always thought you were a tough old sea dog."

Salty lashed back, "I fear no man or beast, you overgrown cabin boy."

Keno fired back, "If that's the case, why is your peg leg shaking so much?"

Salty replied, "It's shaking because that bloody cross in my hollowed out leg thinks it's time to go home."

Keno laughed and said, "You'd better stay out of the weather. The Tucker Cross loves this kind of weather. If a lightening bolt strikes that old peg leg of yours you'll be visiting Davy Jones's Locker instead of the Triangle."

Salty replied, "There ain't no lightening bolt in the world that can do me in!" Just then a horrific bolt struck near the Unfinished Cathedral. Salty just about jumped out of his leg. He looked around, and seeing Keno smiling, got up and moved to a safer spot saying, "My back was getting a little sore sitting there. This spot looks much more inviting."

Keno smiled and said, "It sure does. Mind if I join you?" Salty nodded his head in approval while Keno moved next to Salty.

Meanwhile, Portagee and Cooter were enjoying walking along Government Hill Road in the rain. They had passed Tobacco Bay. Cooter thought that this was the spot where Captain Drax had ambushed him in the Triangle. Although it was dark and looked very different, Cooter was perfectly right. This was the spot where Captain Drax murdered the entire crew of the confederate blockage running ship, except for Cooter, Bubba and Buford. As they cleared the top of the hill, Portagee pointed out the Unfinished Cathedral. Cooter commented, "That old church looks like it should be the Triangle, not here."

Portagee replied, "Well, since it's a one way gateway to the Triangle, it must think it is part of the Triangle." They walked for another ten minutes when they were within earshot of the old church. Portagee started to yell so, Cooter signaled him to be quiet.

He whispered to Portagee, "We don't know whether it's friend or foe in that church. I'll give a hog call. If Salty's in there he'll let us know." Cooter started snorting and carrying on like a wild hog. Portagee did everything he could to hold back his laughter, as he didn't want to upset Cooter.

Then from within the church they both heard Salty yelling back, "I know that's you Cooter. Get your big butt in here before someone shoots it off!"

Cooter smiled and said, "You old hound dog. Glad to see you and Keno made it here." Cooter and Portagee quickly ran into the church and caught up with their friends. Cooter told Salty and Keno about their near death experience and eventual escape. After listening to Cooter, one might think they had just destroyed Scarzo's entire pirate crew, ship and choppers all at once. All Salty and Keno really cared about was that Cooter and Portagee were safe. It didn't matter how Cooter embellished the story.

Portagee leaned over to Keno and whispered into his ear, "I'll tell you what really happened later. It's really just as exciting."

Salty added, "Boys, it's time for us to go home." He sat down and took his wooden peg leg off; he unscrewed the top and reached inside pulling out the Tucker Cross. Salty tossed it to Portagee and said, "Here it is, do your thing."

Portagee caught the cross and said, "Now hold on Salty. It's not going down that way."

Salty replied, "What the hell do you mean, not going down?"

Portagee responded, "Keno and I have decided to go back with you two. Right now, we think Michael, Graham and Sam may be in the Triangle. We haven't seen them for a couple of days. Also, with these modern day pirate goons running around here, it might be good to escape into the Triangle for a couple of days. That's why we're going with you two, OK?"

Cooter chimed in, "Come on you old sea dog! Let our friends come with us. We can always send them back when they have worn out their welcome."

Salty caved in and added, "All right you bloody nags! You can come. Now let's get out of here before something bad happens."

Keno laughed and said, "Salty, I think we've already seen enough bad things for one day."

Portagee stood up with the Tucker Cross in his left hand, and said, "We need to be outside of the Cathedral and be ready to re-enter through the west archway. Although it's not a gale force storm tonight, hopefully it's strong enough to open the gateway to let us pass through. Oh yes, one other thing, I think we should all hold hands while we pass through."

Cooter and Salty looked at each other slightly confused. Then Cooter asked, "Why in the blazes do we have to do that? Are we going to get lost?" Both Portagee and Keno knew that there was no way of knowing where in the Bermuda Triangle they would show up, since this was a one-way gateway. There was no gateway on the other side to match this one so there was no way of knowing where they would emerge. It could be in the ocean, a cave, or a shipwreck.

Knowing this, Keno responded, "Sometimes you can get whipped around a bit. We just want to keep us together." Salty and Cooter both accepted that statement from Keno. Otherwise Cooter, who couldn't swim, might have second thoughts about going back. They all lined up in single file, one behind the other holding hands. Keno was first, followed by Cooter, then Salty, and lastly Portagee holding the cross up high with his left hand. Portagee turned the cross in the direction of the archway of the Cathedral. Within seconds the fireworks display kicked in. The green lights began emanating from the entrance, while lightening began to strike at the archway. The gateway was beginning to open, but the opening was not going to be very large. It was clear that they would have to move fast and bend over at the waist to get through.

The time was right. Portagee yelled, "Go for it dudes!" With that, Keno started running for the archway pulling the others behind him. The electronic waves were going crazy. As each of them passed through the archway, a combination of green explosions and small lightening bolts struck the stone archway. As Portagee made the final pass through, a series of rapid greens explosions fired. Then abruptly, there was calm.

The vacuum created on the outside of the Triangle sucked the four into the Bermuda Triangle in seconds. There were mild explosions as each of them passed into the Triangle rolling head over heels. Once in the Bermuda Triangle, they each hit an object with such force that they were knocked out cold. Keno was the first to come to. Everything was very fuzzy, the lighting was poor, and it smelled damp and old. It finally came to him he was in the hold of a ship. As he moved around to find the others, the old timbers creaked and moaned. Keno went over to Portagee first and shook him, trying to wake him up. As Portagee began to move around Keno said, "Portagee, we're back and you won't believe this."

Portagee looked up and asked, "Believe what?"

Keno whispered back, "We're in an old shipwreck somewhere around the island."

Then out of the clear blue, Salty spoke up," I've got bloody bad news for you two. This is no wreck. It's a real pirate ship with real pirates."

Keno fired back, "How do you know that Salty?"

Salty replied, "Just look around. See those old treasure chests? Plus look, there are fresh bananas hanging up in the corner."

Portagee added, "Oh crap, if these are pirates, we're in deep trouble."

"I think we just jumped out of the frying pan and into the fire and look my new bat is busted to pieces," Cooter spoke up.

Salty turned to Cooter and saying, "Well it's nice to have you join us."

Cooter looked at Portagee and Keno and asked, "How in the hell did we get here? I thought we would come out in the exact same spot that we entered."

Portagee replied, "We left out one little detail. The Cathedral gateway was a one-way gateway. Once you enter, you might pop out anywhere on the island."

Cooter just shook his head, saying, "Let's see if we can get the hell out of here. I'll climb up the ladder and take a look see."

While Cooter climbed up the ladder, Portagee looked down and saw the Tucker Cross lying on the floor. He picked it up and tossed it to Salty saying, "Salty, stow this baby away for safe keeping. We may need it later." Salty knew what to do, and back into the leg it went. By now Cooter was up on deck looking around. He slid back down the ladder and hit the floor on his butt with a thump.

Salty looked at him and said, "Are you trying to alert the whole ship that we're down here in the ship's hold?"

Cooter stood up and said, "I don't think that's a problem. We're home alone, but the real surprise is that we're anchored just off our home on St.

George's. The pirates must be looking for what's left of the lost treasure."

Salty replied, "That's great. You already moved the treasure so when these cutthroat pirates figure that out they're going to...."

Keno interrupted saying, "Make us walk the plank?"

Cooter added, "I wish, but if these pirates are anything like Captain Drax, they'll run us through and eat our hearts."

Portagee started talking hysterically in Portuguese. Keno could understand only one of every twenty words.

Finally, Salty said, "Let's get up top and sneak over the back of the ship."

Cooter added, "Ok, but remember one of us can't swim a lick." One after the other, they climbed up the ladder to the deck. They started looking around for the best way to get off the ship without being seen.

Meanwhile, back in the village, Scorpion and her crew were ransacking the entire village looking for the Spinners and the power source. Scorpion was ready to strike and kill anyone who might get in her way. Ever since she arrived on the island, one bad thing after another had happened. Then it hit her. She turned around like a bolt of lightening and screamed as she pointed back to the ship, "I feel the power. It's on board the ship." Just then, Portagee stuck his head up to look over the side. Scorpion drew out her cutlass and yelled, "There they are. Back to the ship and we'll skin them alive." The entire crew started running, screaming and yelling towards their longboats on the shore.

Portagee quickly turned around and said, "Guys, I think the pirates just saw me."

Cooter turned back to Portagee and asked, "What in hell would make you think that?"

Portagee snapped back, "Oh, I don't know. Just look over my shoulder." Cooter walked over and looked. To his horror, he saw the entire crew getting into their longboats.

Cooter promptly yelled, "Salty, do you think we can fire these cannons off in the next thirty seconds?"

Salty cried back, "Do bears crap in the woods? You bet we can. Come on boys, help me prime two of these old cannons." In an instant the four were priming and loading two cannons. They were ready to fire them in less than thirty seconds. There was only one problem. There were four longboats heading towards the ship and they were spread out too far for one cannon shot to take out two longboats at a time. Cooter fired his cannon first, and hit the front of one of the longboats. The longboat tipped over, but most of the pirates survived.

Salty saw that the cannon shot was off the mark and said, "What a terrible shot. No wonder the South lost the war. Watch this you bloody landlubber. Here's how you do it." He fired the cannon and made a direct hit on one of the remaining longboats. The longboat blew to pieces leaving no survivors. It was too late to reload. The remaining pirates had already tied up alongside the ship, and were climbing up the side. Salty yelled, "Back up everyone! There's going to be one hell of a fight in a few seconds." Salty and Cooter had picked up two sabers and were now backed up against the opposite rail on the ship. Portagee and Keno were behind them.

As the pirates came over the side and started moving towards the four, Cooter yelled, "Come on you cutthroats, meet your maker!"

Scorpion jumped on board the ship. She drew out her pistol and said, "I think you sea scum better drop those sabers before I signal my mates to blow holes through your little friends." Salty turned to his side. He realized that there were two pirates behind them, just over the side of the ship, pointing pistols at the back of Portagee and Keno's heads.

Salty turned to Cooter and said, "Drop your sabers, it's over." Cooter did what he was told and threw down his saber. Salty quickly followed suit behind him.

Meanwhile, Michael, Sam and Graham had reached high ground on St. David's Island and had seen the entire ordeal by looking through the old telescope they had found onboard the longboat. Sam said, "What do we do now? I think the pirates have captured Portagee, Keno, Cooter and Salty."

Michael asked, "Where did they come from?"

Sam replied, "That really doesn't matter right now. Our friends are in trouble." All three stared in the direction of the pirate ship, not knowing what to do next to help their friends.

Scorpion walked over to the four. She reached Cooter first. When she approached, Cooter stood up and said, "Missy, you sure do remind me of a sweet little thing I left back home in the war. Is your name Clarabell?" Scorpion moved closer to Cooter, so close that Cooter was starting to get a little nervous. He had never been so close to such a beautiful woman before.

Scorpion slowly moved her stinger hand up Cooter's arm. She whispered into his ear, "So you think I'm beautiful do you?"

Cooter nodded his head and replied, "Yes, my little southern bell." Scorpion smiled and acted like she was about to kiss him. However, without any hesitation she quickly kneed him in the groin and slashed his face with her stingers. Cooter was lying on the deck crippled with pain and bleeding profusely.

Scorpion screamed down at him as she was kicking him with her boots, "You bloody idiot! You're a dead man! You've just felt my scorpion sting across your ugly face." She turned to her crew and said, "Throw him overboard. Let him die."

Portagee broke loose from the pirate who was holding him and ran over to Scorpion pleading, "Please don't throw him overboard. He can't swim."

Scorpion looked down at Portagee laughing and said, "Good, then he'll die quicker. Throw him overboard now!" With that, three crewmembers picked up Cooter and threw him over the gunwale. Since it was now dark, you could only hear Cooter's splash and moans. Scorpion looked back at Portagee and said, ""Don't worry my little one, the poison venom will probably kill him before he drowns." She turned and yelled, "Throw these three in the hold and chain them up!" As Salty, Portagee and Keno were being dragged below, Scorpion looked up to the black sky and screamed, "I can feel the power. It's strong here, but where is it?" She then stormed up to the bridge and yelled at one of her crewmembers to bring her a bottle of rum.

Meanwhile, in the ship's hold, the three were locked up in chains. Keno looked over to Salty and asked, "Do you think Cooter has a chance to swim to shore?"

Salty hug his head and replied, "No, he's gone now we've lost a good friend tonight. That evil woman will pay for this, I guarantee you that mates." Nothing else was said. It was dark and they all felt hopeless. They would wait to see what the morning would bring.

Salty didn't know it, but he was dead wrong about Cooter. When Cooter was thrown overboard, his head and chest landed on a piece of debris from one of the wrecked longboats. However, he was mostly paralyzed unable to move because of the venom. His head and shoulders were being kept afloat which prevented him from drowning. As the night wore on, Cooter slowly gained back body movement. He was able to paddle himself towards St. David's Island. As the numbness wore off, he began to feel the pains from his injuries. Cooter was a survivor. He was determined to make his way to shore. After hours of floating and paddling, he finally made it to shore at Emily's Bay at St. David's Island. Cooter knew he could not stay on the beach in the daylight hours, just in case the pirates were looking for him. He slowly pulled himself up on the beach and clawed his way towards the dense brush. He hoped to hide under the brush out of sight until he recovered. As he was crawling under the brush his head cracked something very solid. Cooter looked up and said, "Well I'll be dog gone. It's one of our longboats. That means some of my buddies are around these parts." He felt slightly comforted knowing that his friends might be close by. Now that he was under cover, his body just gave out. Cooter dozed off and was out like a light.

~16~

WHO'S AFTER WHAT?

Darkness had set in at Ferry Reach by the time the Pilgrims made it back to the speedboat with their captors. Scarzo looked up as his goons dragged Buford up close to the boat. He ordered, "Drop him there on the beach. His friends can take care of him. One of you, stay on guard over our guest while the other one goes with Axil to find some firewood. We'll have a nice bonfire tonight and toast marsh mallows with our new found friends." Then he laughed as he laid back in the soft cushioned seat of his speedboat. By now, Jason and Bubba had arrived and sat down next to Buford.

Jason looked up and pleaded, "I need to tend to my friend. He's bleeding and needs help. Will you cut my hands loose?"

Scarzo looked up, smiling, "Amigo, I don't trust you, you're the smart one." He looked over to his goon and yelled out, "Cut loose the other one. He'll behave himself," while pointing to Bubba.

Scarzo's goon walked over to Bubba and kicked him onto his side. Reaching down with his knife, he cut the plastic strap, saying, "Gringo, go to your friend. But remember, if you try anything I'll shoot you down like a dog." Bubba quickly jumped up and ran over to Buford to help him out.

Jason turned to Scarzo and said, "Thanks." Scarzo turned his head ignoring him. The bonfire had been burning for a couple of hours. Scarzo and his men had plenty to eat, but never shared a morsel with the Pilgrims. Sitting on the exposed beach as the fire blazed did not seem to bother Scarzo. He must have felt that his superior weapons could handle any surprise attack. Having the big bonfire was almost an invitation for trouble, but Scarzo could care less.

The Spinners had been sitting for hours overlooking the bay, keeping an eye on the Venom from St. David's Island. Finally Graham said, "I'm getting very hungry. Can we go back down to the longboat and find some grub?"

Sam replied, "That's a good idea. Michael, why don't you stay here? You keep an eye on that pirate ship while we fetch some food and water."

Michael turned and said, "Aye, aye, Captain." With that, the two Spinners went down the hill to Emily's Bay where the longboat was beached.

As they got closer, Graham signaled Sam to stop. He whispered; "What's that sound down there by the longboat? It almost sounds like somebody groaning." He drew out his saber and continued towards the longboat. When they were within a few feet, the noise stopped. Graham said, "You'd better get out of that boat or I'll run you through, you scum."

A broken voice came right back saying, "Bring it on you Yankee lover."

Sam looked at Graham, reached over to make him lower his arm and said, "That's Cooter and he sounds like he's in bad shape." They both ran over to the longboat and dragged Cooter out from under the branches. When they got Cooter out in the open Sam asked, "Coot, what in the world happened to you?"

Cooter looked up and smiled, "I just got my butt kicked by the most beautiful woman I've seen in over two hundred years."

Sam replied, "Well, I thought I was the most beautiful girl in the Triangle."

Cooter added, "Well dang it, you know what I mean, Miss Sam."

Sam laughed saying, "I know. Oh Cooter, I forgot to introduce you to Graham."

Cooter looked up at Graham asking, "Don't tell me you're another Yankee?"

Graham smiled, "No sir, I'm just another friendly Bermudian."

Sam said, "That's enough talking. Let's get Cooter off the beach and back up the hill." They grabbed some supplies and helped Cooter back up the hill where Michael was. Michael was amazed to see Cooter.

After they had eaten, Cooter told them what had happened to him and Salty. He also brought them up to speed on how they came back to the Triangle with Portagee and Keno, and how they were now all prisoners of Scorpion.

Michael asked, "What does this Scorpion want? What's left of the lost treasure?"

Cooter replied, "I don't reckon she's after the treasure. She's possibly looking for the power source of the Triangle. She's some type of Voodoo queen."

"Does she want the Tucker Cross?" asked Sam.

Cooter thought for a second and replied, "Yes, if that gives her the power of the Triangle."

Graham interrupted, "But where in the world is the cross?"

Cooter smiled and said, "Oh it's safe for now. Salty has it safely tucked away in his peg leg."

Michael said, "We have no idea where Jason, Spence, Bubba and Buford are, but we do know where Salty, Portagee and Keno are. We must try to help them escape." Michael and the others didn't know that they had already lost their good friend Spence.

Cooter replied, "They're too strong on the ship. We can't make a move until they move onto land. We'll just have to follow them like a pack of wolves and wait for Scorpion to make a mistake. Believe me, I found out the hard way. She is not one to mess with. Sam, you stay clear of her she won't want another pretty face around."

Keno questioned, "Scorpion's on a ship and we're on land. How are we going to follow her?"

Cooter said, "Don't forget, my cousins and I used to track Union soldiers for old General Stonewall Jackson during the war. That ships not going out to sea. We'll just keep out of sight on the shore and follow her. Tomorrow's going to be a long day. We'd better get some shuteye." With that, they all turned in for the night. Grizzly and Bear curled up beside Sam and Michael.

The sun rose early the next morning. It was going to be another beautiful day in the Triangle. Scarzo was the first one up at Ferry Reach that day. As soon as he lit up his cigar, he walked over to Jason and gave him a hard kick in the ribs. Jason rolled over in pain. His moan woke everyone else on the beach. Scarzo looked around and said, "Well, I see your friend made it through the night. You're a pretty good nurse."

Jason looked up and replied, "No thanks to you."

Scarzo laughed, then turned away. As he walked towards the speedboat he said, "Come on Gringos, daylight's burning. We're going treasure hunting today." He climbed into the speedboat while Axil and the other thugs helped Jason, Bubba and Buford into the back of the speedboat. Scarzo turned around and said, "My friend Jason, you come up and sit by me. You can be my navigator. Mr. ex-pilot Axil, you sit behind him with your weapon pointed at the back of his head, just in case he gets any funny ideas. Jason, my good friend, kindly direct me to the treasure."

Jason pointed to the west and said, "It's a long way from here. We're going to the Great Sound." Bubba and Buford looked at each other wondering what Jason had up his sleeve. Scarzo, asking no more questions, threw the throttle forward. They were blasting through the waves in seconds. Scarzo was thinking about the riches that were awaiting him, while Jason was hoping to run Scarzo out of gas.

Activity aboard the Venom was slow that morning. Many of the crewmembers had drunk themselves into a stupor on rum and home-brewed grog from the previous night. Scorpion had also put herself into a Voodoo trance trying to locate the power source of the Triangle. Salty, Keno and Portagee had been awake since before dawn, but as they were chained down in the hold, they were helpless to move about. Finally, Scorpion made her way up to the bridge of the ship. After looking around for a while she screamed down to a crewmember, "Get those prisoners topside! I have some more questions for them." Several crewmembers slipped down the steep stairs into the hold. Once there, one of them unlocked the prisoners from the chain, but left them in their leg irons. Because of Salty's peg leg, the leg irons were clamped to Salty's good leg with one end to Portagee's leg and the other end to Keno's leg.

The crewmember yelled at them, "Get your bloody butts on deck! The captain demands your presence." Salty mumbled some words in disgust at him, then started moving towards the stairs. As he passed, the crewmember grabbed him by the shoulder and said, "Mate, what was that you said?"

Salty replied, "I said, yes sir, that's all." Portagee, Keno and Salty slowly climbed up the steep stairs one after the other. When they reached the deck they were taken to the bridge and made to stand in front of Scorpion.

Scorpion looked them over saying, "It's nice of you shipmates to join me this beautiful morning. I hope for your sakes we're going to make better headway today." Salty looked her straight in her blood red eyes and started to say something, but before it could come out Keno jerked his leg as hard as he could, sending Salty to the deck. Keno realized that Salty was about to say something that would probably get himself killed.

Keno dropped to his knee and whispered, "Salty, I'm sorry, you OK?"

Salty looked up at Keno saying, "I'm fine, I just lost my balance."

Scorpion laughed adding, "Your young friends are watching out for you, you worthless dog." Salty decided to keep his mouth shut as Keno helped him back up. Scorpion walked up to Salty and said, "When I get close to you, I sense a power. What are you hiding from me, old man?"

Salty replied, "Nothing captain, maybe it's my animal magnetism."

Scorpion snapped back, "Don't get cocky with me you old goat, or I just might let you join the zombie world." She raised her left hand and curled her stingers tightly until venom started dripping from them. She realized her prisoners knew nothing about the power source of the Triangle. She was obviously wasting her time with them. She said, "Keep these fools on deck and keep an eye on them." She turned to her crew and yelled, "Pull up the anchor and set sail. We'll move along the shoreline and watch for suspicious activity."

The crew went scrambling to do Scorpion's bidding. The ship went slowly up the north shoreline of St. David's and through the narrow channel of Ferry Reach. As they neared opening of the Castle Harbour Bay, Scorpion began to receive mixed signals. She began to chant and made unusual body gestures. She quickly snapped out of her state. Scorpion pointed towards the south saying, "Head for that small cove over there near that dense jungle." She was pointing towards Tom Moore's Jungle. Keno and Portagee silently looked at each other knowing that this might present an opportunity to escape. Scorpion was not being drawn to the jungle by the force she had been feeling. Instead, it was a feeling of a great evil being that was living in the jungle. Even if it was the devil himself she was ready to enter into a pact with him. Scorpion was right. As the ship drew closer to the shore of the jungle, a very evil being was watching them through the dense jungle.

The Spinners and Cooter were so exhausted from the night before. By the time Sam woke up, the Venom had left St. George's Harbour. Sam was in a panic, yelling, "Wake up, wake up, the pirate ship has left! What are we going to do?"

Cooter sat up and said, "Now hold on Miss Sam. Don't get your knickers in a twist. I reckon they sailed north. From Ferry Reach they'll go along the North Shore or turn south into Castle Harbour."

Michael said, "By the time we get over to the Ferry Reach area, they'll be long gone. We won't know which way they went."

Coot, as usual, smiled and said, "I bet you a possum pie that Grizzly and Bear and I can find the ship before night fall, right pups?" Both labs came running over to Cooter and of course he gave them some jerky.

"OK," said Graham, "how are we going to find the ship?"

Cooter replied, "Very simple, we're going to cut across St. David's as the crow flies to Castle Harbour. By the time we get there with the aid of our trusty telescope, we should be able to spot those bloody pirates as they clear Ferry Reach."

Sam jumped up and down and said, "What are we waiting for? We need to get moving now!" Everyone quickly got up and moved in a due south direction. The labs were so excited running through the bush, you would have thought they were tracking a flock of geese. The small group had labored through the dense bush for almost an hour. They had no luck finding any hog trails on this part of St. David's. Finally they came through to a clearing on the shoreline of the island. The labs were romping up and down the beach while the Spinners and Cooter were trying to find some sign of the pirate ship.

Graham finally sat down in the sand and said, "Well, I guess they went the other way. Now we'll never catch up to them."

Sam was still looking through the telescope when she said, "Don't be too sure of that guys. Looks to me like a ship is just coming around the southwest tip of St. David's." She was right. However the ship was on a due south course.

Michael then said, "Look, they must be heading towards Tom Moore's Jungle. That's good news. We can head down to Cooper's Island and island hop across to Castle Point, then on up to the jungle."

Graham jumped in and said, "Let's get going before they see us."

Everyone started to move out at a fast pace, except Cooter. He stood there and yelled, "Wait just a dang blasted minute! If you think I'm going swimming again after last night you're daft."

Sam stopped and turned around and said, "Come on Coot I promise we'll help you across the narrows."

Cooter shook his head from side to side and said, "No I ain't going to do it and that's final."

Graham asked, "Then what are we going to do?"

Cooter responded, "You young ones go ahead the way you already planned. I'm going back to the longboat and going to row myself around."

Sam asked, "You sure, Coot?"

Cooter replied, "Yep, I'm sure." He went over and hugged each of the

Spinners and waved them on. Cooter turned around, pulled out his saber and started whacking away at the bush.

Michael yelled out, "Coot, why don't you take Grizzly and Bear with you to keep you company?"

Cooter replied, "If you don't mind, that's a bloody good idea."

Sam said, "They love boats."

Cooter smiled and yelled, "Come on pups, let's go for a ride." Grizzly and Bear went running after Cooter. When they caught up to them, he gave them both a big pat on the head and some jerky. Then, within seconds, Cooter and the labs were out of sight.

Michael, Graham and Sam turned away. They walked down the beach at a fast pace towards Cooper's Island. The ocean was fairly calm so their swim from island to island went fairly quickly. They made it to Castle Point in less than an hour. They were at least two hours away from Tom Moore's Jungle. It was going to be exhausting moving through the bush, but hopefully they would find a hog trail on the way to make the going easier.

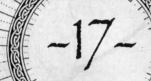

~17~

RUMBLE IN THE JUNGLE

RUMBLE IN THE JUNGLE

The Venom was now closing in on the bay that bordered Tom Moore's Jungle on its northeast side. This jungle is very unique for both Bermuda and the Triangle. It is extremely dense in tree growth and over ninety percent of the jungle area is shaded by this dense growth. The trees are not very tall, making the ceiling of the jungle very low to the ground. In many places you have to bend over to walk through. The jungle has several hog trails that zigzag from left to right, up and down the terrain. Because the sun cannot penetrate through the ceiling growth and the fact that a compass doesn't work in the Triangle, you never have a clue which direction you're heading. To make matters even worse, there are many what would appear to be small hills, which are really wickedly sharp rock formations that you would normally find on rocky shorelines. One slip on these rocks could easily mean a fall to your death. There are also small marshes and land-locked salt water ponds with who knows what swimming in them, barracuda and giant eels to say the least. Then there are the caves scattered all over the jungle. Most have water in the bottoms of them. Many of them you can enter, but watch out for the stalagmites and stalactites. They can be very dangerous if you hit your head or if you happen to fall on one. Some of these caves are so well hidden that if you slipped on the damp ground and fell through one of the concealed openings, you could be lost forever. This was truly one of the spookiest places in the Triangle and the Spinners knew it.

The Venom dropped her anchor in the shallow bay just off the shoreline of Tom Moore's Jungle. The water was so clear and shallow at this spot that Scorpion decided to forgo the longboats and just wade through the water to get ashore. Scorpion's crew was beginning to thin out. She had never heard back from her first mate at Ferry Reach and she had lost a longboat full of crew in St. George's Harbour. She decided to keep half her crew aboard ship and the other half would follow her into the jungle. Scorpion also made sure her prisoner, Salty, accompanied her into the jungle. A power seemed to emanate from him, which she could not understand. As she entered the fringe of the jungle she could feel an evil force. This caused her to smile. She feared nothing and would embrace any evil force she might encounter. Scorpion barked out commands to her crew, "Two of you take the lead and scout ahead, but keep within fifty feet! As for my peg leg buccaneer, you stay just in front of me. I want to keep my eyes on you and the two young boys can bring up the rear."

Salty replied, "You sea hag, you'd better be careful here. A wild bear may tear you to shreds."

Scorpion already had her fill of Salty, she drew out her cutlass and poked it into Salty's back saying, "There are no bears in the Triangle, so shut your mouth unless I speak to you."

"Yes captain," replied Salty. Salty asked, "What are we here for, lost treasure?"

Scorpion snapped back, "You fool, I can find treasure anywhere, I want the power of the Triangle."

Salty replied, "Oh." Then he looked down at his peg leg wondering if the cross had anything to do with her search.

The small band entered the jungle, in single file, starting down the first hog trail they encountered. As they walked along, Portagee whispered to Keno, "Now that the chains are off our legs and only our hands are tied we could easily escape."

Keno turned back to Portagee and said, "Two problems. What about Salty? He's up front and secondly where do we go?"

Portagee scratched his head and said, "I can't think of everything." Nothing else was said. They just kept walking along with neither one having a clue where they were going. Just out of sight through the dense jungle, someone or something was watching their every move.

Sam, Graham and Michael had been moving up the shoreline for over an hour. Not being on a hog trail slowed down the progress immensely. As they rounded a rock protrusion on the shoreline, they noticed the pirate ship anchored in the bay. Peeking over the top of the rock formation Sam said, "I wonder how long they've been there? I don't see any longboats on the shore."

Michael replied, "The ship looks fairly deserted. There's not a lot of crew on her."

Graham commented after looking through the telescope, "The shoreline over there looks like it's been disturbed."

Sam added, "If we sneak around to that part of the shoreline, they might see us from the ship."

Michael suggested, "Well, if we just sit here we'll never find them. Let's move around just inside the jungle and see if we can spot tracks or signs." They agreed on this plan and crept into the jungle, circling around to the landing spot. Staying in the jungle and out of sight, the Spinners looked around for clues.

Pretty soon Graham pointed down to the muddy ground and whispered, "Look here. This looks like a peg leg print."

Michael said, "You're right. Let's be sure and see if we can find the shoe prints of Keno and Portagee."

Sam then reminded the others, "They should be easy to find because all the pirates will have smooth prints and Keno and Portagee will probably have some type of sports shoe on with distinctive tread."

Sure enough, within a couple of minutes Graham found some, "Holy smokes, this one must be Keno's size thirteen bear print, and look there, that must be Portagee's size eight. Well at least we know they're O.K. What are they doing here? Are they looking for the lost treasure?"

Michael answered, "That's the only thing that makes sense. They must think the treasure is buried here. I wonder if it really is?"

"It really doesn't matter. We'd better follow them and wait for a chance to get our buddies back," added Graham. They agreed and slowly and as quietly as possible, they went down the hog trail that Scorpion was on.

Scorpion and her party had walked for what seemed to be miles through the hot, humid jungle. In reality they hadn't walked a mile yet. The two scouts were much further ahead than they were supposed to be. They were passing through a jagged rocky area when one of them heard a noise in the bush. He stopped, signaled his mate to stop and commanded, "Who the hell is out there? Show your face mate or I'll blow your bloody head off." He waited a minute then lowered his musket and said to his mate, "I guess I was bloody well hearing things."

Before he could turn around a large coconut spiked with eight-inch cedar barbs came swinging through the trees and imbedded itself right into the pirate's chest. The sudden impact caused the pirate to pull the trigger on his musket. The shot fired harmlessly into the ground. He was killed instantly and ended up dangling in the air, swinging back and forth across the hog trail, impaled to the spiked coconut. The other pirate began screaming and fired his musket out of panic in the direction where the spiked ball had come from. As the musket smoked cleared, the pirate saw a black figure spreading apart the bushes and vines as he cleared the jungle. It was a one-eyed figure with scars all over his menacing face.

The pirate screamed, "You're the devil!" He turned to run back down the trail. No sooner had he began to run, than he felt a heavy thud in his back and then excruciating pain. He stopped and looked down at his chest. The sharp point of a spear was sticking out of his chest. Within seconds he fell dead to the ground, face first with the spear handle sticking out of his back. The dark figure looked down at him and smiled. He clicked his boots and disappeared back into the jungle.

Within minutes, Scorpion and her crew and prisoners had found the spot where her scouts had been killed. Scorpion was vexed, but at the same time she smelled the scent of evil all around her. She reached into her pocket and flipped some dust into the air chanting, "Oh evil one, come and join me. I will share the power of the Triangle with you." While she was chanting and ranting, Salty was staring at her. He had never seen anything like this in all his years.

Keno turned to Portagee and said, "We're not going to make it out of this jungle alive."

Portagee, still shaking a bit, replied, "As soon as we get a chance, we are out of here."

Scorpion turned back to the others and said, "We're wasting time. Let's get going." She snapped at one of her crew to take the lead. Then everyone passed by the two dead pirates and went on down the trail.

The Spinners also heard the shots. At first they didn't know whether to run towards the shots or away from them. Michael spoke up, "We have to go on unless we hear them heading back this way. We now need to be extra careful. Someone up the trail is firing their muskets."

Graham added, "Yeah, all we have are these sabers."

Sam quickly responded, "Don't worry. In this jungle no one's going to fire off a good shot. Now let's move out." With that, they cautiously moved out along the hog trail.

About fifteen minutes later they came across the scene where the two pirates had been ambushed. Graham was first to speak, "Whoever killed these pirates made their weapons here in the jungle."

Michael turned to Sam and said, "Sam, you might want to keep moving." Sam nodded her head and did not stop to look at the pirates. After leaving the small clearing Michael added, "Well, at least we know Portagee, Keno and Salty are still all right."

"I hope you're right," replied Graham. They continued up through the rocks and left the bodies behind them.

Scorpion and her band finally came to a very small clearing. To one side was a very jagged, rocky hillside. At the base of this rock formation was an entrance to a cave. The cave entrance was just as jagged as the rest of the formation. It was about four feet wide and five or six feet high. No more than two people could enter the cave at a time. It was clear the floor of the cave was about ten feet down from the entrance, but it was too dark to tell if there were stone steps down to the floor. As Scorpion stood in front of the entrance, she could feel the evil she was looking for was inside the cave. Next, she stepped back twenty paces and commanded one of her pirates to throw a couple of torches into the cave. She yelled out, "Evil one, come out and join me! You have two choices. Join me or die. You have until those torches burn out, then my men will fill that cave full of musket shots. Then we'll throw in a keg of black powder and blow you and this cave to hell." All was quiet in the cave. The only noise you could hear was the light wind blowing through the entrance. Scorpion was getting impatient. She yelled into the cave, "You've had your chance!" She turned to her crew and waved them forward, commanding, "Mates, on the count of three, fire those muskets into the cave. One, two."

Then from within the cave a voice spoke out, "Fraulein, don't shoot, I'm coming out with my hands up."

Portagee and Keno looked at each other in shock. Portagee said, "It can't be! You said he was killed by Captain Drax."

Keno responded, "He was, I saw him shot."

It appeared to Keno and Portagee that the voice they heard was that of Stryker Von Hammer, a Nazi SS submarine commander. He was a ruthless cold-blooded killer. He had lost his left eye in a shrapnel explosion in the invasion of France in 1940. Stryker's submarine was on a spy mission to the United States and was lost in the Devil's Triangle in 1944. It was thought that Captain Drax had shot and killed him a year ago, at the Battle of St. George's.

Just then, the dark figure stepped out of the cave. His face was scarred with only one eye. He was dressed in an old Nazi SS black uniform. With his hands raised straight up, he stepped forward to within a few feet of Scorpion and stopped. Scorpion looked at him and said, "You have the mark of the devil on your face. What is your name? Speak up quickly before I have my mates blow a hole through your head."

The dark figure looked Scorpion in the eyes and said, "I'm Stryker." Then he quickly dropped his arms, releasing daggers he had concealed in his hands. Each dagger struck its intended targets, two of Scorpions crewmembers, directly in the heart. They collapsed and died instantly. Before Stryker could move, Scorpion jumped forward, sinking all five stingers from her left hand into his neck. With her right hand, she opened her palm, which had a yellow powder in it and blew it into Stryker's face. Stryker flinched backward in severe pain and started cursing in German. He fell over and slid back into the cave.

Scorpion smiled and said, "Well, Stryker when you awake, you'll be one of my zombie slaves. You will be worth fifty men when we find the power source." She yelled at her remaining crew to go into the cave and bring Stryker back out.

While all this was going on, Salty saw an opportunity to escape. He spun around on his peg leg and kicked one of Scorpion's legs out from under her, dropping her to the ground. He turned to Portagee and Keno and yelled, "Get the hell out of here!" Then he started running back up the hog trail as fast as he could.

Meanwhile Portagee and Keno took off like lightening bolts and were out of sight in seconds. Salty started up the steep hill, but before he could clear it, Scorpion got to her feet and lunged at him catching his peg leg. She jerked on it so forcefully that the strap holding it to Salty's upper leg snapped. The leg came off and Salty rolled back down the hill into the remaining pirates. As Scorpion stood up she was shaking the peg leg so violently at Salty that the end of the leg snapped off and the Tucker Cross fell onto the ground in front of Scorpion. Scorpion looked down at the cross, bent over and picked it up. She immediately felt the power of the cross and placed it in a leather bag on her hip. She turned to her remaining six crewmembers and yelled, "Two of you, go quickly after those prisoners and bring them back dead or alive, I really don't care which." She looked at Salty and said, "Now I know why I felt a power when you were around. This must be a key to something and I'm betting it's the Triangle." Scorpion bent over to Salty and blew the mysterious yellow powder in his face. Salty immediately started choking and coughing and rolling around. She grabbed Salty and lifted him up on one leg. She said, "Old man, I don't need you anymore." Scorpion then dug one of her stingers into Salty's neck and shoved him, like a tin soldier, into the cave. She added, "You can die in there." Scorpion then took Salty's peg leg in both hands and snapped it into two pieces by cracking it over her thigh. By now, the other four crewmembers had pulled Stryker from the cave. They made a makeshift stretcher to carry him back to the ship. Scorpion signaled them to follow her and said, "Let's get the bloody hell out of this sweat hole. Follow me back to the ship. Maybe on the way back, we'll find our other prisoners." The greatly reduced pirate band left the clearing, winding their way back to the bay along the hog trails.

Sam, Graham and Michael were slowly and cautiously moving along. They were trying to be very careful not to be seen by the pirates. They were also drawing blanks figuring out how to rescue their friends. As they were getting ready to go around a very sharp bend, Sam waved her hands in the air and said, "Stop, listen, can you hear that noise?"

Michael whispered, "Yeah, whatever it is, it's heading in our direction." The sound was getting closer and closing in very quickly.

Graham, in panic mode, cried out, "Oh crap, whatever it is, it's running right at us! Let's get out of here fast." They all started to run in the other direction, but it was too late. A blur of figures came running around the bend and ran smack into the Spinners. Everyone crashed and fell down.

Michael jumped up and drew his saber yelling, "You pirates aren't going to get us without a fight!"

Keno stood up and said, "Oh yeah? I think I'll just kick your butt right now." It was unbelievable. All the Spinners were together again. They quickly hugged each other.

Portagee interrupted the reunion by saying, "I think we'd better get moving. The pirates may be chasing us. In fact, Salty was behind us. I don't think he made it. Plus the pirates have guns. Oh, and by the way, we just saw Stryker and he looks meaner than ever."

Sam cringed and said, "You saw Stryker?" Sam had a very bad run in with Stryker and his Nazi troops and was scared to death of him.

Keno replied, "Yes, but we have to get moving before it's too late."

They took off running again. Just as they ran over a small rise in the trail, they heard a musket fire and the shot whizzed by Graham's head. "Holy crap! They're trying to kill us," screamed Graham as they ran for their lives. Finally, after about ten minutes of running, they stopped to listen for the pirates.

Michael panted, "I think we wore them out. They must have stopped for a rest. Does anyone know where we are? I'm lost."

Portagee replied, "Not a clue, but this big pond looks familiar." It was a sizable salt-water pond fed by the ocean.

Sam said, "If I'm right, the edge of the jungle is over there somewhere on the other side of this pond."

Michael asked, "That's good, but how do we get over there?"

Graham smiled saying, "Why not swim?"

Sam snapped back, "Sure, do you have any idea what might be in there?" Before anyone could respond they heard sounds coming from both directions of the hog trail.

Keno said, "Oh great! Now those cutthroat pirates are going to gut us."

Sam yelled, "You want a bet!" Then she dove into the pond and started swimming. By now, both pirates were in full view coming from either direction. The one with the musket pointed it at the Spinners and the other was swinging his cutlass. All four guys tried to dive into the pond at the same time. Portagee, being the smallest, got knocked down. By the time he got back up, the pirate with the cutlass was grabbing at his leg. Portagee finally jumped into the pond, but the problem was that the pirate was still hanging on to his leg. Sam had made it to the opposite bank of the pond and was climbing out. Keno, Michael and Graham were about half way across the pond and were being encircled by several creatures in the water swimming around them, biting their legs under the water.

Meanwhile, Portagee was fighting for his life with the pirate. They were rolling around under water. Portagee noticed, out of the corner of his eye, that the creatures swimming in the water with them were giant eels with razor sharp teeth. He knew they were attracted to shiny objects from his long years of fishing with his father. Portagee reached into his pocket and pulled out his Spinners key chain. Having the gyro device on it, he knew it would spin in the water. Being shiny it would attract the eels. He grabbed at the pirate's ear and with the quick release snap of the key chain, clipped it on the pirates hoop earring. Portagee kicked the pirate in the face and started swimming for his life. The pirate went after Portagee swimming underwater. The faster he swam, the faster the key chain spun. The three eels were instantly attracted to the spinning object and went for the pirate. Within seconds they were ripping at the pirates face and neck. The water turned red with blood. The pirate surfaced and screamed for his life, but within a minute, he sank below the surface of the water. The other pirate on the bank fired at the eels trying to help his mate, but it was too late.

On the other bank the Spinners were helping each other out of the water before the eels turned on them again. Michael, Keno and Graham were bleeding from their bites, but that didn't slow them down. Michael went back to help Portagee along so he could reach the bank quicker. As soon as they cleared the water, they slipped back in the jungle and out of sight.

After five minutes of scratching their way through the dense jungle, they came to a small clearing. Sam looked at Michael, Keno and Graham. Seeing their wounds she said, "We need to get out of here and tend to those bites before they get infected." She then turned to Portagee and asked, "How did you survive not getting bitten when that pirate you were fighting was attacked and killed by the eels?"

Portagee was still a little shaken, but tried to collect himself as he replied, "I baited the poor pirate with my Spinners key chain, by attaching it to his earring. Then the eels went for the bait."

Michael got up and went over and patted Portagee on the back and said, "Good thinking dude, but isn't this about the third Spinners key chain you've lost?" Portagee smiled and nodded his head. After resting for a few minutes, the Spinners moved out and were lucky to find a hog trail. Within twenty minutes they were able to clear the jungle.

Scorpion and her crew had almost made it out of the jungle when she met the lone pirate who had been tracking the prisoners at a trail junction. Scorpion could tell all was not well, so she said, "Well, you scum, what happened to your mate and where are the prisoners?"

The pirate started to tremble. He replied, "Giant eels killed him, captain."

Scorpion was now mad. She screamed, "What in the devil was he doing with eels and where are my prisoners?" She then backhanded, him knocking him to the ground.

The pirate cried out, "It's not my fault. By the time we caught up to the prisoners, there were five of them. They jumped into a large pond to get away from us. My mate jumped into the pond after them and was attacked by eels and killed. I fired at them and maybe hit one."

Scorpion yelled back, "How did two become five? You're nothing but a bloody liar." She kicked him in the side several times. Scorpion turned and started to walk along the trail at a much faster pace. Without looking back, she yelled, "I'm wasting my time talking to this mangy dog, let's go. He can stay or follow us. It really doesn't matter." Scorpion made it back to the bay where her ship anchored off shore. She was first to wade into the bay with her cutthroats close behind her, carrying Stryker on the stretcher.

Off from a distance, their movements were being watched by Cooter. He had avoided detection by rowing the long boat along the shoreline staying out of sight of the lookout in the crow's nest on the Venom. Cooter had seen Scorpion and her crewmates carrying someone on a stretcher, but he couldn't tell who it was. While he was waiting, he also had to make sure the labs didn't bark at the pirates. Just to make sure, he went ahead and rowed to shore, pulling the long-boat up under some overhanging bushes. He moved ashore and into the jungle to keep concealed. Cooter started talking to the labs, "What do you pups think happened to our friends? I didn't see them come back with that witch and her goons. Maybe they're still on the ship, but I bet not. Maybe they left them in the jungle. What do you two think?" Grizzly and Bear didn't have much to say. They just wagged their tails and wanted to set off to track something in the jungle. Finally, the pirates were aboard the ship. Cooter thought it was a good time to start tracking his friends. With two hunting dogs he knew the tracking would be much easier, but he needed something to give them for the scent. Then it hit him. He had some of the money that Salty had won and handled playing Crown and Anchor at Cup Match. He pulled the bills out of his pocket and called the labs over to him saying, "Here guys, smell this, it's Salty. Go find him." He clapped his hands and Grizzly and Bear tore off through the jungle. Cooter knew labs were bird dogs, but he was sure they could help track down Salty. If they found him, Keno and Portagee would be there too.

Cooter was struggling to keep up with the labs. The dense jungle was hard to navigate. Finally, they crossed a hog trail and the labs picked up the scent of Salty. They went running down the trail barking their heads off. Cooter knew they were on the trail. He had seen quite a few sets of tracks on the damp trail. The Spinners tracks were especially easy to spot because of the modern day tread. He was a bit confused, as there seemed to be too many sets of Spinner tracks. He dismissed that from his head and went running after the labs.

Cooter was so far behind Grizzly and Bear that he could hardly hear their barking. Plus he was getting tired. He finally had to sit down and rest for a while. While he was sitting there staring at the trees, he drifted off, remembering the swamps of Louisiana. He sure did miss the hunting for possums and deer and his momma's home 'cookin' of jambalaya. Then, as quickly as he'd left reality, he came back. Something stuck in a tree caught his attention. He stood up and pulled out his dagger and started digging at it. Sure enough, it was a musket ball; it couldn't have been stuck in the tree for more than a couple of hours.

Cooter said, "Well I'll be danged. Whoever fired this musket ball was shooting at something in the opposite direction from where the labs went." He scratched his head, put the ball in his pocket and went on after the labs. He finally came to a clearing. He could see the labs barking at the entrance of a cave. Cooter was surprised the labs wouldn't go in. Maybe it reminded them of the black hold in the ship they were trapped in. At any rate, Cooter went over to the cave entrance and yelled, "I got my musket primed and cocked, so if there's anyone down there you'd better come out now before I blow your bloody head off."

"Like hell you will. If I could get my bloody butt up, I would kick your big southern butt." Cooter knew it was Salty. He had to be hurt or why would he be down in the cave? Cooter went down into the dark cave, and sure enough, there was Salty sitting on the cave floor bleeding from the neck and missing a leg.

Cooter helped Salty up questioning, "Did that little witch girl kick your butt too?"

Salty replied, "Yeah. It took her and all her cutthroats to throw me down here. By the way, where's that musket you were going to shoot into the cave with?"

"I lied," replied Cooter. When they cleared the cave, Cooter sat Salty down on a rock to rest. Grizzly and Bear came running over to Salty and began licking his whiskers. Salty was happy to see the labs and his old friend Cooter. Cooter looked around. Seeing the broken peg leg he asked Salty, "What in blue blazes happened here?"

Salty replied, "You won't bloody well believe it? The pirates captured Stryker, the kids escaped, I got my butt kicked, and Scorpion found the cross."

Cooter was shocked, "You said captured Stryker?" Salty nodded his head. Cooter added, "He was dead!"

Salty snapped back, "Well, now he's undead as in zombie."

Cooter responded, "I think that witch broke your wooden leg over your head. You're still confused."

"No, it's the truth," replied Salty.

Cooter looked around again saying, "Did you kill theses pirates?"

Salty replied, "No, believe it or not, Stryker did. Then Scorpion nailed him."

Cooter said, "Ok she's got the cross. She's looking for power so she must be heading for Shark Hole. Let me make you a new wooden leg out of that small cedar tree over there. Then we'll get out of this jungle and head in the direction of Shark Hole. Maybe we'll run into the Spinners on the way." As soon as Cooter finished the wooden leg, they made their way towards Shark Hole.

~18~

ONE MAN'S JUNK IS ANOTHER
MAN'S TREASURE

ONE MAN'S JUNK IS ANOTHER MAN'S TREASURE

Scarzo and his thugs had been cruising along the North Shore of the island enjoying the ride, viewing the pristine unspoiled coastline. It was even more appealing that he was on his way to pick up a fortune in lost treasure. On the other hand Jason, Bubba and Buford were sitting in the back seat staring at AK47s staring at them. They did not appear to have the same enjoyment of the boat cruise. As the speedboat was passing Clarence's Cove, Bubba leaned over to Jason and whispered, "Is this your plan? To bail out here and escape back to our old camp?"

Jason whispered back, "Keep your rebel butt down and don't do anything stupid. I'll let you know when the time is right."

Bubba smiled and said, "O.K., I got it. You're going to tell me when to do something stupid, right?"

Jason laughed and nodded his head. Axil interrupted them, "You two keep your mouths shut or I'll come over there and shove this AK47 down your throat."

Buford had been napping, but Axil had disturbed his nap. He looked up at Axil and said, "Listen, you vulture, I might decide to take my chances and git up and shove that new fangled rifle down your throat." He then started to get to his feet, but before he could, Bubba grabbed his arm and jerked him back down into his seat.

Then Bubba said, "I promised your momma when we left for the war I would take care of you cuz so shut up, sit back and enjoy the ride."

Axil laughed, "Your mate is right. Your momma wouldn't want me to take care of you, would she?" He jerked back the firing bolt and pointed the assault weapon at Buford. Buford wanted to get up and kick his butt, but he decided retreating was the better part of valor and with that he would live to fight another day.

As the speedboat passed around Spanish Point, Scarzo yelled back to the others, "Gringos, where to now?"

Jason yelled back as he pointed, "Stay on a southwesterly course and stay in the middle of the sound. We need to avoid the hidden reefs." He winked at Bubba.

Scarzo turned to Axil and asked, "Should I believe this gringo?"

Axil replied, "Beats me. I'm from St. George's I'm not used to these waters."

Scarzo then turned back to Jason and said, "Remember if you lie, you die." Next he turned around and headed in the direction Jason had suggested. It took about fifteen minutes for the speedboat to get to the point in the sound that Jason gave directions for. Scarzo then stopped the boat. He yelled back at Jason, "OK smart guy, where now?"

Jason just pointed and said, "Now go due east. See all those islands over there? The big one farthest from us is Hinson's Island. That's where we're going, boss man."

Scarzo was now madder than ever. He turned around and jumped over the seat and landed a few feet in front of Jason. Scarzo pulled out his pistol and pointed it at Jason saying, "You take me for a fool! This is a joy ride for you. You're just wasting my time. When we get to this Hinson's Island, the lost treasure better be there. I swear if it's not. I will personally put a bullet through your head."

Jason smiled, "Don't worry boss, your wildest dreams will come true there."

Both Bubba and Buford were wondering what Jason was up to. Hinson's Island was where they stored emergency supplies a couple of years ago, just in case the Nazis or pirates overran their settlement at Spanish Point. They had not been close to the island since last year, when they had rescued the Spinners from the Nazis. The Pilgrims had stored food, water, blankets, a longboat and most importantly muskets, black powder, musket balls and sabers on the island. Now all they had to do was to figure out how to escape when they got to the island without talking to each other.

When they were within a couple hundred yards of Hinson Island, Jason pointed towards the narrows between Hinson Island and Watling Island. He then said, "Keep to the middle of the narrows. We need to land just on the other side of the tip of the island." Scarzo was so busy operating the speedboat he missed seeing Jason giving Bubba and Buford the thumbs up. As the boat went through the narrows, Scarzo slowed down to make sure they stayed clear of any reefs just under the surface. Just when he was getting ready to turn the speedboat towards Hinson's Island, Jason jumped up and screamed, "Look out on the port side!" While everyone was looking out to the port side of the boat Jason jumped up on the seat and back flipped into the water. Bubba and Buford were quick to follow each jumping off opposite sides of the boat. Buford was swimming towards Watling Island as a diversion, while Bubba and Jason were swimming towards Hinson's Island. The speedboat glided through the water for at least another twenty feet before Scarzo could get his wits about him and turn the boat around. He turned the boat towards Watling Island so the first person they saw swimming was Buford.

Scarzo yelled, "Shoot that Gringo!" His men fired everything they had at Buford. The air was filled with smoke from the gunfire and the water was being riddled with bullets. Buford sunk out of sight while the water around him turned red with blood. Scarzo stood up as they trolled by where Buford sank under the water. He then said, "One of those American fools is dead now. Let's get the other two and then find the treasure." They had turned the boat back around facing Hinson's Island, but there was no sign of Jason or Bubba.

Axil said, "They must have swum ashore. It's a small island. We can find them."

Scarzo was now beet red. He looked at Axil and said, "No, stupid, I thought they flew away. We'd better find them or this island will be the last place you see alive." They quickly made land on the northern point of Hinson's Island. Scarzo and his three goons tied the speedboat up to a palm tree that was gracefully arching over the waters edge. He then yelled out, "Spread out about fifty paces apart! We'll move towards the center of the island and find the cowards." They moved along very slowly not wanting to miss Jason and Bubba or fall into some type of trap.

Bubba and Jason were now half way across the island. Finally Bubba waved at Jason to stop. He needed to catch his breath. He asked, "Jason, I never got a chance to see if Buford made it. All I can remember is hearing all that firing. It gave me a flashback of the Battle of Bull Run. Do you think they bushwhacked Buford?"

Jason looked over at Bubba and said, "I don't honestly know Bubba. They sure fired enough rounds at him to kill a herd of elephants. All we can do now is pray he made it. Right, now we better get our butts moving, I'm sure they're following us."

"OK, let's move out," replied Bubba. The two needed to get over to the southeast corner of the island where they had built a very small stone hut that was stocked with their emergency supplies. The pilgrims had code-named it

'Island Trading'. They also had a small punt hidden under some bushes there that they might be able to use to escape to the main island. It took them another five minutes to get to the stone hut. Bubba kicked in the small cedar door that had some writing on it and to their surprise the hut had been ransacked. The food and blankets were gone as was most everything else. Bubba looked over at Jason and asked, "Who the hell would do this?"

Jason replied, "I don't know Bubba, but keep looking. Did they leave any weapons?"

After looking for a while, Bubba jumped up and said, "By jiggers look here." He picked up an old cap and ball pistol, a bayonet and a saber.

Jason then said, "I'll take the saber. The rest is yours." They left the hut. As they stepped out bullets were striking everything around them. Both men quickly dropped to the ground behind the stone hut.

Bubba looked over at Jason and said, "This reminds me back in the war when me and Coot were trapped by Yankee soldiers in Dead Man's Canyon."

Jason asked, "So what happened? How did you escape?"

Bubba replied, "No they killed us."

Jason said, "What?"

"I'm just having fun with you," replied Bubba. Jason peered over the hut and was immediately shot at again.

As he dropped back down he said, "I don't think these killers are playing with us Bubba."

Bubba replied, "You're right. I'll cover you while you pull that punt there down over that little rise and get it in the water. Then I'll catch up to you."

"You sure?" asked Jason.

Bubba grinned saying, "Git your butt out of here before I change my mind." He pulled the hammer back on the pistol jumped up and yelled, "You damn pirates take this one for General Robert E. Lee!" He fired his pistol a split second later, nailing one of the goons right between the eyes. Meanwhile, Jason was dragging the punt down to the shoreline and getting it in the water. Bubba had dropped back down behind the hut and was reloading his pistol. He jumped back up to take his second shot, but as his head cleared the hut, Scarzo started firing his AK47 on fully automatic. The bullets hit all over the hut causing stone fragments to explode all around Bubba. The fragments temporarily blinded Bubba. As he fell to the ground, his pistol misfired. He pulled out his bayonet, but it was too late. Axil rounded the side of the hut and nailed him in the forehead with the butt of his automatic rifle. The other goon and Scarzo ran after Jason. Jason was rowing for his life. As soon as Scarzo and the goons started shooting at him, he knew he would have to dive into the water and try to swim underwater to the shore if he could. Seconds after he bailed out of the punt, Scarzo riddled it with over fifty bullets.

As the punt began to sink, Scarzo said to his goon, "He's probably dead. Let's go back and see what's left of our southern friend." By the time they got back to the stone hut, Bubba was sitting there with Axil pointing his Ak47 at him. Scarzo said, "My friend, you're still with us so where is the treasure?"

Bubba looked up at him and said, "Well it ain't here, stupid."

Scarzo smiled and said, "Gringo, I know that now and I know you're going to show us.

Bubba piped back, "Like hell I will."

Axil started to whack him again. However Scarzo raised his hand and said, "Wait Axil, have compassion for our friend. He just lost two of his best friends. Help him up and let's go back to the boat." Axil and the other goon helped Bubba and pushed him in the direction of the boat. When they were back in the boat, they fired up the engines and roared back towards the middle of the sound.

Jason had made it to shore. He was lucky that there were some bushes overhanging the water, which allowed him to swim undetected and covered his exit out of the sound and onto the shore. He was able to get up high enough to see Bubba being captured by Scarzo and his goons.

As he watched them speed off towards the centre of the sound, he thought that they may be heading back to Harrington Sound. He wondered if Bubba would tell them where the treasure was hidden, after all it was not worth loosing one's life over. Jason began to think of Buford and wondered if he had made it to Watling Island. He could see the island from here, but could not see any sign of life. Jason wanted to move as quickly as he could across the central part of the island to try to warn the others about Scarzo and maybe help Bubba, but he could not do that. His military training was haunting him right now. He had been trained that no man was to be left behind after a battle or an incursion. He would have to swim back to Hinson's Island, then swim on over to Watling

Island and at least try to find Buford, or recover his body if possible. Jason went back down to the shoreline as soon as he thought it was safe. He dove into the sound. He seemed to be swimming in slow motion compared to when Scarzo was shooting at him.

Finally, when he made it to Hinson's Island, he went back to the stone hut to see if there were any medical supplies. Jason still wondered who in the world had found their small hidden stash. The only answer was that maybe the Nazis had found it a long time ago, on one of their hunting trips. At any rate, it didn't really matter anymore. As he dug through the mess, he found an old white shirt that might be good for a bandage. He had already checked the cap and ball pistol, but it was ruined from the misfire as the barrel was split wide open. Jason hoped Bubba wasn't hurt when that happened. The black powder might come in handy he thought, so he took the powder horn, but that was about it.

Jason jogged across the island until he made it to the northern shore. Then, as before, he waded into the water trying to protect the shirt and powder horn. He started swimming towards Watling Island. As he was swimming, he tried to keep his eyes on the sound's bottom, making sure Buford's was not submerged. He finally made it to the tiny island, but was too tired to move away from the beach. He needed to rest for a bit. While he was laying there with his eyes closed, he heard a stirring in the nearby bushes. Jason jumped up to look and to his surprise it was a baby hog. How in the world did he ever get out to this tiny island, he wondered. As he sat back down he heard a voice through the bushes, "What in the Sam hill are you doing here, hunting that harmless baby hog?"

Jason knew that voice. It was Buford. He jumped back up and yelled, "You old hound dog, I thought you were dead."

Buford walked over and gave Jason a hug saying, "You think those new fangled weapons can do me in, a solider of the Confederate States of America?"

Jason replied, "I guess not, but by the looks of you, they came close." Buford did have a few cuts and scrapes on his head and arms from where bullets had grazed him. Jason said, "Let's swim north to shore from here and get back to the main island. Then I'll bandage you up. After that, we'll cut back across the middle of the island and try to warn the others."

Buford replied, "That's O.K., but where's my cuz?"

"He's O.K. Scarzo got the best of him when his pistol misfired. By now, he's probably leading them to the treasure," Jason answered. The two walked over to the north shore of the tiny island, slipped into the water and swam for the main island. After reaching the main island, which the Spinners would have known as Hamilton, they patched up Buford's wounds and headed towards Harrington Sound on the hog trails.

Scarzo's speedboat was back in the centre of the Great Sound. He killed the engines, turned around to Bubba and asked, "OK Gringo, which way to my treasure? And if you think for a minute you're going to BS me, then think again. Your death will be excruciatingly slow and painful." Bubba knew they had already accomplished what Jason had set out to do and that was to use up most of Scarzo's gas. He also knew the treasure wasn't worth dying for and without the Tucker Cross, these pirates weren't going anywhere.

Bubba replied, "Ok, OK, the treasure is back in Harrington Sound in the southern corner of a cave we found there."

Scarzo looked over at Axil and asked, "Is this Gringo telling the truth this time?" Axil scratched his head for a minute.

Bubba quickly spoke up, "What's the matter, you got fleas?"

Axil then snapped back, "Shut up or I'll blow your head off. Besides, now that I think about it, there's no cave where he said there was. The only thing there is Devils Hole."

Scarzo asked, "What the hell is Devils Hole?"

Axil said, "Well, it's a small pit where sharks and turtles live. It's a tourist attraction in Bermuda."

Scarzo turned back to Bubba and pointed his pistol at him insisting, "So tell me now, which finger do you want blown off first?"

Bubba yelled out, "Wait a minute! You called it a pit. Maybe in your world it was a cave at one time and the roof collapsed?" Scarzo turned back to Axil and stared waiting for an answer.

Axil, now a little nervous, said, "He might be right. I do remember back in school that it was a cave and the roof collapsed over a hundred years ago."

Scarzo turned around and said, "Show me the way to this Devils Hole and the treasure." It was going to be a long drive. The others sat back and relaxed, except for Bubba. Axil still had his AK47 trained on him. Scarzo pulled out another Cuban cigar, lit it up, and was back to daydreaming about finding the treasure.

At this point, the Venom was sailing in the direction of the North Shore. Scorpion could only use her instincts as to where to go, until Stryker came around. Being impatient, she finally went below to check on him. Once there, she could tell he was beginning to stir. She took her stingers and ran them up and down his arm to wake him up. Finally, Stryker opened up his one glazed eye and said, "Who are you and where am I?"

Scorpion looked deep into Stryker's eye as her hypnotic powers put him into a trance when she said, "You're on board my ship, the Venom, and you're my undead slave. Yes, you're a zombie. You will do my bidding without question. Your only thoughts are to do what I command. You will fight like a tiger when I so command. No one can hurt you except me. You're already a zombie."

Stryker looked at her and saluted, "Heil Hitler." Scorpion was puzzled by the response. She had never heard those words before. What she didn't know was that Stryker was already half mad and had already been brained-washed years ago by Adolf Hitler who was his master.

Scorpion pierced his arm with one of her stingers and said, "No, I'm your master. My name is Scorpion, repeat it!"

Stryker repeated, "Yes, my master, Scorpion."

"Very good you bloody idiot, now sit up," she commanded.

Stryker sat up and said, "What, my master?"

Scorpion replied, "I'm looking for the power source for the Triangle. I believe this has something to do with it, what can you tell me slave?"

Stryker's one good eye almost popped out of his head at the sight of the Tucker Cross. He responded, "Yes, that was mine for a while. It was taken from me. Its power comes from Shark Hole."

Scorpion evilly smiled and suggested, "Stryker, you must show me where this Shark Hole is."

Stryker replied, "Yes master." Stryker stood up, went over to the steep stairs and walked up them. Scorpion was quick to follow him up to the top deck. Stryker stood on the bridge and pointed in the direction of the north shore saying, "We have to leave this place and head west until we get to an inlet. Then we will enter the inlet into a large sound." Suddenly he stopped and just stared.

Scorpion replied, "Very good, my zombie slave. We will find the power of the Triangle together." She turned to her new second in command and said,

"Stay the course, call me when we get to the inlet." She then went down into her cabin, leaving Stryker staring into the unknown.

~19~

X MARKS THE SPOT

X MARKS THE SPOT

With everyone converging on Harrington Sound, it was clearly going to be a day of destiny or destruction in the Triangle. Scarzo, on his treasure hunt, would easily be the first party to enter Harrington Sound with his lightening fast speedboat. The speedboat tore across the whitecaps as they followed along North Shore. Approaching the halfway point between the Great Sound and Harrington Sound, Scarzo leaned over and whispered into Axil's ear, "Do you think the gringo is telling the truth?"

Axil replied, "Not sure, but I think so. Why?"

Scarzo replied, "Having him on board now is wasting fuel, if he was really telling the truth."

"You thinking of killing him?" asked Axil.

Scarzo replied, "No, I thought it would be more fun just throwing him overboard at high speed and watching him bounce across several waves before he could try to swim to shore. Plus, if he was lying, we can always come back and get the bum."

"Sounds like a plan to me," responded Axil.

Scarzo added, "I'll call the gringo up here to me. When he comes up here, I'll make a sharp turn with the boat and good bye gringo." Scarzo turned around and yelled back to Bubba, "Hey gringo, come up here. I need to ask you a question."

Bubba got up from his seat and started to climb over the seat in front of him. Just as he was stepping over the seat Scarzo made a sharp left turn. Bubba never had a chance. Before he knew what was happening he was flying backwards off the speedboat and went skipping across the water like a flat pebble. Scarzo and his goons were laughing their heads off. Scarzo yelled back, "Hope you can swim, gringo. Watch out for the sharks." Without a second thought, the speedboat roared along the North Shore.

Bubba felt like he had just been shot from a cannon. Having no control over his body, he was spinning at what felt like a hundred miles an hour. It felt like he was bouncing off concrete each time he hit the water. Finally he came to a stop. All he could see was the speedboat off in the distance, getting smaller every second. Bubba was sore, but he didn't think he had any broken bones. At any rate, he didn't have time to think about it. He needed to swim for the shore as fast as he could. He was afraid that they might try to come back for him or even try to run him over. Being close to shore, it only took Bubba about five minutes to swim there.

As he crawled ashore, he rolled over on his side and lay motionless like a beached whale. While lying there, he was trying to think what the hell had just happened. Why would they kick him overboard like that? They didn't even shoot him first. What if he had lied to them about the location of the treasure? Well, that was water over the bridge now. He would have to get to his feet and try to warn the others, in case they were already in Harrington Sound.

Bubba cleared through the bushes without much trouble. He was in familiar territory and he knew there was a hog trail up ahead that would take him over to Harrington Sound. His only problem was the fact that he didn't have a weapon. He felt naked without some kind of weapon. As he walked along, he kept thinking about Buford, whether he was really killed and if Jason had made it to shore safely or not. Even though he was tired and sore, he kept moving forward. Occasionally, he would stop and grab a banana off the wild banana trees.

The Spinners had already made it to Harrington Sound. They were trying to keep close to the shoreline, but at the same time trying to stay out of sight from anyone that might be in the sound already. The boy's wounds were fairly superficial and nurse Sam had helped them clean them up as best she could without any medical supplies. As they walked along, Portagee said, "Can you believe Stryker is still alive?"

Sam replied. "No, and I hope I never see him again. He scares the 'you know what' out of me."

They were only about a half mile away from Shark Hole when Michael looked back across the sound, "Look, there's Scarzo's speedboat. He's still in the sound or has come back for something."

Graham piped up, "Yes, he's back for us. He must still be looking for the treasure and he still believes we know where it is."

Sam added, "Well, if he's got the treasure, he's doesn't have the Tucker Cross so he won't be leaving the Triangle anytime soon."

Keno jumped into the conversation, "Look, he's not heading to Shark Hole at all. It looks like he's going in the direction of Devils Hole. What do you think he's up to?"

Michael suggested, "You can bet it's not good, whatever it is." He pulled out the old telescope and looked at the speedboat saying, "Looks to me like there's only three of them left. I think I see Scarzo, Axil and one of Scarzo's thugs. That's all."

Portagee added, "If Cooter got a hold of them with his cricket bat like he did in St. George's, I'm surprised any of them made it back. You should have seen Coot. He nailed two of Scarzo's thugs with the cricket bat and knocked them off their rental scooters."

Graham laughed adding, "I hope they had insurance for the scooters."

Sam said, "I think we'd better go and find out what Scarzo's doing over at Devils Hole. In fact, if I remember when we were over there last year, we didn't even see Devils Hole."

Graham said, "I think the reason why you didn't see it was that it's still a cave with a roof on it."

Portagee added, "I think he's right."

Michael said, "Well, let's go find out." The Spinners were more cautious than ever not knowing who might show up next. It seemed strange to walk past Shark Hole without stopping. They crept along just above the tree line so as not to be seen by anyone else. Furthermore, they tried to keep a watch on Scarzo and his speedboat.

Scarzo, Axil and Scarzo's one remaining goon were now going much more slowly trying to follow the curvature of the southwestern corner of Harrington Sound. Scarzo was beginning to get impatient. He mumbled, "That damn gringo lied to us. There's no cave here. We should have killed him."

Axil responded, "Hold on, mate. We may not be there just yet. With all this growth around here, it might be hard to spot the cave. It should be almost right smack in the very southwest corner."

"All right then, we'll keep going," grumbled Scarzo. The boat had finally reached the far corner of the sound. Scarzo ran the speedboat up into a small sandy rocky spot and yelled back to his goon, "Get your butt out of the boat and tie us up to that old cedar tree over there. Now start looking for a cave entrance." Scarzo sat back to relax for a while. He lit up a new Cuban cigar and pulled out a bottle of tequila.

Axil looked over at Scarzo and asked, "Mate, can I have a drink? I'm getting awfully thirsty."

Scarzo took a big swig and suggested, "I might let you have the worm in the bottle." He then laughed and chugged down some more.

Meanwhile, the Spinners had crept close enough to hear what Scarzo and Axil were talking about. They were on a small hillside listening from above. Keno was first to speak out, "They are looking for the treasure. The Pilgrims must have hidden in Devils Hole Cave."

Sam added, "Looks to me like they're not looking very hard. Scarzo and Axil are more interested in drinking and smoking than finding the treasure. Look, that poor goon of his doesn't have a clue what to look for."

Michael said, "We'd better lay back for a while until we can figure out what's going on."

While the Spinners were watching the activity at Devils Hole, they failed to see the Venom enter the small inlet at Flatt's that leads to Harrington Sound. Scorpion could see the Sound for the first time as they closed in on it. Stryker stood silently on the bridge staring at the Sound in front of the ship. As they approached, one of Scorpion's crew members came running up to her yelling, "Captain, that tiny inlet is too small for our ship to pass through."

Scorpion pulled out her telescope and surveyed both sides of the channel. She yelled, "Drop the sails and turn us broadside to the inlet!" Scorpion had seen that both shorelines of the channel were limestone. She was going to widen the channel very quickly with her cannons. Scorpion yelled, "Train two cannons each on the limestone shorelines of the inlet. Be ready to fire in five minutes on my command!" The crew scurried about deck getting the cannons ready to fire.

The first mate turned to Scorpion reporting, "Captain, the cannons are ready, awaiting your command."

Scorpion yelled, "Fire!" Within seconds, the four cannons fired, blasting the limestone shorelines to pieces. The explosions echoed all over Harrington Sound. The crew reloaded the cannons and fired again causing even greater devastation on the shorelines.

Scarzo and Axil just about jumped out of their skins when they heard the explosions. Scarzo screamed, 'What the hell was that?"

Axil got to his feet and yelled, "I don't know, but we're sitting ducks here!"

Scarzo screamed, "Come on, let's get out of here before we're trapped!" Then they heard four more explosions in rapid order from the direction of Flatt's Inlet. Scarzo yelled at Axil, "Untie us from the tree. Let's leave, now!"

Axil jumped out of the speedboat and untied the boat from the tree. He yelled towards the bush, "We're shoving off now. You'd better get your butt down here or you'll be left behind." Just then Scarzo's thug came running through the bushes. He helped Axil shove the boat back into the water. They both jumped aboard. Within seconds, Scarzo had the boat in reverse and then, once in deep water, he turned the boat around and shot out like a bat out of hell towards Shark Hole.

The Spinners had seen everything after the first series of explosions. Graham said to the others, "Look at that dog running with his tail between his legs." He was pointing to Scarzo's speedboat.

Portagee chimed in, "I bet he's going to go over to Hall's Island to hide there until he figures out what is going on."

Sam asked, "Speaking about what is going on, what is that pirate ship firing at? Looks to me like they're shooting at nothing."

Keno said, "Maybe they're just target practicing."

Sam replied, "I don't think so. Cannon balls and black powder are scarce here."

Michael had been watching the pirate ship through the telescope. He eventually spoke up, "I know what they're doing. They're trying to widen the inlet so the ship can pass through into Harrington Sound."

Graham replied, "You've got to be kidding. Let me see."

Michael tossed Graham the telescope adding, "See for yourself."

Graham looked over, saying, "I don't believe it." Just then four more massive explosions blasted off in rapid succession. Graham added, "I do believe it. In fact, look they might be trying to enter the inlet right now."

Graham was right. Scorpion had called off any more cannon shots. She felt that they had blown away enough of the shoreline to enter the sound. Scorpion commanded the sails to be raised. She slowly maneuvered the old ship around to enter the inlet. At first, all seemed to be progressing well, but then there was an awful scraping sound as the boat beached itself on a solid reef. Scorpion started screaming at he crew, "Someone get below and make sure we're not taking on any water!" Within a couple of minutes one of her crew returned from below deck to inform her that there appeared to be no damage done to the ship. Scorpion replied, "Good, but we're stuck here now until high tide when the ocean flows back into the sound again." As expected Scorpion was so mad at herself she couldn't see straight. She could feel the power from within the Harrington Sound, but couldn't reach it yet.

Graham had been watching the pirate ship for quite a while. He said to the others, "I don't think they will be entering the sound anytime soon. They appear to be stuck on a reef or something. They won't be going anywhere until high tide frees them."

Sam added, "Well, that's interesting. I wonder if we should go down to Devils Hole and see what Scarzo was looking for."

Michael added, "We might as well, but someone needs to stay here as a lookout to warn us if anyone is coming."

Portagee spoke up, "Leave me with the telescope and I'll keep a look out." They all agreed and Graham handed Portagee the telescope. The four Spinners headed down the hillside towards Devils Hole, leaving Portagee on look out.

Meanwhile Jason and Buford were still a long ways off from the Sound, trekking across the central portion of the main island. In fact they were so far away that they never heard any of the cannon shots. Bubba had heard the cannon shots. He reckoned they must be coming from the pirate ship. He thought that maybe, with luck, the cannons were being fired at Scarzo's speedboat.

Salty and Cooter were on their way down the strip of island that was between Harrington Sound and Castle Harbour. They too had heard the cannons and wondered who was on the receiving end. Grizzly and Bear had picked up the tracks of the Spinners. They were so anxious to find their new friends that they picked up speed and charged down the hog trail that the Spinners had been on hours earlier. Cooter yelled at them, "Grizzly, Bear you come back now, ya hear! Halt! Now git back here right this minute."

Salty poked Cooter in the ribs saying, "What do you think you're doing? These dogs aren't soldiers you bloody goofball. They're not going to stop if you yell halt. Besides it's too late now. They're long gone after the kids."

Cooter asked, "Well, what in the world are we going to do now?"

Salty replied, "Simple. The dogs are tracking the kids and you're going to track the dogs."

Cooter snapped back, "Oh that's great! Now I'm a dang dog tracker. Don't tell my cousins, you hear?"

Salty smiled, "Don't worry my friend, your secret is safe with me." They picked up speed and continued down the hog trail.

The Spinners' thinking had been correct. Scarzo had hidden the speedboat behind Hall's Island. They had hidden the boat on the east side of the island and made their way over to the west side. From there, they could easily see the pirate ship in the inlet. Scarzo was a bit nervous about facing a pirate ship full of cannons. Even though they still had their AK47s, one direct cannon ball hit would take all of them and their speedboat out. While they were waiting, Scarzo looked over to his goon and asked, "As we hastily left Devils Hole, I forgot to ask you if you found the cave entrance."

The goon replied, "I think I was close to it. I found what looked like an opening covered with brush and palm leaves."

"Very good. When the coast is clear, we'll head back, pick up the treasure and get out of this hell hole," replied Scarzo.

Axil said, "I hate to ask the question, but how exactly are we going to get out of this place anyway?"

Scarzo pulled out his pistol and said, "Well Mr. Smart Butt, when I figure that out, you'll be the first to know." He pointed the pistol in Axil's face, pulled the hammer back and said, "What else would you like to know?"

Axil was quick to respond, "Nothing, nothing at all."

Scarzo lit up his cigar and said, "Good, we'll wait a little longer."

The Spinners were down in the area where they would have expected to find Devils Hole. There was only one problem. They could not find it. After about twenty minutes of searching and coming up empty, Keno said, "Maybe we're nuts. Devils Hole must be over there somewhere." He pointed in a southern direction. The others looked the same way. When Sam turned back around to say something to Keno was gone.

Sam asked the others, "Where did Keno go?" Michael and Graham were just standing there with blank looks on their faces. "Come on where did he go?" she repeated. Then as she walked over to where Keno was standing, she saw a hole in the ground. She quickly yelled into it, "Keno, are you down there?"

"Yes," a voice responded.

Sam then asked, "Are you hurt?"

Keno replied, "No. I just feel so stupid. Does anybody have a match? I think there are some torches down here."

Michael pulled out a small box of wooden matches that he had picked up when they were getting supplies in the Pilgrim's village. Michael said, "Heads up Keno."

Keno yelled back, "Be careful. There's lots of water down here."

"All right," Michael replied. Then he dropped the matchbox through the hole.

The matches hit Keno on the head. They bounced down the rocks towards the water. Keno dropped to his hands and knees and began feeling around for them. Luckily the box of matches had stopped just inches from the water. Keno managed to grab them and lit a torch. He looked around and exclaimed, "Holy Moses! This cave is incredible. It's not very large, but you won't believe it." Now with torches lit, it was easy to step through the cave entrance onto a set of natural rock steps and go down into the cave. Graham, Michael and Sam went down into the cave in search of the treasure.

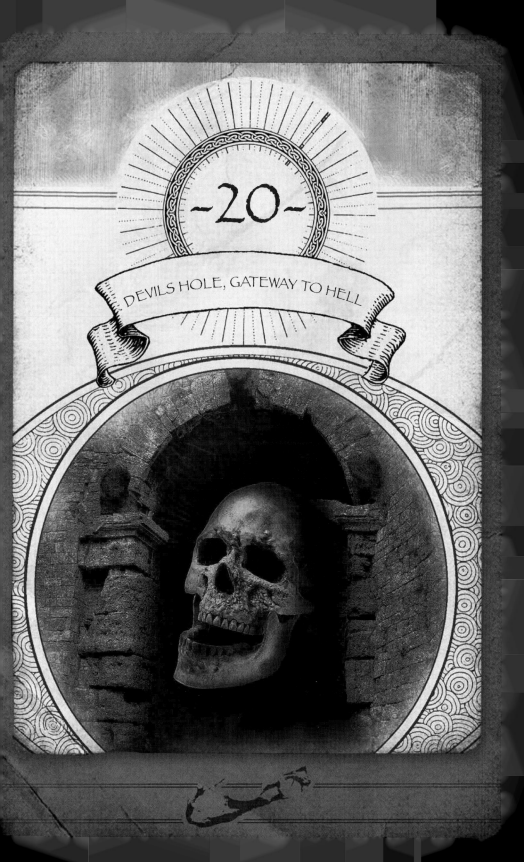

~20~

DEVILS HOLE, GATEWAY TO HELL

DEVILS HOLE: GATEWAY TO HELL

Scarzo decided he had waited long enough. It appeared as though the pirate ship was going to be stuck on the rocks for some time to come. The three-some shoved off from Hall's Island and went on a direct course back to Devils Hole.

The Spinners were exploring the cave hoping to come across the treasure. Keno spotted a narrow passageway hidden in the back of the cave. He yelled out, "Check this out! I wonder if the treasure is hidden down this passage."

Michael replied, "Wait for me. I'll go with you." Michael followed Keno into the passage. The passage made a near ninety-degree turn before opening up into a very spacious room.

Once the two were in the room, Keno yelled back down the passage, "It's a cool room, but there's nothing in here except us."

Sam answered, "That's OK. I found the treasure. Come on back."

Michael and Keno rushed back into the room where Sam was. Finally Michael said, "All right Sam, where is it?" Sam smiled and looked down to the centre of the cave that was full of water. She held her torch above the water.

Keno said, "Wow! It's in the bottom of the pond."

Michael added, "Go for it Keno! Swim down and grab a chest."

"Are you nuts? See those sharks swimming down there?" cried Keno.

Everyone laughed. Sam said, "I think Scarzo may have a problem recovering the treasure."

Meanwhile, Portagee had been so engrossed watching the Venom stuck on the rocks that he hadn't even noticed that the speedboat was two thirds the way back to Devils Hole. In fact, if he hadn't hear the loud speedboat engine he might have never seen it. As soon as Portagee saw the speedboat he went into a panic. He was not sure if he could get to Devils Hole before Scarzo. Portagee went running down the hill on a hog trail as fast as he could. The speedboat had made it to the shoreline of Devils Hole. Scarzo yelled out, "Tie the boat up to that cedar tree! Let's get going and find this treasure. We won't have much time before the pirates clear the inlet."

Portagee was just a step ahead of Scarzo. He jumped into the cave and slid down the rocky stairs. Just as he was about to slide into the pond, Graham reached out and grabbed him by the arm warning, "Hey buddy, you going swimming with the sharks?"

Portagee was still panicking, "Scarzo, he'll be here in any minute."

Sam said, "Let's get back in that small passage. Maybe he won't find us back there." Within thirty seconds all the Spinners made their way through the passage and back into the spacious room. They snuffed their torches on the cave floor and waited in silence.

Scarzo, Axil and his one remaining thug stumbled across the entrance to the cave. Scarzo looked into the dark hole and said, "Axil, pickup some of that dried up brush. We'll set it on fire and kick it down the hole. That way we'll see what we're getting into."

Axil did as he was told. In a few minutes he fashioned the brush into a huge ball. Axil held it over his head while Scarzo lit it with his lighter. When Axil dropped the ball into the hole, a large flame lit up the cave. Scarzo looked at Axil saying, "Get your butt down there and take my associate with you." Both men went down into the cave. Once down there they found a couple of torches and lit them. They then signaled Scarzo to come down. Once down in the cave, Scarzo asked, "Where the hell is the treasure?"

Axil replied, "I don't know. I don't see any sign it."

Scarzo snapped, "Keep looking. It must be down here somewhere." Axil looked around the perimeter of the cave and found the passageway beyond which the Spinners were hiding. He started crawling down the passage when Scarzo yelled again at him to come back quickly. The Spinners relaxed slightly. Axil backed out of the passage and returned to Scarzo. Scarzo pointed towards the bottom of the pond and said," There it is. Look at all those chests down there in the bottom of that pond. If it weren't for all those sharks, I'd jump in and bring some of that treasure to the surface."

Scarzo told his goon to go back to the speedboat and grab some of his deep sea fishing gear. Scarzo would try fishing for the treasure. A few minutes later, the goon returned with the equipment. The fishing line was high tensile stainless steel and could easily handle the weight of some of the treasure chests. Within twenty minutes Scarzo had four chests pulled to safety.

Portagee decided to take a peek at what was going on. He saw what Scarzo was doing and inched back to the hidden room. He turned to the other Spinners and whispered, "He's using a fishing line to pull those chests out of the water."

Sam whispered back, "Oh great. He'll be there all day doing that. We're going to be stuck down here forever." What Sam didn't know, was that it was now high tide. The Venom had just broken loose and had cleared the small inlet at the entrance to Harrington Sound.

Scarzo tossed the fishing pole to his goon and said, "You fish for a while, while Axil and I haul these chests to the boat. I also desperately need a cigar." Scarzo climbed out of the cave while Axil passed up all four treasure chests. They began to drag them through the bush towards the speedboat. Meanwhile, when the goon cast his line into the pond, Portagee decided to take another peek. As he poked his head out to see what was going on, he accidentally sneezed from the damp, stuffy air.

The goon jumped and yelled, "Who goes there?"

Portagee without thinking answered, "Nobody." Then he started back peddling into the passageway. The goon jumped up and grabbed his AK47 in one hand, while still holding the pole in the other. Before he knew what hit him, a shark bit the hook and ran with it. The goon was pulled into the pond before he could scream for help. Instantly, the hungry sharks went into a feeding frenzy and attacked Scarzo's goon. His watery screams could not be heard outside the cave, but the Spinners knew exactly what was happening.

Sam screamed out, "When Scarzo comes back he's going to be looking for his man. What are we going to do?"

Michael replied, "I think when he sees the water full of blood, he'll know what happened."

Scarzo and Axil had just loaded the last chest onto the boat when there was a huge explosion in the bushes just twenty feet from them. The explosion knocked both Scarzo and Axil off their feet. Scarzo, a bit dazed, sat up and yelled over to Axil, "What was that?"

Axil pointed to the northwest and said, "I think it was that ship firing at us." Just then, another explosion hit the water only ten feet behind the boat.

Scarzo screamed, "Get your butt in the boat! Let's get the hell out of here before they hit us!"

Axil jumped in the boat and asked, "What about our mate back in the cave?"

Scarzo threw the speedboat in full reverse and snapped, "What about him? He's on his own now. Plus, the treasure is ours. Forget about him." He threw the engine into forward and gunned it.

Scorpion had never seen anything like this before. A boat that could out-run a cheetah, she wanted one. She also knew it was not the day to be distracted. She would deal with that boat later. Although she did sense a power source in the eastern corner of the Sound, there was a compelling power drawing her to the southern corner, which was Devils Hole. Scorpion yelled to her crew, "Stay the course! Anchor over there where that boat pulled out. Get as close to shore as you can, then drop anchor. We'll take the longboats ashore." Within a few minutes the Venom anchored alongside of Devils Hole. Before she left the ship, she spoke to her skeleton crew remaining onboard. "Guard this ship with your lives and if that lightning boat comes back, blast it out of the water." She climbed over the gunwale of the ship, and down into the longboat. As soon as her crew was in the longboat, they shoved off and rowed towards Devils Hole.

The Spinners had heard the explosions outside, but had no idea what was going on. All had been quiet now for about fifteen minutes. Finally Sam said, "Guys, I think maybe it's time we made a move out of here."

Michael agreed, "Sam's right. Let's get out while we can." Everyone crawled out behind Michael, down the passageway back into the first cave. Michael turned to Portagee and said, "Portagee, you're the smallest. Climb up there and stick your head out. Tell us what you can see."

Portagee replied, "Cool." Then he scrambled up the natural steps of the cave and peered out. He whispered back down, "The coast looks clear, just give me a minute. I'll check out the bush to make sure Scarzo's speedboat has left."

Michael replied, "That works for us, go for it." Portagee scrambled out of the cave and within ten seconds the Spinners heard musket fire. At least four shots were fired.

Sam cried out, "Oh my God! Someone has shot Portagee." No sooner had she spoken than they heard voices and some movement above them.

Graham said, "Quick, we'd better get back into the hidden room." The four remaining Spinners ran and then crawled back into the passageway and through to their hiding place.

Scorpion and her crew were approaching the cave entrance. She held up her stinger hand and yelled, "Stop you fools! What in hell were you firing at?"

Her first mate spoke up, "We thought we saw someone running through the bush."

"Well, did you hit him?" asked Scorpion.

Her first mate replied, "I'm not sure, captain. Do you want me to go find out?"

"No, forget it," replied Scorpion. "The force is so strong here it's almost intoxicating. It's coming from over there." She pointed down into the Devils Hole Cave. She added, "Bring up the zombie. He will go down into the cave first." Several pirates brought Stryker to the cave. Scorpion commanded, "My slave, go down into the cave and destroy anything you find."

Stryker turned to Scorpion and said, "Yes master." He climbed down into the cave. Stryker walked around the cave, but in his state, he would never find the hidden passageway where the Spinners had retreated. Scorpion waited for a few minutes, but her impatience caught up with her. Before going into the cave, she turned around and screamed at her crew, "Half of you stay here and form a ring around the cave entrance. No one is to pass. Shoot first and ask questions later! The rest of you follow me. Bring those torches and light them now."

As Scorpion entered the cave, she could feel the power drawing on all of her senses. She had never felt this force before. When everyone had entered the cave Scorpion commanded, "I want this pond lit up with your torches. Zombie, you come stand next to me." Stryker walked back to stand near Scorpion.

Inside the hidden room, the Spinners could hear the sounds and movement from the front cave. Keno whispered, "They must have the whole ship's crew down here. What are we supposed to do now?"

Sam whispered back, "Nothing, unless you think you're ready to take on an army of pirates." Keno shook his head and fell silent.

The front room of the cave was now fully illuminated. One could easily see the sharks swimming around in the deep water, with the treasure chests at the bottom. Scorpion could care less about the treasure. She attempted to communicate with the dark underworld. Just as she was beginning to drift into her trance, Michael moved a little and his footing slipped on the damp stones. Michael fell onto his side. He tried to muffle the pain that he felt from the loose rocks digging into his side. Just as quickly as this happened, Scorpion's blood red eyes popped open. She screamed, "There are intruders in this cave. Find them at once!"

The pirates began searching high and low around the cave until finally one pirate found the hidden passageway. He signaled to the first mate who ran over to him then stuck his torch into the passageway. He reached back and took the musket from the pirate. He pointed it into the passageway way and fired it. The shot echoed throughout the cave. Anybody would have thought that a cannon had been fired off in the cave. The musket ball ricocheted down the passageway and into the hidden room, finally dropping to the floor. The Spinners were lucky. They had been almost lying down and the first mate had fired the shot high. The first mate then screamed into the passageway, "You have ten seconds to come out before we fire ten more musket rounds. What will it be?"

The Spinners all looked at each other knowing it was certain death to stay where they were. Michael yelled back, "We're coming out! Hold your fire. We're unarmed." They dropped their sabers and daggers and left them behind as they followed Michael out of the hidden room. As each Spinner emerged into the front room, they were each grabbed by a pirate and taken over to Scorpion. Michael was the first to be introduced to Scorpion if you could call it that.

Scorpion looked at Michael and said, "These are just children! I never expected this. I sense that you are the spokesperson for the others?"

Michael responded, "Just let us go. The treasure is yours."

Scorpion laughed back, "We don't want the treasure you fool. It's the power and the force of the underworld I seek. Forget about being let go, we can always use slaves." She looked over at the other Spinners and noticed Sam and said, "Bring the little princess over to me."

Michael grabbed at Scorpion and screamed, "You witch, leave her alone!" As soon as Michael spoke up, Scorpion backhanded him in the face. She raised her stinger hand snarling, "You'd better listen to me right now boy. One more word out of you and these poisonous scorpion stingers will end your worthless life."

Sam cried back, "Michael, shut up."

Scorpion smiled and said, "I see the princess is the smart one." Sam was now standing in front of Scorpion who instantly became jealous. She did not like the presence of any beautiful female near her. Under normal circumstances she would have killed Sam on the spot, but today she had different plans for her. Scorpion added, "Take the princess over to my right side. We will save her for later." Scorpion looked at the other Spinners and said, "Sit them down. If they so much as move, run your daggers through their hearts." She was ready to go back in her trance.

As she did, Keno poked Graham in the side and whispered, "What's this witch doing?"

Graham replied, "I think she's summoning the demons from the underworld."

Keno whispered back, "She's nuts." Before he could finish, the pirate guarding him poked the dagger he was holding and pricked Keno's neck with it. Keno realized he was being warned to shut up.

Scorpion stood silently with her eyes closed. She finally opened them looking somewhat perplexed. She could feel the strong force in the room, but didn't have a clue as to how to use it. While she was standing there, she felt the leather bag on her hip begin to shake. She had totally forgotten about the cross. She opened the bag and took the cross out. The room glistened in a green glow from the emeralds embedded in the cross. The Spinners were shocked that Scorpion had possession of the Tucker Cross. They wondered what had happened to Salty. Even Stryker seemed to come out of his trance for a few seconds. Scorpion could see there was some sort of connection with the cross and the force in the Triangle. She held the cross with both hands up over her head and pointed it in the direction of the centre of the cave where the green laser beam focused in the middle of the pond. Scorpion started chanting and commanding the underworld and those zombie spirits to join her.

Michael then whispered to Graham, "I have a bad feeling about this. I hope this isn't another gateway back to our world." No sooner had he finished speaking than the water in the pond began to spin like a giant whirlpool and steam began to rise from the surface of the pond. The sharks were going crazy attacking each other. The pond turned blood red in color.

Stryker yelled out, "The end is near!" Without hesitation, he jumped into the blood red whirlpool and was sucked under in a flash. Sam stumbled backwards almost slipping and falling in herself.

Scorpion started screaming, "Give me the power of the Triangle now, oh dark ones!" Then the floor of the cave started shaking violently. Several of the pirates had fallen into the pond and were instantly engulfed, sinking out of sight. The earth stopped shaking as quickly as it had started. Then a mega explosion took place under the pond, blowing the water up to the top of the cave and splashing back down over the Spinners and the pirates. Scorpion backed away from the edge of the pond signaling the others to do the same. She sensed something was about to happen.

Just as if lightning had struck, the bottom of the pond dropped out taking the treasure and the sharks with it. For a couple of seconds it got eerily quiet and then the inside of the cave began to glow red. There were explosions coming from deep in bottom of the cave where the pond used to be. A glowing red substance and lightning strikes from the depths of the earth were now making their way to the surface.

The cave started shaking again, causing several more pirates to fall into the fire pit. The Spinners backed up to the walls of the cave as far as they could, not wanting to fall into the death pit. Scorpion was convinced that the red substance in the bottom of the pit was the force of the Triangle coming towards her.

Keno looked over at Michael and Graham and yelled, "Holy crap! This witch has just awakened the extinct volcano beneath Harrington Sound. She's going to get us all killed."

Michael yelled back, "By the time Scorpion figures out what is going on, it'll be too late. We have to get out of here now!"

Graham replied, "We're never going to get by the pirates. Besides, Sam is on the other side of the room.

Scorpion turned to the pirates holding Sam and commanded, "Now the underworld demands a sacrifice. We must throw the princess into the pit. Bring her to me." Michael, Graham and Keno realized they had to do something quickly, but what?

~21~

DESTRUCTION OF THE TRIANGLE

DESTRUCTION OF THE TRIANGLE

Back on the surface, Portagee had been trying to keep an eye on the cave from the hillside just to the east. He had felt the ground tremor beneath his feet and was worried for his friends' safety. There were now only a couple of pirates left guarding the cave entrance. Two had fallen into the cave, and two had fled for their lives. Portagee still had no idea how to rescue his friends.

While he was trying to devise a plan he heard something rustling through the bushes. He was trapped. There was no time to move. He would have to stand there and fight. He stood up, pulled out his dagger and yelled, "Bring it on, you scum buckets!" Before he could make a move, two large creatures jumped out of the bushes and knocked Portagee over onto his back. Portagee thought this was the end. That is, until he started getting licked in the face by Grizzly and Bear. Portagee was ever so happy to see his four-legged friends. He wondered how he might get rid of the remaining two pirates guarding the cave. It took a few minutes to calm the two labs, as they were so excited to see him. While he was petting them he wondered what had happened to Cooter. Did he fall in the ocean and drown, or what? He would have to figure that out later. He was ready to move quietly down the hillside with Grizzly and Bear and get much closer to the pirates.

Portagee had a simple plan, but if it failed it would probably get him shot. He was just about twenty feet from the clearing where the cave entrance was. He held tightly onto the dogs and began screaming bloody murder like he was being attacked. He yelled out, "Please don't kill me, help, help! They're ripping me to pieces!" The two pirates walked towards the bush from which all the racket was coming. Portagee set the labs free and started running with them, yelling, "Grizzly bears, Grizzly bears they're chasing me trying to kill me! Look out Grizzly bears!"

Then right above the pirates, Grizzly and Bear jumped out of the bush growling and barking. They knocked the pirates over before they knew what had hit them. They scrambled to their feet leaving their muskets. They screamed for their lives and ran out through the bush. Portagee called the dogs back and gave them each a big hug. He commanded them to sit while he crawled up to look into the entrance of the cave. By the time he got there, he could see Sam being dragged over to Scorpion. When he looked into the pit, he saw what he thought was a lava flow heading their way. Portagee knew that he and the labs were going to have to make another surprise attack. As he stood up to go get the labs, the ground shook again, knocking him to the ground. He got back to his feet, as he knew there was very little time. Besides he wasn't so sure that Grizzly and Bear would enter the cave with the terrible sulfur smell that was pumping out of the entrance. Portagee went over to the labs saying, "Come on pups, there's a nasty wild cat down there."

Scorpion reached over and took Sam from the two pirates. She said, "My little princess, the forces of the dark rejoice with your sacrifice." With the strength of three women, she lifted Sam straight overhead while still holding the cross.

Sam yelled at her, "You witch, put me down!"

Scorpion ignored her and screamed, "Grant me the power. I am giving you your sacrifice!" She shifted forward to throw Sam into the fiery pit. Portagee knew he had to move at lightning speed. He ran and jumped into the cave with Grizzly and Bear charging right behind him. As Portagee hit the first step, he lost his balance and went sliding down the stairs on his back, headfirst. Just as Scorpion was beginning to release Sam, Portagee's head and shoulders slid between her legs.

Portagee looked up at Scorpion and yelled, "BOO!" The force of his impact knocked her legs straight out from under her. The sudden jolt made her release Sam. Sam began falling head first into the pit. Just as she was slipping over the edge of the pit, Grizzly and Bear grabbed one of Sam's pant legs with their teeth. This bought Portagee enough time to turn over and grab hold of Sam's belt. By now the other three Spinners were running towards Sam and Portagee.

Half way there, Michael yelled, "Look, Scorpion dropped the cross!" It was lying by the edge of the pit. Scorpion was regaining her wits. She could see Michael running to get the cross.

She kicked it with her boot sending it over the edge. She cackled and declared, "If I can't have the power, neither will you."

Michael yelled at Graham, "Grab my arm! I'm going for the cross." He jumped over the edge of the pit, grabbing the cross in mid air with his right hand. Graham grabbed at Michael's left hand, but it slipped away.

He yelled back at Keno and said, "Grab my ankles Keno!" Keno lunged forward and grabbed Michael's ankles at the last second, causing Michael to bump his head against the pit's wall. Thank goodness Keno was super strong.

He began pulling Michael and Graham back up the side of the pit wall. While the Spinners were moving to the side of the cave, another tremor hit the cave, causing more pirates to fall into the lava pit. It appeared the cave was about to self-implode.

Portagee yelled, "The Devils Hole Cave roof collapsed back in our world and I think it's ready to collapse here!" The Spinners and the labs clawed their way out of the cave as quickly as they could. No sooner than they made it to safety than another explosion from deep within the cave, rocked everything. The ground shook violently and the weakened roof of the cave collapsed on the remaining pirates and Scorpion. Scorpion looked up just in time to see a sharp stalactite drop directly on her. It pierced her chest. She fell over the edge of the pit and was burned alive in the lava flow.

The Spinners and the labs collapsed at the edge of Devils Hole, which was truly a Devil's Hole now. Ash and smoke were emitted from of the hole like a spewing volcano. The Triangle was definitely damaged and could very well self-destruct. As the Spinners lay on the ground trying to catch their breath, Graham looked down the hole and said, "It looks like to me like Scorpion re-activated one of the ancient dormant volcanoes of Bermuda." Now all the Spinners had to do was to try to figure out how to seal this vent hole off again before a full eruption occurred.

-22-

CANNON BALLS & VOLCANOES

CANNON BALLS AND VOLCANOES

As the Spinners sat around the newly created volcanic vent hole, they had some tough decisions to make. Sam spoke up first, "We have to seal off the volcano vent somehow, plus we have to keep an eye out for Scarzo and Axil. They're still running around the Triangle with their automatic weapons."

Michael added, "How can we seal off Devils Hole? We would need some powerful excavating equipment and dynamite."

Graham chimed in, "Well, out there on the ship, I know they have black powder."

Portagee interrupted, "Wait, wait, I know. We'll use the cannons to blow open a channel to Devils hole just like Scorpion did, to widen the inlet. Then, we'll let the sea water cool and seal off the volcano vent."

Sam said, "That's a great idea. It's going to be one heck of an impact when that seawater hits that hot lava. That leaves us with one more problem, boys."

"What's that?" Michael asked.

"Well," said Sam, "that pirate ship still has pirates on it. As soon as they figure out that Scorpion is dead, they might want to set sail and leave the Island."

Michael responded, "Yes, I see what you mean. That does pose a problem."

Sam said, "So, we have to fool them into leaving the ship. We will sneak onboard and seize control of it."

Keno asked, "Well Sammy, how are we going to do that?"

Sam didn't like being called Sammy, but she replied anyway, "Well Mr. Smart Butt, since you're the biggest one here, you're going to dress up like a pirate and convince them to leave their ship and come ashore."

Keno blasted back, "So where's my pirate outfit?"

Sam smiled and pointed down in Devils Hole. Keno couldn't believe what he was hearing, "You think I'm going back down there to take the clothes off of a dead pirate?"

Graham responded, "No, you won't have to. Michael and I will do it for you. We'll find the biggest one down there for you. Come on Michael, let's go. Somebody has to do it." Michael got up. He and Graham walked back down what was left of the stairs. It was different now with the roof of the cave totally gone. It was a little hot and it was difficult to breathe from all the smoke and sulfur fumes. They got lucky and found a pirate who was close enough to Keno's size whose clothes were in pretty good shape. He must have died from inhaling too much sulfur. Once done, they climbed out of the pit and threw Keno his new wardrobe. Keno was still unhappy, but he went to the bush and put the outfit on anyway. When he came out, he looked just like a real pirate. Unfortunately he smelled like one to. The pirate who had worn these clothes must not have had a bath in a very long time.

Portagee said, "Keno, you may be my best friend, but no hugs today, OK?"

Keno grumbled, "OK, now what?"

Sam waved for the rest of the Spinners to come over. Michael, Portagee, Keno and Graham went over to find out what the plan was. After listening, they agreed that it could work and even in the worst case scenario there was very little chance of anyone getting hurt. They knew what needed to be done and they quickly moved out.

Keno had to sit in the bush in front of Devils Hole to wait for a signal from the other Spinners that they were in place. Meanwhile, the rest of the Spinners and Grizzly and Bear moved up the shoreline and had sneaked down to the water. They slipped into the water and swam over to Turtle Island, which was only about thirty yards away from where the ship was anchored. As soon as they were well hidden on the tiny island, Graham made the sound of a Kiskadee, a beautiful black and yellow native bird of Bermuda. Keno moved into action. He cleared the bush and walked down to the shoreline. He yelled, pointed the musket into the air and fired it. The remaining crewmembers came running to the side of the ship facing the Devils Hole area. Keno tried to talk as hoarsely as he could. He yelled out, "Mates, the captain says get your bloody butts over here right now. We've got a problem!" Keno turned raising his musket high with one arm and went running into the bush yelling and screaming.

Once out of sight he picked up the other musket that had been left behind by the pirates when they ran from Grizzly and Bear. He fired it into the air. Keno looped back to watch the ship from the bush up on the shoreline. The plan appeared to be working. The four remaining crewmembers lowered a longboat into the water, climbed down the side of the ship with their muskets and cut-lasses, and shoved off for the shore. The four pirates rowed as fast as they could. They didn't want Scorpion to take out her wrath on them. Within five minutes they made it to shore and pulled the longboat up on the beach. They ran up into the bush looking for Scorpion and the rest of the crew.

As soon as the Spinners saw the pirates leave the beach, they jumped into the sound from Turtle Island. They swam as fast as they could towards the Venom. Even the labs were right behind them. Keno moved into action. All four of the longboats were clustered together on the beach. He ran over to each of the longboats and started punching holes in the sides of them with the butt of one of the muskets. Once he had done that, he threw the muskets into the Sound, dove into the water, and started swimming as quickly as he could towards the Venom.

Meanwhile, the Spinners had reached the Venom. Michael said, "I'll climb up the side of the ship with Graham. Sam, you and Portagee stay here with the labs so they won't swim away." They scurried up the side of the ship.

Once they got on deck, Graham threw down two ropes and yelled, "Tie each of the ropes to the labs and we'll pull them up." Portagee and Sam tied Grizzly and Bear to the ropes.

Sam gave the ropes a tug and yelled, "Pull them up!" Within thirty seconds Michael and Graham had the two labs on deck. When they shook the water off their fur, Michael and Graham got drenched.

Graham yelled down to Portagee and Sam, "Grab hold of the ropes and we'll pull you up next." By the time the two were on the deck, Keno was waiting for them to throw him a rope.

Keno yelled up, "Move it guys! I think I'm on borrowed time. The pirates might be on their way back by now."

Graham laughed and yelled back, "Here's your rope, but don't worry. Those pirates won't be coming back until they find Scorpion, and we all know that's going to take a while."

As soon as Keno stepped on deck, Sam threw a bundle of clothes at him saying, "Here Keno, I'm pretty sure you want you old clothes back."

Keno laughed saying, "You got that right, baby cakes." Keno went below deck and changed as quickly as he could. He looked around just to make sure there were no other pirates still on board. Soon they were all gathered back at the bridge.

Michael said, "The first cannon shot we fire will tip off the pirates that we've taken over their ship. They'll be some sort of livid and will come at us with all they've got."

Sam thought for a second and said, "Maybe not. If they think we're firing at them instead of firing at the ground, they may decide to head for the hills."

Graham replied, "I hope you're right. If they decide to attack this ship, we'll never get the anchor up fast enough or hoist the sails in time to make a run for it. Our only chance will be to jump overboard and swim for our lives."

Michael responded, "Let's hope you're not right and we can learn how to fire these cannons fairly soon."

Portagee spoke up, "Don't worry. Keno and I helped Cooter and Salty fire these same cannons at the pirates in their longboats back in St. George's."

Graham said, "Well, let's get busy. Show the rest of us how to fire these monsters." Michael teamed up with Keno on one of the cannons, while Sam and Graham joined Portagee on one of the others. Luck was with the Spinners that day. All four of the cannons on this side of the ship were already loaded. They must have been loaded from the firing session back at Flatt's Inlet earlier on.

Portagee took the first stab at firing one of the cannons. He took his time, setting what he thought was the right angle for firing the cannon over the bush and into Devils Hole. He had hoped to scare the pirates. He was ready. He looked around and yelled, "Fire in the hole!" Then he lit the short fuse. Within a split second, the cannon made a deafening explosion and the cannon rocked back a couple of feet knocking Portagee off his feet. Portagee jumped up and shouted, "Do you think I scared them?"

Sam laughed, "Only if they were at the Royal Naval Dockyard. That cannon ball went so far I didn't even see it make landfall."

Keno said, "Well one thing is for sure. Now they know we're here." He went to one of the other cannons and yelled over to Portagee, "Watch this mate." Keno lowered the angle of the cannon, lit the fuse, jumped out of the way and stuck his fingers in his ears. The cannon fired with the same force as the first cannon but this time it blasted through the bush and appeared to score a direct hit into Devils Hole. There was not only the explosion of the cannon ball; there was also a separate explosion from the lava pit. They could hear the pirates screaming and cursing. They spotted movement in the bush that appeared to be the pirates running away from the ship, and deep into the main island. The

Spinners jumped up and down, cheering. Now they would have the time they needed to blast away the rock and sand in front of Devils Hole, in the hopes of creating a channel to it.

Sam said, "Let's get these cannons reloaded. Oh, and don't forget to keep checking in the opposite direction for a surprise visit from Scarzo."

The Spinners started firing one cannon after another, blasting a trench through the rocks, dirt, and sand in front of Devils Hole. It was reasonable to assume that the Spinners would probably use up the entire firepower of the Venom trying to accomplish this engineering long shot feat.

Jason and Buford were getting close to Harrington Sound. They came across a hog trail that they were pretty sure would get them to the Sound. They had been concerned when they heard the cannons firing and saw a steady cloud of smoke coming from the same area. As they moved along, they heard someone coming up from behind them on the same trail. Buford signaled Jason to follow him off the trail and hide behind a fallen cedar tree. Whoever this person was, he or she was in a big hurry because they were running. As the person shot by Jason and Buford, Jason slid his saber out across the trail and tripped whoever it was. Buford jumped out and yelled, "Remember the South!"

The two men started rolling over the trail and finally the intruder spoke out, "You fight like a damn sissy, Yankee."

Buford stopped dead in his tracks. It was Bubba. Buford jumped up to give Bubba a hug and said, "I figured they used you for shark bait, cuz."

Bubba laughed saying, "They tried. They kicked me out of the boat and left me for dead. By the way what's all this cannon firing going on? It's non-stop."

Jason replied, "Can't help you Bubba. We were just trying to figure it out ourselves." Then out of the clear blue, they heard voices coming up the trail from the other direction. Jason said, "Based on their accents, it sounds like pirates are heading this way."

One of the pirates saw Jason and yelled out, "Kill those bloody scum buckets!" They drew their cutlasses and pistols and went running up the trail screaming after the Pilgrims.

"Oh great!" cried Bubba. "All I have is a stick for a weapon."

Buford said, "I wish I had a stick."

Jason yelled, "Boys, it too late to hide. Here they come!" Jason turned and ran straight for them yelling, "Geronimo!"

Bubba turned to Buford and asked, "What the hell is Geronimo?"

Buford raised his shoulders and went running after Jason yelling, "Geronimo!" Not to be outdone Bubba did the same.

The poor pirates didn't know what hit them. They should have run back towards the cannons instead of running into some crazies yelling, "Geronimo." At any rate, it didn't matter much. Jason cut two of the pirates down with his saber in seconds, while Bubba ran his wooden spear through another. The last pirate threw down his cutlass and ran off into the bush. When it was over, Jason plopped down on the ground shaking his head saying, "I don't know what got into me. I just made up my mind that I was tired of these pirates killing my friends over the last few days."

Buford said, "That's OK. But what's a Geronimo?"

Jason laughed and said, "I'm sorry. Geronimo was an Apache warrior chief from the Old West. Soldiers going into battle would scream his name to build up their courage and scare the hell out of their enemies. Speaking of enemies, I think we'd better get moving in the direction of that cannon fire."

Bubba added, "You're right, but first let's help ourselves to some of these weapons. I'm tired of feeling naked." The three helped themselves to the fallen pirates' weapons and headed on down the trail.

Back at the Venom, the Spinners were having some luck blasting out a channel to connect the sound with Devils Hole. It was becoming obvious that they might run out of cannon balls before they broke through to Devils Hole. The cannons were almost too hot to fire. While they were waiting, Graham said, "We're close, but no cigar, I don't think we're going to make it."

Michael said, "Well then, what are we going to do? Just let this Triangle self destruct because of this volcano is about to erupt?"

Portagee said, "I have an idea. We still have lots of kegs of black powder, just not enough cannon balls."

Keno replied, "Yes, so what?"

Portagee smiled and said, "We need to lower the last longboat into the sound, fill it with kegs of black powder and take it over to Devils Hole. We'll blow up several kegs on both sides of the remaining rock that blocks us from forging the channel."

Sam asked, "What about the pirates?"

Michael replied, "I think they're long gone now."

Keno asked Portagee, "How are we going to get the kegs to blow at the same time?"

"That's easy," replied Portagee. "We'll take two ropes of equal length and coat them with black powder. We put one end into a keg of black powder and lead the other end off to a safe place that's equidistant from the other side. Then do the same on the other side. So, when we light the powder coated rope they will start at the same time and reach the kegs simultaneously."

Sam responded, "I don't know if it will really work, but it sounds like a good shot."

They got moving. Keno and Michael lowered the last longboat into the Sound while Sam, Graham and Portagee rolled black powder kegs over the side that the longboat was on. They tied ropes around the kegs and lowered them one by one into the longboat. After loading eight kegs into the longboat, they lowered themselves and the labs down. They made it to shore and began rolling the kegs into place on each side of the remaining rock blockage. Portagee and Graham worked on the two fuses from each set of kegs, making sure they were of equal length and met exactly in the middle. The fuses were covered with black powder and ready to be lit. Now the question was: who was going to light it while the others were running for cover? Finally everyone agreed that Michael was the fastest on his feet, so he would light the fuse. Sam hugged Michael and said, "Listen up, Michael, we'll be waiting for you behind those rocks over there. Light the fuse then get your butt out of there. Portagee figures you have about thirty seconds."

Michael replied, "Don't worry, Sam. I can run like the wind. You guys get moving. I'll give you a couple of minutes to get in place." The Spinners moved over behind the massive rocks with the labs and waited for Michael to light the fuse. Michael could see that his friends were in the clear. He ran up the hill where the two rope fuses met. Michael took one final look to make sure he was certain of his exit route. He then took the torch and dropped it on the fuses and immediately ran down the hill. At the bottom of the hill he had to jump over a small ravine and then make a final run towards the rock formation where every-one was hiding. Michael was making good time.

However, without warning, another tremor struck, causing Michael to loose his balance, He stumbled and twisted his ankle. He hit the ground striking his head on a rock. Michael was out cold. With the other Spinners hiding behind the rocks no one saw that Michael had fallen. The fuses were within ten feet of the powder kegs. Grizzly sensed that Michael was in trouble. If Michael was left where he had fallen, the debris and the force from the explosion would surely kill him. Finally Grizzly broke away from Keno and went charging over the hill after Michael. The Spinners now knew Michael must be in trouble. Grizzly had already reached Michael and was pulling him by his shirt collar back up the hill. With only seconds to go, Graham and Keno knew there was no way Grizzly would make it to cover with Michael before the explosion. Keno and Graham jumped over the top and reached down. They grabbed Michael by the arms with Grizzly still pulling on his collar. Just as the black powder kegs exploded, Keno, Graham and Grizzly pulled Michael over the rocks to safety. Flying rocks, dirt and water totally choked the air. The explosion was so massive one would have thought an atomic bomb had just exploded.

When the smoke, dust and dirt had cleared, the Spinners peeked over the top of the rocks to see what had transpired. To their amazement, the channel was now open and water was gushing through into Devils Hole. Thousands of gallons of water colliding with the lava flow created steam clouds shooting over a thousand feet into the air. Meanwhile Sam slid back down the hill to check on Michael. He was stirring and trying to sit up. Sam put her hand on Michael's forehead and said, "Hang in there big guy. Its OK, I think we've slowed down the lava." Over the next hour the steam and dust settled and began to dissipate. It appeared that the millions of gallons of seawater had cooled the lava and sealed off the volcano for good.

The Spinners had to turn their attention to Scarzo, not knowing where he was and what he was up to. They loaded into their longboat and rowed back to the Venom. Once aboard, they realized the anchor had to be raised, the sails had to be hoisted and the cannons needed to be reloaded. Sam volunteered first, "I'll take care of the anchor, you guys take care of the sails."

Michael asked, "You sure about that Sam?"

Sam winked and said, "Yes."

Michael then said, "Let's do it."

The guys went over and started working on the sails with Portagee's assistance. Sam picked up the ship's axe then walked over to the anchor's rope. She hacked away at the rope. The other Spinners watched her in amazement. Finally she severed the rope and it slid into the Sound with the anchor. Sam turned to the others and said, "Well, we don't need an anchor. Scarzo might be here in the Sound, so let's get moving."

The sails were up now. It was not very pretty, but they were catching some of the wind. Because of Portagee's background with fishing boats, he took command of the bridge and was steering the old ship. The Spinners agreed that Scarzo would probably be somewhere around Shark Hole since that was his only way back home. Sam was at the stern of the ship watching through the old telescope. All was clear except that she noticed something very unusual from Shark Hole. Sam turned and yelled at the others, "Come quick! Look at Shark Hole." Portagee tied down the wheel to maintain their course then he and the others quickly joined Sam. Sam proceeded, "Look, the gateway is wide open without the cross opening it and there's no storm to deal with." The events at Devils Hole from using the cross, to Scorpion's spells and chants and the volcano activity must have triggered the gateway to open.

Keno added, "For all we know, Scarzo has already returned through the gateway by now."

Portagee interrupted, "I don't think so. Look over there coming out from behind Hall's Island." It was Scarzo's speedboat bee lining at high speed towards Shark Hole. Portagee raced to the ship's bridge yelling, "I'll bring the ship about and we'll give them our broadsides. Get the cannons ready!" The other Spinners ran to the cannons and readied them for firing.

Sam yelled, "Fire cannon one!" Keno fired the first cannon, but they missed by a mile. Sam yelled again, "Fire cannon two!" This time Michael fired, but with the same results. The cannon ball exploded fifty yards behind the speedboat.

Graham spoke up, "It's useless. They're going too fast. We'll never hit them."

Meanwhile, on the speedboat, Scarzo and Axil were laughing at what they thought were pirates firing at them. Scarzo said, "Those fools can't catch us. The gateway is wide open and we'll be through in a few minutes with our treasure." They were within fifty yards of the gateway when the engine in the boat started sputtering. Then in the next second, the engine died. Scarzo looked down at the gas gauge and yelled, "Damn! We're out of gas." Jason's plan, going on a wild goose chase to the Great Sound, using up fuel, had worked after all!

Axil looked up and said, "No problem. At this rate we're floating directly towards the gateway. We'll be there in a couple of minutes."

Back on the Venom, Graham screamed out, "Look, they stopped! They must have run out of gas. Let's nail them now."

Sam jumped up and said, "Boys, let a girl show you how it's done." The guys all laughed, but stood back nevertheless and watched Sam reload the cannon. She yelled, "Fire in the hole!" The cannon fired, Scarzo and Axil could hear the ball screaming through the air on a direct course towards them.

Axil yelled, "It's going to hit us!"

Scarzo smiled and said, "Not a chance." In the next instant, the ball struck the front of the speedboat flipping it over and throwing Axil and Scarzo in the Sound. Back on the ship, the Spinners were jumping up and down knowing they had scored a direct hit.

Meanwhile, back at the sinking speedboat, Scarzo and Axil were swimming for their lives. The water was teaming with sharks. Axil yelled to Scarzo, "There are sharks everywhere, what do we do?"

Scarzo turned back to Axil and yelled, "Feed them, my friend."

Axil replied, "Feed them what?" Scarzo smiled, he pulled out his pistol and shot Axil in the chest. The blood in the water caused an instant feeding frenzy. Scarzo turned around and swam towards the Shark Hole gateway.

The Spinners were in shock having witnessed Scarzo shoot and kill Axil just to save his own skin. Portagee asked, "What do we do now? Scarzo's getting away." They already knew the answer, nothing. Scarzo was going to escape. Scarzo laughed as he entered the gateway. His presence in the gateway caused a series of green explosions and lightning bolts to emanate from the cave, and as quickly as it started it was over. Scarzo had escaped from the Triangle.

Michael was very upset as he said, "Well, at least he had to leave the treasure behind."

Sam added, "By the time we get back Scarzo and his goons will be long gone."

With nothing else to do the Spinners thought about their friends. As they were about to bring the ship about, they heard yelling from the shoreline. It was Cooter and Salty waving and yelling at them.

Portagee barked out, "Mates, we're coming for you. Hold your horses." He would anchor the ship just off Millhouse Bay and pick up their friends.

-23-

HOME IS WHERE YOU FIND IT

HOME IS WHERE YOU FIND IT

With the departure of Scarzo, and as the volcano returning to its dormant state, life was calm again in the Triangle, at least for the moment. The volcano in Devil's Hole had swallowed up the "Lost Treasure". Jason, Bubba and Buford finally made their way back to St. George's Village. The Spinners and the Pilgrims took time to remember the friends they had lost in the recent past. They also rejoiced in the addition of their newfound friends, Grizzly and Bear. The two labs had bunked up with Salty in his hut. The added benefit from Salty being the village cook also had its upside for the labs.

Several of Scorpion's pirates were hiding on the island. The Pilgrims would be in a constant state of alert just in case they got out of control. Once again Salty reminded the others that he too, had once been a pirate.

Mother Nature had not been cooperative for the Spinners. Without a good storm, the Shark Hole gateway would not open enough to allow them to leave the Triangle. The plus side of this was that the Spinners had spent the last ten days enjoying the Triangle without the threat of pirates and other evil beings.

The following morning, the Spinners were awakened early by Salty's dinner bell. To make matters worse, it was raining. It looked like a storm was brewing. Everyone gathered at the mess hut for breakfast in the morning. While everyone was eating, Jason spoke up, "Morning everyone. Today looks like the day Mother Nature will help us get our friends back home." Several of the Spinners booed at Jason. Jason continued, "I know, we'll miss you all too, but after breakfast we're going to take the longboats and head to Shark Hole to see if we can get you back to your families today." After breakfast, everyone loaded up the longboats and began the journey back to Harrington Sound.

After several hours, they finally arrived at Shark Hole. Jason had been right. A gale force storm now struck the island. As the Spinners got ready to go home, everyone said their goodbyes with lots of hugs. Bubba and Cooter stood on each side of Shark Hole, holding torches to help the Spinners see more clearly as they entered the cave. Grizzly and Bear had also been set ashore. They were barking as the Spinners entered the cave in their longboat. Jason was in his longboat holding the Tucker Cross while Salty tried to stabilize their position with the oars. This time, because the pilgrims were short of a longboat, the Spinners would have to dive into the cave from their longboat and swim into the gateway.

Jason aimed the Tucker Cross at the Shark Hole entrance. Within seconds the fireworks display kicked in. The green lights emanated from the entrance while lightning began to strike at the cave. The gateway was going to open very wide today. As soon as the green explosions began, Jason signaled the Spinners to hustle. As usual, Sam was the first to dive into the water and swim into the gateway. As she passed through, more green explosions occurred. Within seconds Michael, Graham, Keno and Portagee followed Sam into the gateway. Explosions filled the cave as each one of them passed through. As the last of them exited, Cooter yelled out, "Ya all come back soon! Ya hear? Oh, and bring me back one of those cricket bats."

Meanwhile, back in Bermuda as each of the Spinners entered, more green explosions occurred. They were all a bit dazed as they came out of the Triangle. While they were making sure one another was OK, a voice from just outside the cave said, "Well mates, it's about bloody time you came back. I've been waiting for you."

Sam instantly panicked and screamed to the others, "It's Scarzo, he's here to get us!"

The voice spoke again, "No baby, it's me, your daddy. I knew you would come back this afternoon with such a big storm brewing." Sam swam out of the cave to where Inspector Savage was waiting for her on the rock ledge outside. The inspector gave her a big hug then offered her a beach towel to dry off. He yelled at the others to hurry up and get out of the water. They moved up to the abandoned cottage just up the hillside from Shark Hole to dry off and talk to the Inspector.

Sam was first to speak up, "Daddy, you're supposed to be in England. Scarzo escaped from the Triangle. How did you know where we were?"
The Inspector laughed saying, "OK, OK, slow down. One thing at a time. When I heard the five of you were missing, I took a leave of absence from my training trip in the UK and came back home to assure the other parents that you would all be fine. Once we found the two crashed choppers in the ocean just off of Fort St. Catherine, we put two and two together and decided the shoot-out at the Shinbone and the crashes must be related. We knew the choppers must have come from a ship offshore. So the Harbour Patrol and the US Coast Guard tracked down their ship twenty miles off shore. By the way, did I say it was a stolen US Navy stealth ship?"

Sam interrupted, "Yes, daddy, but Scarzo's a killer and he's on the loose."

Inspector Savage smiled and remarked, "Oh, yes. He did pop out of the Triangle a couple of weeks ago. I just happened to be waiting here for you guys when he made his appearance. While he was disoriented, I jumped in the water and snatched his pistol. I managed to cuff him before he knew what had hit him. He's now in jail facing about every kind of charge imaginable. If he ever gets out of Westgate Prison, the US government intends to extradite him. So tell me Sam, did the Spinners save the Triangle from the forces of evil?"

Sam smiled. She winked at her friends and replied, "No, daddy. It was just another beautiful day in paradise."

THE ADVENTURE CONTINUES:

Episode III

ALREADY IN BOOK STORES:

Spinner's

The Lost Treasure of Bermuda

Episode I

ISBN: 1-894916-60-3